Adventures among Books

Andrew Lang

Adventures among Books

ISBN: 978-1-64799-566-9

CONTENTS

PREFACE

Of the Essays in this volume "Adventures among Books," and "Rab's Friend," appeared in Scribner's Magazine; and "Recollections of Robert Louis Stevenson" (to the best of the author's memory) in The North American Review. The Essay on "Smollett" was in the Anglo-Saxon, which has ceased to appear; and the shorter papers, such as "The Confessions of Saint Augustine," in a periodical styled Wit and Wisdom. For "The Poems of William Morris" the author has to thank the Editor of Longman's Magazine; for "The Boy," and "Mrs. Radcliffe's Novels," the Proprietors of The Cornhill Magazine; for "Enchanted Cigarettes," and possibly for "The Supernatural in Fiction," the Proprietors of The Idler. The portrait, after Sir William Richmond, R.A., was done about the time when most of the Essays were written—and that was not yesterday.

CHAPTER I

ADVENTURES AMONG BOOKS

I

In an age of reminiscences, is there room for the confessions of a veteran, who remembers a great deal about books and very little about people? I have often wondered that a Biographia Literaria has so seldom been attempted—a biography or autobiography of a man in his relations with other minds. Coleridge, to be sure, gave this name to a work of his, but he wandered from his apparent purpose into a world of alien disquisitions. The following pages are frankly bookish, and to the bookish only do they appeal. The habit of reading has been praised as a virtue, and has been denounced as a vice. In no case, if we except the perpetual study of newspapers (which cannot fairly be called reading), is the vice, or the virtue, common. It is more innocent than opium-eating, though, like opium-eating, it unlocks to us artificial paradises. I try to say what I have found in books, what distractions from the world, what teaching (not much), and what consolations.

In beginning an autobiographia literaria, an account of how, and in what order, books have appealed to a mind, which books have ever above all things delighted, the author must pray to be pardoned for the sin of egotism. There is no other mind, naturally, of which the author knows so much as of his own. On n'a que soi, as the poor girl says in one of M. Paul Bourget's novels. In literature, as in love, one can only speak for himself. This author did not, like Fulke Greville, retire into the convent of literature from the strife of the world, rather he was born to be, from the first, a dweller in the cloister of a library. Among the poems which I remember best out of early boyhood is Lucy Ashton's song, in the "Bride of Lammermoor":—

> "Look not thou on beauty's charming,
> Sit thou still when kings are arming,
> Taste not when the wine-cup glistens,
> Speak not when the people listens,
> Stop thine ear against the singer,
> From the red gold keep thy finger,

Vacant heart, and hand, and eye,
Easy live and quiet die."

The rhymes, unlearned, clung to my memory; they would sing themselves to me on the way to school, or cricket-field, and, about the age of ten, probably without quite understanding them, I had chosen them for a kind of motto in life, a tune to murmur along the fallentis semita vitæ. This seems a queer idea for a small boy, but it must be confessed.

"It takes all sorts to make a world," some are soldiers from the cradle, some merchants, some orators; nothing but a love of books was the gift given to me by the fairies. It was probably derived from forebears on both sides of my family, one a great reader, the other a considerable collector of books which remained with us and were all tried, persevered with, or abandoned in turn, by a student who has not blanched before the Epigoniad.

About the age of four I learned to read by a simple process. I had heard the elegy of Cock Robin till I knew it by rote, and I picked out the letters and words which compose that classic till I could read it for myself. Earlier than that, "Robinson Crusoe" had been read aloud to me, in an abbreviated form, no doubt. I remember the pictures of Robinson finding the footstep in the sand, and a dance of cannibals, and the parrot. But, somehow, I have never read "Robinson" since: it is a pleasure to come.

The first books which vividly impressed me were, naturally, fairy tales, and chap-books about Robert Bruce, William Wallace, and Rob Roy. At that time these little tracts could be bought for a penny apiece. I can still see Bruce in full armour, and Wallace in a kilt, discoursing across a burn, and Rob Roy slipping from the soldier's horse into the stream. They did not then awaken a precocious patriotism; a boy of five is more at home in Fairyland than in his own country. The sudden appearance of the White Cat as a queen after her head was cut off, the fiendish malice of the Yellow Dwarf, the strange cake of crocodile eggs and millet seed which the mother of the Princess Frutilla made for the Fairy of the Desert—these things, all fresh and astonishing, but certainly to be credited, are my first memories of romance. One story of a White Serpent, with a woodcut of that mysterious reptile, I neglected to secure, probably for want of a penny, and I have regretted it ever since. One never sees those chap books now. "The White Serpent," in spite of all research, remains introuvable. It was a lost chance, and Fortune does not forgive. Nobody ever interfered with these, or indeed with any other studies of ours at that time, as long as they were not prosecuted on Sundays. "The fightingest parts of the

2

Bible," and the Apocrypha, and stories like that of the Witch of Endor, were sabbatical literature, read in a huge old illustrated Bible. How I advanced from the fairy tales to Shakespeare, what stages there were on the way—for there must have been stages—is a thing that memory cannot recover. A nursery legend tells that I was wont to arrange six open books on six chairs, and go from one to the others, perusing them by turns. No doubt this was what people call "desultory reading," but I did not hear the criticism till later, and then too often for my comfort. Memory holds a picture, more vivid than most, of a small boy reading the "Midsummer Night's Dream" by firelight, in a room where candles were lit, and some one touched the piano, and a young man and a girl were playing chess. The Shakespeare was a volume of Kenny Meadows' edition; there are fairies in it, and the fairies seemed to come out of Shakespeare's dream into the music and the firelight. At that moment I think that I was happy; it seemed an enchanted glimpse of eternity in Paradise; nothing resembling it remains with me, out of all the years.

We went from the border to the south of England, when the number of my years was six, and in England we found another paradise, a circulating library with brown, greasy, ill-printed, odd volumes of Shakespeare and of the "Arabian Nights." How their stained pages come before the eyes again—the pleasure and the puzzle of them! What did the lady in the Geni's glass box want with the Merchants? what meant all these conversations between the Fat Knight and Ford, in the "Merry Wives"? It was delightful, but in parts it was difficult. Fragments of "The Tempest," and of other plays, remain stranded in my memory from these readings: Ferdinand and Miranda at chess, Cleopatra cuffing the messenger, the asp in the basket of figs, the Friar and the Apothecary, Troilus on the Ilian walls, a vision of Cassandra in white muslin with her hair down. People forbid children to read this or that. I am sure they need not, and that even in our infancy the magician, Shakespeare, brings us nothing worse than a world of beautiful visions, half realised. In the Egyptian wizard's little pool of ink, only the pure can see the visions, and in Shakespeare's magic mirror children see only what is pure. Among other books of that time I only recall a kind of Sunday novel, "Naomi; or, The Last Days of Jerusalem." Who, indeed, could forget the battering-rams, and the man who cried on the battlements, "Woe, woe to myself and to Jerusalem!" I seem to hear him again when boys break the hum of London with yells of the latest "disaster."

We left England in a year, went back to Scotland, and awoke, as it were, to know the glories of our birth. We lived in Scott's country, within four miles of Abbotsford, and, so far, we had heard nothing of it. I remember going with one of the maids into the cottage of a kinsman of hers, a carpenter; a delightful place, where there was sawdust, where our first fishing-rods were fashioned. Rummaging among the books, of course, I found some cheap periodical with verses in it. The lines began—

> "The Baron of Smaylhome rose with day,
>   He spurred his courser on,
> Without stop or stay, down the rocky way
>   That leads to Brotherstone."

A rustic tea-table was spread for us, with scones and honey, not to be neglected. But they were neglected till we had learned how—

> "The sable score of fingers four
>   Remains on that board impressed,
> And for evermore that lady wore
>   A covering on her wrist."

We did not know nor ask the poet's name. Children, probably, say very little about what is in their minds; but that unhappy knight, Sir Richard of Coldinghame, and the Priest, with his chamber in the east, and the moody Baron, and the Lady, have dwelt in our mind ever since, and hardly need to be revived by looking at "The Eve of St. John."

Soon after that we were told about Sir Walter, how great he was, how good, how, like Napoleon, his evil destiny found him at last, and he wore his heart away for honour's sake. And we were given the "Lay," and "The Lady of the Lake." It was my father who first read "Tam o' Shanter" to me, for which I confess I did not care at that time, preferring to take witches and bogies with great seriousness. It seemed as if Burns were trifling with a noble subject. But it was in a summer sunset, beside a window looking out on Ettrick and the hill of the Three Brethren's Cairn, that I first read, with the dearest of all friends, how—

> "The stag at eve had drunk his fill
> Where danced the moon on Monan's rill,
> And deep his midnight lair had made
> In lone Glenartney's hazel shade."

Then opened the gates of romance, and with Fitz-James we drove the chase, till—

4

"Few were the stragglers, following far,
That reached the lake of Vennachar,
And when the Brig of Turk was won,
The foremost horseman rode alone."

From that time, for months, there was usually a little volume of Scott in one's pocket, in company with the miscellaneous collection of a boy's treasures. Scott certainly took his fairy folk seriously, and the Mauth Dog was rather a disagreeable companion to a small boy in wakeful hours.[1] After this kind of introduction to Sir Walter, after learning one's first lessons in history from the "Tales of a Grandfather," nobody, one hopes, can criticise him in cold blood, or after the manner of Mr. Leslie Stephen, who is not sentimental. Scott is not an author like another, but our earliest known friend in letters; for, of course, we did not ask who Shakespeare was, nor inquire about the private history of Madame d'Aulnoy. Scott peopled for us the rivers and burnsides with his reivers; the Fairy Queen came out of Eildon Hill and haunted Carterhaugh; at Newark Tower we saw "the embattled portal arch"—

"Whose ponderous grate and massy bar
Had oft rolled back the tide of war,"—

just as, at Foulshiels, on Yarrow, we beheld the very roofless cottage whence Mungo Park went forth to trace the waters of the Niger, and at Oakwood the tower of the Wizard Michael Scott.

Probably the first novel I ever read was read at Elgin, and the story was "Jane Eyre." This tale was a creepy one for a boy of nine, and Rochester was a mystery, St. John a bore. But the lonely little girl in her despair, when something came into the room, and her days of starvation at school, and the terrible first Mrs. Rochester, were not to be forgotten. They abide in one's recollection with a Red Indian's ghost, who carried a rusty ruined gun, and whose acquaintance was made at the same time.

I fancy I was rather an industrious little boy, and that I had minded my lessons, and satisfied my teachers—I know I was reading Pinnock's "History of Rome" for pleasure—till "the wicked day of destiny" came, and I felt a "call," and underwent a process which may be described as the opposite of "conversion." The "call" came from Dickens. "Pickwick" was brought into the house. From that hour it was all over, for five or six years, with anything like

---

[1] "Mauth" is Manx for dog, I am told.

5

industry and lesson-books. I read "Pickwick" in convulsions of mirth. I dropped Pinnock's "Rome" for good. I neglected everything printed in Latin, in fact everything that one was understood to prepare for one's classes in the school whither I was now sent, in Edinburgh. For there, living a rather lonely small boy in the house of an aged relation, I found the Waverley Novels. The rest is transport. A conscientious tutor dragged me through the Latin grammar, and a constitutional dislike to being beaten on the hands with a leather strap urged me to acquire a certain amount of elementary erudition. But, for a year, I was a young hermit, living with Scott in the "Waverleys" and the "Border Minstrelsy," with Pope, and Prior, and a translation of Ariosto, with Lever and Dickens, David Copperfield and Charles O'Malley, Longfellow and Mayne Reid, Dumas, and in brief, with every kind of light literature that I could lay my hands upon. Carlyle did not escape me; I vividly remember the helpless rage with which I read of the Flight to Varennes. In his work on French novelists, Mr. Saintsbury speaks of a disagreeable little boy, in a French romance, who found Scott assommant, stunningly stupid. This was a very odious little boy, it seems (I have not read his adventures), and he came, as he deserved, to a bad end. Other and better boys, I learn, find Scott "slow." Extraordinary boys! Perhaps "Ivanhoe" was first favourite of yore; you cannot beat Front de Boeuf, the assault on his castle, the tournament. No other tournament need apply. Sir Arthur Conan Doyle, greatly daring, has attempted to enter the lists, but he is a mere Ralph the Hospitaller. Next, I think, in order of delight, came "Quentin Durward," especially the hero of the scar, whose name Thackeray could not remember, Quentin's uncle. Then "The Black Dwarf," and Dugald, our dear Rittmeister. I could not read "Rob Roy" then, nor later; nay, not till I was forty. Now Di Vernon is the lady for me; the queen of fiction, the peerless, the brave, the tender, and true.

The wisdom of the authorities decided that I was to read no more novels, but, as an observer remarked, "I don't see what is the use of preventing the boy from reading novels, for he's just reading 'Don Juan' instead." This was so manifestly no improvement, that the ban on novels was tacitly withdrawn, or was permitted to become a dead letter. They were far more enjoyable than Byron. The worst that came of this was the suggestion of a young friend, whose life had been adventurous—indeed he had served in the Crimea with the Bashi Bazouks—that I should master the writings of Edgar Poe. I do not think that the "Black Cat," and the "Fall of the House of Usher," and the "Murders in the Rue Morgue," are very good reading for a boy who is not peculiarly intrepid. Many a bad hour they gave me, haunting me, especially, with a fear of being prematurely buried, and of waking up before breakfast to find myself in a coffin. Of all the books I devoured in that year, Poe is the only author whom I wish I had reserved for later consideration, and whom I cannot conscientiously recommend to children.

I had already enjoyed a sip of Thackeray, reading at a venture, in "Vanity Fair," about the Battle of Waterloo. It was not like Lever's accounts of battles, but it was enchanting. However, "Vanity Fair" was under a taboo. It is not easy to say why; but Mr. Thackeray himself informed a small boy, whom he found reading "Vanity Fair" under the table, that he had better read something else. What harm can the story do to a child? He reads about Waterloo, about fat Jos, about little George and the pony, about little Rawdon and the rat-hunt, and is happy and unharmed.

Leaving my hermitage, and going into the very different and very disagreeable world of a master's house, I was lucky enough to find a charming library there. Most of Thackeray was on the shelves, and Thackeray became the chief enchanter. As Henry Kingsley says, a boy reads him and thinks he knows all about life. I do not think that the mundane parts, about Lady Kew and her wiles, about Ethel and the Marquis of Farintosh, appealed to one or enlightened one. Ethel was a mystery, and not an interesting mystery, though one used to copy Doyle's pictures of her, with the straight nose, the impossible eyes, the impossible waist. It was not Ethel who captivated us; it was Clive's youth and art, it was J. J., the painter, it was jolly F. B. and his address to the maid about the lobster. "A finer fish, Mary, my dear, I have never seen. Does not this solve the vexed question whether lobsters are fish, in the French sense?" Then "The Rose and the Ring" came out. It was worth while to be twelve years old, when the Christmas books were written by Dickens and Thackeray. I got hold of "The Rose and the Ring," I know, and of the "Christmas Carol," when they were damp from the press. King Valoroso, and Bulbo, and Angelica were even more delightful than Scrooge, and Tiny Tim, and Trotty Veck. One remembers the fairy monarch more vividly, and the wondrous array of egg-cups from which he sipped brandy—or was it right Nantes?— still "going on sipping, I am sorry to say," even after "Valoroso was himself again."

But, of all Thackeray's books, I suppose "Pendennis" was the favourite. The delightful Marryat had entertained us with Peter Simple and O'Brien (how good their flight through France is!) with Mesty and Mr. Midshipman Easy, with Jacob Faithful (Mr. Thackeray's favourite), and with Snarleyyow; but Marryat never made us wish to run away to sea. That did not seem to be one's vocation. But the story of Pen made one wish to run away to literature, to the Temple, to streets where Brown, the famous reviewer, might be seen walking with his wife and umbrella. The writing of poems "up to" pictures, the beer with Warrington in the mornings, the suppers in the back-kitchen, these were the alluring things, not society, and Lady Rockminster, and Lord Steyne. Well, one has run away to literature since, but where is the matutinal beer? Where is the back-kitchen? Where are Warrington, and Foker, and F. B.? I have never met them in this living world, though Brown, the celebrated reviewer, is familiar to me, and also Mr. Sydney Scraper, of the Oxford and Cambridge Club. Perhaps back-kitchens exist, perhaps there are cakes and ale in the life literary, and F. B. may take his walks by the Round Pond. But one never encounters these rarities, and Bungay and Bacon are no longer the innocent and ignorant rivals whom Thackeray drew. They do not give those wonderful parties; Miss Bunnion has become quite conventional; Percy Popjoy has abandoned letters; Mr. Wenham does not toady; Mr. Wagg does not joke any more. The literary life is very like any other, in London, or is it that we do not see it aright, not having the eyes of genius? Well, a life on the ocean wave, too, may not be so desirable as it seems in Marryat's novels: so many a lad whom he tempted into the navy has discovered. The best part of the existence of a man of letters is his looking forward to it through the spectacles of Titmarsh.

One can never say how much one owes to a school-master who was a friend of literature, who kept a houseful of books, and who was himself a graceful scholar, and an author, while he chose to write, of poetic and humorous genius. Such was the master who wrote the "Day Dreams of a Schoolmaster," Mr. D'Arcy Wentworth Thompson, to whom, in this place, I am glad to confess my gratitude after all these many years. While we were deep in the history of Pendennis we were also being dragged through the Commentaries of Caius Julius Cæsar, through the Latin and Greek grammars, through Xenophon, and the Eclogues of Virgil, and a depressing play of Euripides, the "Phœnissæ." I can never say how much I detested these authors, who, taken in small doses, are far, indeed, from being attractive. Horace, to a lazy boy, appears in his Odes to have nothing to say, and to say it in the most frivolous and vexatious manner. Then Cowper's "Task," or "Paradise Lost," as school-books, with notes, seems arid enough to a school-boy. I remember reading ahead, in Cowper, instead of attending to the lesson and the class-work. His observations on public schools were not uninteresting, but the whole English school-work of those days was repugnant. One's English education was all got out of school.

8

As to Greek, for years it seemed a mere vacuous terror; one invented for one's self all the current arguments against "compulsory Greek." What was the use of it, who ever spoke in it, who could find any sense in it, or any interest? A language with such cruel superfluities as a middle voice and a dual; a language whose verbs were so fantastically irregular, looked like a barbaric survival, a mere plague and torment. So one thought till Homer was opened before us. Elsewhere I have tried to describe the vivid delight of first reading Homer, delight, by the way, which St. Augustine failed to appreciate. Most boys not wholly immersed in dulness felt it, I think; to myself, for one, Homer was the real beginning of study. One had tried him, when one was very young, in Pope, and had been baffled by Pope, and his artificial manner, his "fairs," and "swains." Homer seemed better reading in the absurd "crib" which Mr. Buckley wrote for Bohn's series. Hector and Ajax, in that disguise, were as great favourites as Horatius on the Bridge, or the younger Tarquin. Scott, by the way, must have made one a furious and consistent Legitimist. In reading the "Lays of Ancient Rome," my sympathies were with the expelled kings, at least with him who fought so well at Lake Regillus:—

> "Titus, the youngest Tarquin,
> Too good for such a breed."

Where—

> "Valerius struck at Titus,
> And lopped off half his crest;
> But Titus stabbed Valerius
> A span deep in the breast,"—

I find, on the margin of my old copy, in a schoolboy's hand, the words "Well done, the Jacobites!" Perhaps my politics have never gone much beyond this sentiment. But this is a digression from Homer. The very sound of the hexameter, that long, inimitable roll of the most various music, was enough to win the heart, even if the words were not understood. But the words proved unexpectedly easy to understand, full as they are of all nobility, all tenderness, all courage, courtesy, and romance. The "Morte d'Arthur" itself, which about this time fell into our hands, was not so dear as the "Odyssey," though for a boy to read Sir Thomas Malory is to ride at adventure in enchanted forests, to enter haunted chapels where a light shines from the Graal, to find by lonely mountain meres the magic boat of Sir Galahad.

After once being initiated into the mysteries of Greece by Homer, the work at Greek was no longer tedious. Herodotus was a charming and humorous story-teller, and, as for Thucydides, his account of the Sicilian Expedition and its ending was one of the very rare things in literature which almost, if not quite, brought tears into one's eyes. Few passages, indeed, have done that, and they are curiously discrepant. The first book that ever made me cry, of which feat I was horribly ashamed, was "Uncle Tom's Cabin," with the death of Eva, Topsy's friend. Then it was trying when Colonel Newcome said Adsum, and the end of Socrates in the Phaedo moved one more than seemed becoming—these, and a passage in the history of Skalagrim Lamb's Tail, and, as I said, the ruin of the Athenians in the Syracusan Bay. I have read these chapters in an old French version derived through the Italian from a Latin translation of Thucydides. Even in this far-descended form, the tale keeps its pathos; the calm, grave stamp of that tragic telling cannot be worn away by much handling, by long time, by the many changes of human speech. "Others too," says Nicias, in that fatal speech, when—

> "All was done that men may do,
> And all was done in vain,"—

"having achieved what men may, have borne what men must." This is the very burden of life, and the last word of tragedy. For now all is vain: courage, wisdom, piety, the bravery of Lamachus, the goodness of Nicias, the brilliance of Alcibiades, all are expended, all wasted, nothing of that brave venture abides, except torture, defeat, and death. No play not poem of individual fortunes is so moving as this ruin of a people; no modern story can stir us, with all its eloquence, like the brief gravity of this ancient history. Nor can we find, at the last, any wisdom more wise than that which bids us do what men may, and bear what men must. Such are the lessons of the Greek, of the people who tried all things, in the morning of the world, and who still speak to us of what they tried in words which are the sum of human gaiety and gloom, of grief and triumph, hope and despair. The world, since their day, has but followed in the same round, which only seems new: has only made the same experiments, and failed with the same failure, but less gallantly and less gloriously.

One's school-boy adventures among books ended not long after winning the friendship of Homer and Thucydides, of Lucretius and Catullus. One's application was far too desultory to make a serious and accurate scholar.

I confess to having learned the classical languages, as it were by accident, for the sake of what is in them, and with a provokingly

10

imperfect accuracy. Cricket and trout occupied far too much of my mind and my time: Christopher North, and Walton, and Thomas Tod Stoddart, and "The Moor and the Loch," were my holiday reading, and I do not regret it. Philologists and Ireland scholars are not made so, but you can, in no way, fashion a scholar out of a casual and inaccurate intelligence. The true scholar is one whom I envy, almost as much as I respect him; but there is a kind of mental short-sightedness, where accents and verbal niceties are concerned, which cannot be sharpened into true scholarship. Yet, even for those afflicted in this way, and with the malady of being "idle, careless little boys," the ancient classics have a value for which there is no substitute. There is a charm in finding ourselves—our common humanity, our puzzles, our cares, our joys, in the writings of men severed from us by race, religion, speech, and half the gulf of historical time—which no other literary pleasure can equal. Then there is to be added, as the university preacher observed, "the pleasure of despising our fellow-creatures who do not know Greek." Doubtless in that there is great consolation.

It would be interesting, were it possible, to know what proportion of people really care for poetry, and how the love of poetry came to them, and grew in them, and where and when it stopped. Modern poets whom one meets are apt to say that poetry is not read at all. Byron's Murray ceased to publish poetry in 1830, just when Tennyson and Browning were striking their preludes. Probably Mr. Murray was wise in his generation. But it is also likely that many persons, even now, are attached to poetry, though they certainly do not buy contemporary verse. How did the passion come to them? How long did it stay? When did the Muse say good-bye? To myself, as I have remarked, poetry came with Sir Walter Scott, for one read Shakespeare as a child, rather in a kind of dream of fairyland and enchanted isles, than with any distinct consciousness that one was occupied with poetry. Next to Scott, with me, came Longfellow, who pleased one as more reflective and tenderly sentimental, while the reflections were not so deep as to be puzzling. I remember how "Hiawatha" came out, when one was a boy, and how delightful was the free forest life, and Minnehaha, and Paupukkeewis, and Nokomis. One did not then know that the same charm, with a yet fresher dew upon it, was to meet one later, in the "Kalewala." But, at that time, one had no conscious pleasure in poetic style, except in such ringing verse as Scott's, and Campbell's in his patriotic pieces. The pleasure and enchantment of style first appealed to me, at about the age of fifteen, when one read for the first time—

"So all day long the noise of battle rolled
Among the mountains by the winter sea;
Until King Arthur's Table, man by man,
Had fallen in Lyonnesse about their Lord."

Previously one had only heard of Mr. Tennyson as a name.
When a child I was told that a poet was coming to a house in the
Highlands where we chanced to be, a poet named Tennyson. "Is he
a poet like Sir Walter Scott?" I remember asking, and was told, "No,
he was not like Sir Walter Scott." Hearing no more of him, I was
prowling among the books in an ancient house, a rambling old place
with a ghost-room, where I found Tupper, and could not get on with
"Proverbial Philosophy." Next I tried Tennyson, and instantly a new
light of poetry dawned, a new music was audible, a new god came
into my medley of a Pantheon, a god never to be dethroned. "Men
scarcely know how beautiful fire is," Shelley says. I am convinced
that we scarcely know how great a poet Lord Tennyson is; use has
made him too familiar. The same hand has "raised the Table Round
again," that has written the sacred book of friendship, that has
lulled us with the magic of the "Lotus Eaters," and the melody of
"Tithonus." He has made us move, like his own Prince—

"Among a world of ghosts,
And feel ourselves the shadows of a dream."

He has enriched our world with conquests of romance; he has
recut and reset a thousand ancient gems of Greece and Rome; he
has roused our patriotism; he has stirred our pity; there is hardly a
human passion but he has purged it and ennobled it, including "this
of love." Truly, the Laureate remains the most various, the
sweetest, the most exquisite, the most learned, the most Virgilian of
all English poets, and we may pity the lovers of poetry who died
before Tennyson came.

Here may end the desultory tale of a desultory bookish
boyhood. It was not in nature that one should not begin to rhyme
for one's self. But those exercises were seldom even written down;
they lived a little while in a memory which has lost them long ago. I
do remember me that I tried some of my attempts on my dear
mother, who said much what Dryden said to "Cousin Swift," "You
will never be a poet," a decision in which I straightway acquiesced.
For to rhyme is one thing, to be a poet quite another. A good deal of
mortification would be avoided if young men and maidens only kept
this obvious fact well posed in front of their vanity and their
ambition.

In these bookish memories I have said nothing about religion and religious books, for various reasons. But, unlike other Scots of the pen, I got no harm from "The Shorter Catechism," of which I remember little, and neither then nor now was or am able to understand a single sentence. Some precocious metaphysicians comprehended and stood aghast at justification, sanctification, adoption, and effectual calling. These, apparently, were necessary processes in the Scottish spiritual life. But we were not told what they meant, nor were we distressed by a sense that we had not passed through them. From most children, one trusts, Calvinism ran like water off a duck's back; unlucky were they who first absorbed, and later were compelled to get rid of, "The Shorter Catechism!"

One good thing, if no more, these memories may accomplish. Young men, especially in America, write to me and ask me to recommend "a course of reading." Distrust a course of reading! People who really care for books read all of them. There is no other course. Let this be a reply. No other answer shall they get from me, the inquiring young men.

II

People talk, in novels, about the delights of a first love. One may venture to doubt whether everybody exactly knows which was his, or her, first love, of men or women, but about our first loves in books there can be no mistake. They were, and remain, the dearest of all; after boyhood the bloom is off the literary rye. The first parcel of these garrulities ended when the author left school, at about the age of seventeen. One's literary equipment seems to have been then almost as complete as it ever will be, one's tastes definitely formed, one's favourites already chosen. As long as we live we hope to read, but we never can "recapture the first fine careless rapture." Besides, one begins to write, and that is fatal. My own first essays were composed at school—for other boys. Not long ago the gentleman who was then our English master wrote to me, informing me he was my earliest public, and that he had never credited my younger brother with the essays which that unscrupulous lad ("I speak of him but brotherly") was accustomed to present for his consideration.

On leaving school at seventeen I went to St. Leonard's Hall, in the University of St. Andrews. That is the oldest of Scotch universities, and was founded by a papal bull. St. Leonard's Hall, after having been a hospitium for pilgrims, a home for old ladies (about 1500), and a college in the University, was now a kind of cross between a master's house at school, and, as before 1750, a college. We had more liberty than schoolboys, less than English undergraduates. In the Scotch universities the men live scattered, in lodgings, and only recently, at St. Andrews, have they begun to dine together in hall. We had a common roof, common dinners, wore scarlet gowns, possessed football and cricket clubs, and started, of course, a kind of weekly magazine. It was only a manuscript affair, and was profusely illustrated. For the only time in my life, I was now an editor, under a sub-editor, who kept me up to my work, and cut out my fine passages. The editor's duty was to write most of the magazine—to write essays, reviews (of books by the professors, very severe), novels, short stories, poems, translations, also to illustrate these, and to "fag" his friends for "copy" and drawings. A deplorable flippancy seems, as far as one remembers, to have been the chief characteristic of the periodical—flippancy and an abundant use of the supernatural. These were the days of Lord' Lytton's "Strange Story," which I continue to think a most satisfactory romance. Inspired by Lord Lytton, and aided by the University library, I read Cornelius Agrippa, Trithemius, Petrus de Abano, Michael Scott, and struggled with Iamblichus and Plotinus.

These are really but disappointing writers. It soon became evident enough that the devil was not to be raised by their prescriptions, that the philosopher's stone was beyond the reach of the amateur. Iamblichus is particularly obscure and tedious. To any young beginner I would recommend Petrus de Abano, as the most adequate and gruesome of the school, for "real deevilry and pleesure," while in the wilderness of Plotinus there are many beautiful passages and lofty speculations. Two winters in the Northern University, with the seamy side of school life left behind, among the kindest of professors—Mr. Sellar, Mr. Ferrier, Mr. Shairp—in the society of the warden, Mr. Rhoades, and of many dear old friends, are the happiest time in my life. This was true literary leisure, even if it was not too well employed, and the religio loci should be a liberal education in itself. We had debating societies—I hope I am now forgiven for an attack on the character of Sir William Wallace, latro quidam, as the chronicler calls him, "a certain brigand." But I am for ever writing about St. Andrews—writing inaccurately, too, the Scotch critics declare. "Farewell," we cried, "dear city of youth and dream," eternally dear and sacred.

14

Here we first made acquaintance with Mr. Browning, guided to his works by a parody which a lady wrote in our little magazine. Mr. Browning was not a popular poet in 1861. His admirers were few, a little people, but they were not then in the later mood of reverence, they did not awfully question the oracles, as in after years. They read, they admired, they applauded, on occasion they mocked, good-humouredly. The book by which Mr. Browning was best known was the two green volumes of "Men and Women." In these, I still think, is the heart of his genius beating most strenuously and with an immortal vitality. Perhaps this, for its compass, is the collection of poetry the most various and rich of modern English times, almost of any English times. But just as Mr. Fitzgerald cared little for what Lord Tennyson wrote after 1842, so I have never been able to feel quite the same enthusiasm for Mr. Browning's work after "Men and Women." He seems to have more influence, though that influence is vague, on persons who chiefly care for thought, than on those who chiefly care for poetry. I have met a lady who had read "The Ring and the Book" often, the "Lotus Eaters" not once. Among such students are Mr. Browning's disciples of the Inner Court: I dwell but in the Court of the Gentiles. While we all—all who attempt rhyme—have more or less consciously imitated the manner of Lord Tennyson, Mr. Swinburne, Mr. Rossetti, such imitations of Mr. Browning are uncommonly scarce. He is lucky enough not to have had the seed of his flower stolen and sown everywhere till—

"Once again the people
Called it but a weed."

The other new poet of these days was Mr. Clough, who has many undergraduate qualities. But his peculiar wistful scepticism in religion had then no influence on such of us as were still happily in the ages of faith. Anything like doubt comes less of reading, perhaps, than of the sudden necessity which, in almost every life, puts belief on her trial, and cries for an examination of the creeds hitherto held upon authority, and by dint of use and wont. In a different way one can hardly care for Mr. Matthew Arnold, as a boy, till one has come under the influence of Oxford. So Mr. Browning was the only poet added to my pantheon at St. Andrews, though Macaulay then was admitted and appeared to be more the true model of a prose writer than he seems in the light of later reflection. Probably we all have a period of admiring Carlyle almost exclusively. College essays, when the essayist cares for his work, are generally based on one or the other. Then they recede into the

15

background. As for their thought, we cannot for ever remain disciples. We begin to see how much that looks like thought is really the expression of temperament, and how individual a thing temperament is, how each of us must construct his world for himself, or be content to wait for an answer and a synthesis "in that far-off divine event to which the whole creation moves." So, for one, in these high matters, I must be content as a "masterless man" swearing by no philosopher, unless he be the imperial Stoic of the hardy heart, Marcus Aurelius Antoninus.

Perhaps nothing in education encourages this incredulity about "masters" of thought like the history of philosophy. The professor of moral philosophy, Mr. Ferrier, was a famous metaphysician and scholar. His lectures on "The History of Greek Philosophy" were an admirable introduction to the subject, afterwards pursued, in the original authorities, at Oxford. Mr. Ferrier was an exponent of other men's ideas so fair and persuasive that, in each new school, we thought we had discovered the secret. We were physicists with Thales and that pre-Socratic "company of gallant gentlemen" for whom Sydney Smith confessed his lack of admiration. We were now Empedocleans, now believers in Heraclitus, now in Socrates, now in Plato, now in Aristotle. In each lecture our professor set up a new master and gently disintegrated him in the next. "Amurath to Amurath succeeds," as Mr. T. H. Green used to say at Oxford. He himself became an Amurath, a sultan of thought, even before his apotheosis as the guide of that bewildered clergyman, Mr. Robert Elsmere. At Oxford, when one went there, one found Mr. Green already in the position of a leader of thought, and of young men. He was a tutor of Balliol, and lectured on Aristotle, and of him eager youth said, in the words of Omar Khayyam, "He knows! he knows!" What was it that Mr. Green knew? Where was the secret? To a mind already sceptical about masters, it seemed that the secret (apart from the tutor's noble simplicity and rare elevation of character) was a knack of translating St. John and Aristotle alike into a terminology which we then believed to be Hegelian. Hegel we knew, not in the original German, but in lectures and in translations. Reasoning from these inadequate premises, it seemed to me that Hegel had invented evolution before Mr. Darwin, that his system showed, so to speak, the spirit at work in evolution, the something within the wheels. But this was only a personal impression made on a mind which knew Darwin, and physical speculations in general, merely in the vague popular way. Mr. Green's pupils could generally write in his own language, more or less, and could "envisage" things, as we said then, from his point of view. To do this was believed, probably

16

without cause, to be useful in examinations. For one, I could never take it much more seriously, never believed that "the Absolute," as the Oxford Spectator said, had really been "got into a corner." The Absolute has too often been apparently cornered, too often has escaped from that situation. Somewhere in an old notebook I believe I have a portrait in pencil of Mr. Green as he wrestled at lecture with Aristotle, with the Notion, with his chair and table. Perhaps he was the last of that remarkable series of men, who may have begun with Wycliffe, among whom Newman's is a famous name, that were successively accepted at Oxford as knowing something esoteric, as possessing a shrewd guess at the secret.

> "None the less
> I still came out no wiser than I went."

All of these masters and teachers made their mark, probably won their hold, in the first place, by dint of character, not of some peculiar views of theology and philosophy. Doubtless it was the same with Socrates, with Buddha. To be like them, not to believe with them, is the thing needful. But the younger we are, the less, perhaps, we see this clearly, and we persuade ourselves that there is some mystery in these men's possession, some piece of knowledge, some method of thinking which will lead us to certainty and to peace. Alas, their secret is incommunicable, and there is no more a philosophic than there is a royal road to the City.

This may seem a digression from Adventures among Books into the Book of Human Life. But while much of education is still orally communicated by lectures and conversations, many thoughts which are to be found in books, Greek or German, reach us through the hearing. There are many pupils who can best be taught in this way; but, for one, if there be aught that is desirable in a book, I then, as now, preferred, if I could, to go to the book for it.

Yet it is odd that one remembers so little of one's undergraduate readings, apart from the constant study of the ancient classics, which might not be escaped. Of these the calm wisdom of Aristotle, in moral thought and in politics, made perhaps the deepest impression. Probably politicians are the last people who read Aristotle's "Politics." The work is, indeed, apt to disenchant one with political life. It is melancholy to see the little Greek states running the regular round—monarchy, oligarchy, tyranny, democracy in all its degrees, the "ultimate democracy" of plunder, lawlessness, license of women, children, and slaves, and then tyranny again, or subjection to some foreign power. In politics, too, there is no secret of success, of the happy life for all. There is

17

no such road to the City, either democratic or royal. This is the lesson which Aristotle's "Polities" impresses on us, this and the impossibility of imposing ideal constitutions on mankind.

"Whate'er is best administered is best." These are some of the impressions made at Oxford by the studies of the schools, the more or less inevitable "curricoolum," as the Scotch gentleman pronounced the word. But at Oxford, for most men, the regular work of the schools is only a small part of the literary education. People read, in different degrees, according to their private tastes. There are always a few men, at least, who love literary studies for their own sake, regardless of lectures and of "classes." In my own time I really believe you could know nothing which might not "pay" in the schools and prove serviceable in examinations. But a good deal depended on being able to use your knowledge by way of literary illustration. Perhaps the cleverest of my own juniors, since very well known in letters, did not use his own special vein, even when he had the chance, in writing answers to questions in examinations. Hence his academic success was much below his deserts. For my own part, I remember my tutor saying, "Don't write as if you were writing for a penny paper." Alas, it was "a prediction, cruel, smart." But, "as yet no sin was dreamed."

At my own college we had to write weekly essays, alternately in English and Latin. This might have been good literary training, but I fear the essays were not taken very seriously. The chief object was to make the late learned Dr. Scott bound on his chair by paradoxes. But nobody ever succeeded. He was experienced in trash. As for what may be called unacademic literature, there were not many essays in that art. There have been very literary generations, as when Corydon and Thyrsis "lived in Oxford as if it had been a great country house;" so Corydon confessed. Probably many of the poems by Mr. Matthew Arnold and many of Mr. Swinburne's early works were undergraduate poems. A later generation produced "Love in Idleness," a very pleasing volume. But the gods had not made us poetical. In those days I remember picking up, in the Union Reading-room, a pretty white quarto, "Atalanta in Calydon," by A. C. Swinburne. Only once had I seen Mr. Swinburne's name before, signing a brief tale in Once a Week. "Atalanta" was a revelation; there was a new and original poet here, a Balliol man, too. In my own mind "Atalanta" remains the best, the most beautiful, the most musical of Mr. Swinburne's many poems. He instantly became the easily parodied model of undergraduate versifiers.

Swinburnian prize poems, even, were attempted, without success. As yet we had not seen Mr. Matthew Arnold's verses. I fell in love with them, one long vacation, and never fell out of love. He is not, and cannot be, the poet of the wide world, but his charm is all the more powerful over those whom he attracts and subdues. He is the one Oxford poet of Oxford, and his "Scholar Gypsy" is our "Lycidas." At this time he was Professor of Poetry; but, alas, he lectured just at the hour when wickets were pitched on Cowley Marsh, and I never was present at his discourses, at his humorous prophecies of England's fate, which are coming all too true. So many weary lectures had to be attended, could not be "cut," that we abstained from lectures of supererogation, so to speak. For the rest there was no "literary movement" among contemporary undergraduates. They read for the schools, and they rowed and played cricket. We had no poets, except the stroke of the Corpus boat, Mr. Bridges, and he concealed his courtship of the Muse. Corpus is a small college, but Mr. Bridges pulled its boat to the proud place of second on the river. B. N. C. was the head boat, and even B. N. C. did Corpus bump. But the triumph was brief. B. N. C. made changes in its crew, got a new ship, drank the foaming grape, and bumped Corpus back. I think they went head next year, but not that year. Thus Mr. Bridges, as Kingsley advises, was doing noble deeds, not dreaming them, at that moment.

There existed a periodical entirely devoted to verse, but nobody knew anybody who wrote in it. A comic journal was started; I remember the pride with which when a freshman, I received an invitation to join its councils as an artist. I was to do the caricatures of all things. Now, methought, I shall meet the Oxford wits of whom I have read. But the wits were unutterably disappointing, and the whole thing died early and not lamented. Only one piece of academic literature obtained and deserved success. This was The Oxford Spectator, a most humorous little periodical, in shape and size like Addison's famous journal. The authors were Mr. Reginald Copleston, now Bishop of Colombo, Mr. Humphry Ward, and Mr. Nolan, a great athlete, who died early. There have been good periodicals since; many amusing things occur in the Echoes from the Oxford Magazine, but the Spectator was the flower of academic journals. "When I look back to my own experience," says the Spectator, "I find one scene, of all Oxford, most deeply engraved upon 'the mindful tablets of my soul.' And yet not a scene, but a fairy compound of smell and sound, and sight and thought. The wonderful scent of the meadow air just above Iffley, on a hot May evening, and the gay colours of twenty boats along the shore, the poles all stretched out from the bank to set the boats clear, and the sonorous cries of 'ten seconds more,' all down from the green barge to the lasher. And yet that unrivalled moment is only typical of all the term; the various elements of beauty and pleasure are concentrated there."

Unfortunately, life at Oxford is not all beauty and pleasure. Things go wrong somehow. Life drops her happy mask. But this has nothing to do with books.

About books, however, I have not many more confessions that I care to make. A man's old self is so far away that he can speak about it and its adventures almost as if he were speaking about another who is dead. After taking one's degree, and beginning to write a little for publication, the topic has a tendency to become much more personal. My last undergraduate literary discoveries were of France and the Renaissance. Accidentally finding out that I could read French, I naturally betook myself to Balzac. If you read him straight on, without a dictionary, you begin to learn a good many words. The literature of France has been much more popular in England lately, but thirty years agone it was somewhat neglected. There does seem to be something in French poetry which fails to please "the German paste in our composition." Mr. Matthew Arnold, a disciple of Sainte-Beuve, never could appreciate French poetry. A poet-critic has even remarked that the French language is nearly incapable of poetry! We cannot argue in such matters, where all depends on the taste and the ear.

Our ancestors, like the author of the "Faery Queen," translated and admired Du Bellay and Ronsard; to some critics of our own time this taste seems a modish affectation. For one, I have ever found an original charm in the lyrics of the Pleiad, and have taken great delight in Hugo's amazing variety of music, in the romance of Alfred de Musset, in the beautiful cameos of Gautier. What is poetical, if not the "Song of Roland," the only true national epic since Homer? What is frank, natural verse, if not that of the old Pastourelles? Where is there naïveté of narrative and unconscious charm, if not in Aucassin et Nicolette? In the long normally developed literature of France, so variously rich, we find the nearest analogy to the literature of Greece, though that of England contains greater masterpieces, and her verse falls more winningly on the ear. France has no Shakespeare and no Milton; we have no Molière and no "Song of Roland." One star differs from another in glory, but it is a fortunate moment when this planet of France swims into our ken. Many of our generation saw it first through Mr. Swinburne's telescope, heard of it in his criticisms, and are grateful to that watcher of the skies, even if we do not share all his transports. There then arose at Oxford, out of old French, and old oak, and old china, a "school" or "movement." It was æsthetic, and an early purchaser of Mr. William Morris's wall papers. It

20

existed ten or twelve years before the public "caught on," as they say, to these delights. But, except one or two of the masters, the school were only playing at æsthetics, and laughing at their own performances. There was more fun than fashion in the cult, which was later revived, developed, and gossiped about more than enough.

To a writer now dead, and then first met, I am specially bound in gratitude—the late Mr. J. F. M'Lennan. Mr. M'Lennan had the most acute and ingenious of minds which I have encountered. His writings on early marriage and early religion were revelations which led on to others. The topic of folklore, and the development of custom and myths, is not generally attractive, to be sure. Only a few people seem interested in that spectacle, so full of surprises—the development of all human institutions, from fairy tales to democracy. In beholding it we learn how we owe all things, humanly speaking, to the people and to genius. The natural people, the folk, has supplied us, in its unconscious way, with the stuff of all our poetry, law, ritual: and genius has selected from the mass, has turned customs into codes, nursery tales into romance, myth into science, ballad into epic, magic mummery into gorgeous ritual. The world has been educated, but not as man would have trained and taught it. "He led us by a way we knew not," led, and is leading us, we know not whither; we follow in fear.

The student of this lore can look back and see the long trodden way behind him, the winding tracks through marsh and forest and over burning sands. He sees the caves, the camps, the villages, the towns where the race has tarried, for shorter times or longer, strange places many of them, and strangely haunted, desolate dwellings and inhospitable. But the scarce visible tracks converge at last on the beaten ways, the ways to that city whither mankind is wandering, and which it may never win. We have a foreboding of a purpose which we know not, a sense as of will, working, as we would not have worked, to a hidden end.

This is the lesson, I think, of what we call folklore or anthropology, which to many seems trivial, to many seems dull. It may become the most attractive and serious of the sciences; certainly it is rich in strange curiosities, like those mystic stones which were fingered and arrayed by the pupils in that allegory of Novalis. I am not likely to regret the accident which brought me up on fairy tales, and the inquisitiveness which led me to examine the other fragments of antiquity. But the poetry and the significance of them are apt to be hidden by the enormous crowd of details. Only late we find the true meaning of what seems like a mass of fantastic, savage eccentricities. I very well remember the moment when it occurred to me, soon after taking my degree, that the usual ideas about some of these matters were the reverse of the truth, that the common theory had to be inverted. The notion was "in the air," it had already flashed on Mannhardt, probably, but, like the White Knight in "Alice," I claimed it for "my own invention."

These reminiscences and reflections have now been produced as far as 1872, or thereabouts, and it is not my intention to pursue them further, nor to speak of any living contemporaries who have not won their way to the classical. In writing of friends and teachers at Oxford, I have not ventured to express gratitude to those who still live, still teach, still are the wisest and kindest friends of the hurrying generations. It is a silence not of thanklessness, but of respect and devotion. About others—contemporaries, or juniors by many years—who have instructed, consoled, strengthened, and amused us, we must also be silent.

CHAPTER II

RECOLLECTIONS OF ROBERT LOUIS STEVENSON

TUSITALA

We spoke of a rest in a Fairy hill of the north, but he
Far from the firths of the east and the racing tides of the west
Sleeps in the sight and the sound of the infinite southern sea,
Weary and well content, in his grave on the Vaëa crest.

Tusitala, the lover of children, the teller of tales,
Giver of counsel and dreams, a wonder, a world's delight,
Looks o'er the labour of men in the plain and the hill, and the
sails
Pass and repass on the sea that he loved, in the day and the
night.

Winds of the west and the east in the rainy season blow,
Heavy with perfume, and all his fragrant woods are wet,
Winds of the east and the west as they wander to and fro,
Bear him the love of the lands he loved, and the long regret.

Once we were kindest, he said, when leagues of the limitless sea,
Flowed between us, but now that no range of the refluent tides
Sunders us each from each, yet nearer we seem to be,
When only the unbridged stream of the River of Death divides.

Before attempting to give any "reminiscences" of Mr.
Stevenson, it is right to observe that reminiscences of him can best
be found in his own works. In his essay on "Child's Play," and in his
"Child's Garden of Verse," he gave to the world his vivid
recollections of his imaginative infancy. In other essays he spoke of
his boyhood, his health, his dreams, his methods of work and study.
"The Silverado Squatters" reveals part of his experience in America.
The Parisian scenes in "The Wrecker" are inspired by his sojourn in
French Bohemia; his journeys are recorded in "Travels with a
Donkey" and "An Inland Voyage"; while his South Sea sketches,
which appeared in periodicals, deal with his Oceanic adventures.

He was the most autobiographical of authors, with an egoism nearly as complete, and to us as delightful, as the egoism of Montaigne. Thus, the proper sources of information about the author of "Kidnapped" are in his delightful books.

"John's own John," as Dr. Holmes says, may be very unlike his neighbour's John; but in the case of Mr. Stevenson, his Louis was very similar to my Louis; I mean that, as he presents his personality to the world in his writings, even so did that personality appear to me in our intercourse. The man I knew was always a boy.

> "Sing me a song of the lad that is gone,"

he wrote about Prince Charlie, but in his own case the lad was never "gone." Like Keats and Shelley, he was, and he looked, of the immortally young. He and I were at school together, but I was an elderly boy of seventeen, when he was lost in the crowd of "gytes," as the members of the lowest form are called. Like all Scotch people, we had a vague family connection; a great-uncle of his, I fancy, married an aunt of my own, called for her beauty, "The Flower of Ettrick." So we had both heard; but these things were before our day. A lady of my kindred remembers carrying Stevenson about when he was "a rather peevish baby," and I have seen a beautiful photograph of him, like one of Raffael's children, taken when his years were three or four. But I never had heard of his existence till, in 1873, I think, I was at Mentone, in the interests of my health. Here I met Mr. Sidney Colvin, now of the British Museum, and, with Mr. Colvin, Stevenson. He looked as, in my eyes, he always did look, more like a lass than a lad, with a rather long, smooth oval face, brown hair worn at greater length than is common, large lucid eyes, but whether blue or brown I cannot remember, if brown, certainly light brown. On appealing to the authority of a lady, I learn that brown was the hue. His colour was a trifle hectic, as is not unusual at Mentone, but he seemed, under his big blue cloak, to be of slender, yet agile frame. He was like nobody else whom I ever met. There was a sort of uncommon celerity in changing expression, in thought and speech. His cloak and Tyrolese hat (he would admit the innocent impeachment) were decidedly dear to him. On the frontier of Italy, why should he not do as the Italians do? It would have been well for me if I could have imitated the wearing of the cloak!

I shall not deny that my first impression was not wholly favourable. "Here," I thought, "is one of your æsthetic young men, though a very clever one." What the talk was about, I do not remember; probably of books. Mr. Stevenson afterwards told me that I had spoken of Monsieur Paul de St. Victor, as a fine writer, but added that "he was not a British sportsman." Mr. Stevenson himself, to my surprise, was unable to walk beyond a very short distance, and, as it soon appeared, he thought his thread of life was nearly spun. He had just written his essay, "Ordered South," the first of his published works, for his "Pentland Rising" pamphlet was unknown, a boy's performance. On reading "Ordered South," I saw, at once, that here was a new writer, a writer indeed; one who could do what none of us, nous autres, could rival, or approach. I was instantly "sealed of the Tribe of Louis," an admirer, a devotee, a fanatic, if you please. At least my taste has never altered. From this essay it is plain enough that the author (as is so common in youth, but with better reason than many have) thought himself doomed. Most of us have gone through that, the Millevoye phase, but who else has shown such a wise and gay acceptance of the apparently inevitable? We parted; I remember little of our converse, except a shrewd and hearty piece of encouragement given me by my junior, who already knew so much more of life than his senior will ever do. For he ran forth to embrace life like a lover: his motto was never Lucy Ashton's—

"Vacant heart, and hand, and eye,
Easy live and quiet die."

Mr. Stevenson came presently to visit me at Oxford. I make no hand of reminiscences; I remember nothing about what we did or said, with one exception, which is not going to be published. I heard of him, writing essays in the Portfolio and the Cornhill, those delightful views of life at twenty-five, so brave, so real, so vivid, so wise, so exquisite, which all should know. How we looked for "R. L. S." at the end of an article, and how devout was our belief, how happy our pride, in the young one!

About 1878, I think (I was now a slave of the quill myself), I received a brief note from Mr. Stevenson, introducing to me the person whom, in his essay on his old college magazine, he called "Glasgow Brown." What his real name was, whence he came, whence the money came, I never knew. G. B. was going to start a weekly Tory paper. Would I contribute? G. B. came to see me. Mr. Stevenson has described him, not as I would have described him: like Mr. Bill Sikes's dog, I have the Christian peculiarity of not liking dogs "as are not of my breed." G. B.'s paper, London, was to start next week. He had no writer of political leading articles. Would I do a "leader"? But I was not in favour of Lord Lytton's Afghan policy. How could I do a Tory leader? Well, I did a neutral-tinted thing, with citations from Aristophanes! I found presently some other scribes for G. B.

What a paper that was! I have heard that G. B. paid in handfuls of gold, in handfuls of bank-notes. Nobody ever read London, or advertised in it, or heard of it. It was full of the most wonderfully clever verses in old French forms. They were (it afterwards appeared) by Mr. W. E. Henley. Mr. Stevenson himself astonished and delighted the public of London (that is, the contributors) by his "New Arabian Nights." Nobody knew about them but ourselves, a fortunate few. Poor G. B. died and Mr. Henley became the editor. I may not name the contributors, the flower of the young lions, elderly lions now, there is a new race. But one lion, a distinguished and learned lion, said already that fiction, not essay, was Mr. Stevenson's field. Well, both fields were his, and I cannot say whether I would be more sorry to lose Virginibus Puerisque and "Studies of Men and Books," or "Treasure Island" and "Catriona." With the decease of G. B., Pactolus dried up in its mysterious sources, London struggled and disappeared.

Mr. Stevenson was in town, now and again, at the old Saville Club, in Saville Row, which had the tiniest and blackest of smoking-rooms. Here, or somewhere, he spoke to me of an idea of a tale, a Man who was Two Men. I said "'William Wilson' by Edgar Poe," and declared that it would never do. But his "Brownies," in a vision of the night, showed him a central scene, and he wrote "Jekyll and Hyde." My "friend of these days and of all days," Mr. Charles Longman, sent me the manuscript. In a very commonplace London drawing-room, at 10.30 P.M., I began to read it. Arriving at the place where Utterson the lawyer, and the butler wait outside the Doctor's room, I threw down the manuscript and fled in a hurry. I had no taste for solitude any more. The story won its great success, partly by dint of the moral (whatever that may be), more by its terrible, lucid, visionary power. I remember Mr. Stevenson telling me, at this time, that he was doing some "regular crawlers," for this purist had a boyish habit of slang, and I think it was he who called Julius Cæsar "the howlingest cheese who ever lived." One of the "crawlers" was "Thrawn Janet"; after "Wandering Willie's Tale" (but certainly after it), to my taste, it seems the most wonderful story of the "supernatural" in our language.

Mr. Stevenson had an infinite pleasure in Boisgobey,

Montépin, and, of course, Gaboriau. There was nothing of the "cultured person" about him. Concerning a novel dear to culture, he said that he would die by my side, in the last ditch, proclaiming it the worst fiction in the world. I make haste to add that I have only known two men of letters as free as Mr. Stevenson, not only from literary jealousy, but from the writer's natural, if exaggerated, distaste for work which, though in his own line, is very different in aim and method from his own. I do not remember another case in which he dispraised any book. I do remember his observations on a novel then and now very popular, but not to his taste, nor, indeed, by any means, impeccable, though stirring; his censure and praise were both just. From his occasional fine efforts, the author of this romance, he said, should have cleared away acres of brushwood, of ineffectual matter. It was so, no doubt, as the writer spoken of would be ready to acknowledge. But he was an improviser of genius, and Mr. Stevenson was a conscious artist.

Of course we did by no means always agree in literary estimates; no two people do. But when certain works—in his line in one way—were stupidly set up as rivals of his, the person who was most irritated was not he, but his equally magnanimous contemporary. There was no thought of rivalry or competition in either mind. The younger romancists who arose after Mr. Stevenson went to Samoa were his friends by correspondence; from them, who never saw his face, I hear of his sympathy and encouragement. Every writer knows the special temptations of his tribe: they were temptations not even felt, I do believe, by Mr. Stevenson. His heart was far too high, his nature was in every way as generous as his hand was open. It is in thinking of these things that one feels afresh the greatness of the world's loss; for "a good heart is much more than style," writes one who knew him only by way of letters.

It is a trivial reminiscence that we once plotted a Boisgobesque story together. There was a prisoner in a Muscovite dungeon.

"We'll extract information from him," I said.

"How?"

"With corkscrews."

But the mere suggestion of such a process was terribly distasteful to him; not that I really meant to go to these extreme lengths. We never, of course, could really have worked together; and, his maladies increasing, he became more and more a wanderer, living at Bournemouth, at Davos, in the Grisons, finally,

27

as all know, in Samoa. Thus, though we corresponded, not unfrequently, I never was of the inner circle of his friends. Among men there were school or college companions, or companions of Paris or Fontainebleau, cousins, like Mr. R. A. M. Stevenson, or a stray senior, like Mr. Sidney Colvin. From some of them, or from Mr. Stevenson himself, I have heard tales of "the wild Prince and Poins." That he and a friend travelled utterly without baggage, buying a shirt where a shirt was needed, is a fact, and the incident is used in "The Wrecker." Legend says that once he and a friend did possess a bag, and also, nobody ever knew why, a large bottle of scent. But there was no room for the bottle in the bag, so Mr. Stevenson spilled the whole contents over the other man's head, taking him unawares, that nothing might be wasted. I think the tale of the endless staircase, in "The Wrecker," is founded on fact, so are the stories of the atelier, which I have heard Mr. Stevenson narrate at the Oxford and Cambridge Club. For a nocturnal adventure, in the manner of the "New Arabian Nights," a learned critic already spoken of must be consulted. It is not my story. In Paris, at a café, I remember that Mr. Stevenson heard a Frenchman say the English were cowards. He got up and slapped the man's face.

"Monsieur, vous m'avez frappé!" said the Gaul.

"A ce qu'il parait," said the Scot, and there it ended. He also told me that years ago he was present at a play, I forget what play, in Paris, where the moral hero exposes a woman "with a history." He got up and went out, saying to himself:

"What a play! what a people!"

"Ah, Monsieur, vous êtes bien jeune!" said an old French gentleman.

Like a right Scot, Mr. Stevenson was fond of "our auld ally of France," to whom our country and our exiled kings owed so much.

I rather vaguely remember another anecdote. He missed his train from Edinburgh to London, and his sole portable property was a return ticket, a meerschaum pipe, and a volume of Mr. Swinburne's poems. The last he found unmarketable; the pipe, I think, he made merchandise of, but somehow his provender for the day's journey consisted in one bath bun, which he could not finish.

These trivial tales illustrate a period in his life and adventures which I only know by rumour. Our own acquaintance was, to a great degree, literary and bookish. Perhaps it began "with a slight aversion," but it seemed, like madeira, to be ripened and improved by his long sea voyage; and the news of his death taught me, at least, the true nature of the affection which he was destined to win.

28

Indeed, our acquaintance was like the friendship of a wild singing bird and of a punctual, domesticated barn-door fowl, laying its daily "article" for the breakfast-table of the citizens. He often wrote to me from Samoa, sometimes with news of native manners and folklore. He sent me a devil-box, the "luck" of some strange island, which he bought at a great price. After parting with its "luck," or fetish (a shell in a curious wooden box), the island was unfortunate, and was ravaged by measles.

I occasionally sent out books needed for Mr. Stevenson's studies, of which more will be said. But I must make it plain that, in the body, we met but rarely. His really intimate friends were Mr. Colvin and Mr. Baxter (who managed the practical side of his literary business between them); Mr. Henley (in partnership with whom he wrote several plays); his cousin, Mr. R. A. M. Stevenson; and, among other literati, Mr. Gosse, Mr. Austin Dobson, Mr. Saintsbury, Mr Walter Pollock, knew him well. The best portrait of Mr. Stevenson that I know is by Sir. W. B. Richmond, R.A., and is in that gentleman's collection of contemporaries, with the effigies of Mr. Holman Hunt, Mr. William Morris, Mr. Browning, and others. It is unfinished, owing to an illness which stopped the sittings, and does not show the subject at his best, physically speaking. There is also a brilliant, slight sketch, almost a caricature, by Mr. Sargent. It represents Mr. Stevenson walking about the room in conversation.

The people I have named, or some of them, knew Mr. Stevenson more intimately than I can boast of doing. Unlike each other, opposites in a dozen ways, we always were united by the love of letters, and of Scotland, our dear country. He was a patriot, yet he spoke his mind quite freely about Burns, about that apparent want of heart in the poet's amours, which our countrymen do not care to hear mentioned. Well, perhaps, for some reasons, it had to be mentioned once, and so no more of it.

Mr. Stevenson possessed, more than any man I ever met, the power of making other men fall in love with him. I mean that he excited a passionate admiration and affection, so much so that I verily believe some men were jealous of other men's place in his liking. I once met a stranger who, having become acquainted with him, spoke of him with a touching fondness and pride, his fancy reposing, as it seemed, in a fond contemplation of so much genius and charm. What was so taking in him? and how is one to analyse that dazzling surface of pleasantry, that changeful shining humour, wit, wisdom, recklessness; beneath which beat the most kind and tolerant of hearts?

People were fond of him, and people were proud of him: his

achievements, as it were, sensibly raised their pleasure in the world, and, to them, became parts of themselves. They warmed their hands at that centre of light and heat. It is not every success which has these beneficent results. We see the successful sneered at, decried, insulted, even when success is deserved. Very little of all this, hardly aught of all this, I think, came in Mr. Stevenson's way. After the beginning (when the praises of his earliest admirers were irritating to dull scribes) he found the critics fairly kind, I believe, and often enthusiastic. He was so much his own severest critic that he probably paid little heed to professional reviewers. In addition to his "Rathillet," and other MSS. which he destroyed, he once, in the Highlands, long ago, lost a portmanteau with a batch of his writings. Alas, that he should have lost or burned anything! "King's chaff," says our country proverb, "is better than other folk's corn."

I have remembered very little, or very little that I can write, and about our last meeting, when he was so near death, in appearance, and so full of courage—how can I speak? His courage was a strong rock, not to be taken or subdued. When unable to utter a single word, his pencilled remarks to his attendants were pithy and extremely characteristic. This courage and spiritual vitality made one hope that he would, if he desired it, live as long as Voltaire, that reed among oaks. There were of course, in so rare a combination of characteristics, some which were not equally to the liking of all. He was highly original in costume, but, as his photographs are familiar, the point does not need elucidation. Life was a drama to him, and he delighted, like his own British admirals, to do things with a certain air. He observed himself, I used to think, as he observed others, and "saw himself" in every part he played. There was nothing of the cabotin in this self-consciousness; it was the unextinguished childish passion for "playing at things" which remained with him. I have a theory that all children possess genius, and that it dies out in the generality of mortals, abiding only with people whose genius the world is forced to recognise. Mr. Stevenson illustrates, and perhaps partly suggested, this private philosophy of mine.

I have said very little; I have no skill in reminiscences, no art to bring the living aspect of the man before those who never knew him. I faintly seem to see the eager face, the light nervous figure, the fingers busy with rolling cigarettes; Mr. Stevenson talking, listening, often rising from his seat, standing, walking to and fro, always full of vivid intelligence, wearing a mysterious smile. I remember one pleasant dark afternoon, when he told me many tales of strange adventures, narratives which he had heard about a murderous lonely inn, somewhere in the States. He was as good to hear as to read. I do not recollect much of that delight in discussion, in controversy, which he shows in his essay on conversation, where he describes, I believe, Mr. Henley as "Burley," and Mr. Symonds as "Opalstein." He had great pleasure in the talk of the late Professor Fleeming Jenkin, which was both various and copious. But in these noctes coenaeque deum I was never a partaker. In many topics, such as angling, golf, cricket, whereon I am willingly diffuse, Mr. Stevenson took no interest. He was very fond of boating and sailing in every kind; he hazarded his health by long expeditions among the fairy isles of ocean, but he "was not a British sportsman," though for his measure of strength a good pedestrian, a friend of the open air, and of all who live and toil therein.

As to his literary likings, they appear in his own confessions. He revelled in Dickens, but, about Thackeray—well, I would rather have talked to somebody else! To my amazement, he was of those (I think) who find Thackeray "cynical." "He takes you into a garden, and then pelts you with"—horrid things! Mr. Stevenson, on the other hand, had a free admiration of Mr. George Meredith. He did not so easily forgive the longueus and lazinesses of Scott, as a Scot should do. He read French much; Greek only in translations.

Literature was, of course, his first love, but he was actually an advocate at the Scottish Bar, and, as such, had his name on a brazen door-plate. Once he was a competitor for a Chair of Modern History in Edinburgh University; he knew the romantic side of Scottish history very well. In his novel, "Catriona," the character of James Mohr Macgregor is wonderfully divined. Once I read some unpublished letters of Catriona's unworthy father, written when he was selling himself as a spy (and lying as he spied) to the Hanoverian usurper. Mr. Stevenson might have written these letters for James Mohr; they might be extracts from "Catriona."

In turning over old Jacobite pamphlets, I found a forgotten romance of Prince Charles's hidden years, and longed that Mr. Stevenson should retell it. There was a treasure, an authentic treasure; there were real spies, a real assassin; a real, or reported, rescue of a lovely girl from a fire at Strasbourg, by the Prince. The tale was to begin sur le pont d'Avignon: a young Scotch exile watching the Rhone, thinking how much of it he could cover with a salmon fly, thinking of the Tay or Beauly. To him enter another shady tramping exile, Blairthwaite, a murderer. And so it was to

31

run on, as the author's fancy might lead him, with Alan Breck and the Master for characters. At last, in unpublished MSS. I found an actual Master of Ballantrae, a Highland chief—noble, majestically handsome—and a paid spy of England! All these papers I sent out to Samoa, too late. The novel was to have been dedicated to me, and that chance of immortality is gone, with so much else.

Mr. Stevenson's last letters to myself were full of his concern for a common friend of ours, who was very ill. Depressed himself, Mr. Stevenson wrote to this gentleman—why should I not mention Mr. James Payn?—with consoling gaiety. I attributed his depression to any cause but his own health, of which he rarely spoke. He lamented the "ill-staged fifth act of life"; he, at least, had no long hopeless years of diminished force to bear.

I have known no man in whom the pre-eminently manly virtues of kindness, courage, sympathy, generosity, helpfulness, were more beautifully conspicuous than in Mr. Stevenson, no man so much loved—it is not too strong a word—by so many and such various people. He was as unique in character as in literary genius.

CHAPTER III

RAB'S FRIEND

To say what ought to be said concerning Dr. John Brown, a man should have known him well and long, and should remember much of that old generation of Scotchmen to whom the author of "Rab and his Friends" belonged. But that generation has departed. One by one these wits and scholars of the North, these epigoni who were not, indeed, of the heroes, but who had seen and remembered Scott and Wilson, have passed away. Aytoun and Carlyle and Dr. Burton, and last, Dr. Brown, are gone. Sir Theodore Martin alone is left. In her memoir of Dr. Burton—the historian of Scotland, and author of "The Book-hunter"—Mrs. Burton remarks that, in her husband's later days, only Dr. John Brown and Professor Blackie remained of all her husband's ancient friends and coevals, of all who remembered Lockhart, and Hogg, and their times. But many are left who knew Dr. Brown far better and more intimately than the author of this notice. I can hardly say when I first became acquainted with him, probably it was in my childhood. Ever since I was a boy, certainly, I used to see him at intervals, especially in the Christmas vacations. But he seldom moved from Edinburgh, except in summer, which he frequently passed in the country house of certain friends of his, whose affection made much of the happiness of his latest years, and whose unfailing kindness attended him in his dying hours. Living always in Scotland, Dr. Brown was seen but rarely by his friends who resided in England. Thus, though Dr. Brown's sweetness of disposition and charm of manner, his humour, and his unfailing sympathy and encouragement, made one feel toward him as to a familiar friend, yet, of his actual life I saw but little, and have few reminiscences to contribute. One can only speak of that singular geniality of his, that temper of goodness and natural tolerance and affection, which, as Scotsmen best know, is not universal among the Scots. Our race does not need to pray, like the mechanic in the story, that Providence will give us "a good conceit of ourselves." But we must acknowledge that the Scotch temper is critical if not captious, argumentative, inclined to look at the seamy side of men and of their performances, and to dwell on imperfections rather than on merits and virtues. An example of these blemishes of the Scotch disposition, carried to an extreme degree in the nature of a man of genius, is offered to the world in the writings and "Reminiscences" of Mr. Carlyle.

33

Now, Dr. John Brown was at the opposite pole of feeling. He had no mawkish toleration of things and people intolerable, but he preferred not to turn his mind that way. His thoughts were with the good, the wise, the modest, the learned, the brave of times past, and he was eager to catch a reflection of their qualities in the characters of the living, of all with whom he came into contact. He was, for example, almost optimistic in his estimate of the work of young people in art or literature. From everything that was beautiful or good, from a summer day by the Tweed, or from the eyes of a child, or from the humorous saying of a friend, or from treasured memories of old Scotch worthies, from recollections of his own childhood, from experience of the stoical heroism of the poor, he seemed to extract matter for pleasant thoughts of men and the world, and nourishment for his own great and gentle nature. I have never known any man to whom other men seemed so dear—men dead, and men living. He gave his genius to knowing them, and to making them better known, and his unselfishness thus became not only a great personal virtue, but a great literary charm. When you met him, he had some "good story" or some story of goodness to tell—for both came alike to him, and his humour was as unfailing as his kindness. There was in his face a singular charm, blended, as it were, of the expressions of mirth and of patience. Being most sensitive to pain, as well as to pleasure, he was an exception to that rule of Rochefoucauld's—"nous avons tous assez de force pour supporter les maux d'autrui."[2]

He did not bear easily the misfortunes of others, and the evils of his own lot were heavy enough. They saddened him; but neither illness, nor his poignant anxiety for others, could sour a nature so unselfish. He appeared not to have lost that anodyne and consolation of religious hope, which had been the strength of his forefathers, and was his best inheritance from a remarkable race of Scotsmen. Wherever he came, he was welcome; people felt glad when they had encountered him in the streets—the streets of Edinburgh, where almost every one knows every one by sight—and he was at least as joyously received by the children and the dogs as by the grown-up people of every family. A friend has kindly shown me a letter in which it is told how Dr. Brown's love of dogs, his interest in a half-blind old Dandy which was attached to him, was evinced in the very last hours of his life. But enough has been said, in general terms, about the character of "the beloved physician," as Dr. Brown was called in Edinburgh, and a brief account may be given, in some detail, of his life and ways.

---

[2] It is easy to bear the misfortunes of others.

Dr. John Brown was born in Biggar, one of the gray, slaty-looking little towns in the pastoral moorlands of southern Scotland. These towns have no great beauty that they should be admired by strangers, but the natives, as Scott said to Washington Irving, are attached to their "gray hills," and to the Tweed, so beautiful where man's greed does not pollute it, that the Border people are all in love with it, as Tyro, in Homer, loved the divine Enipeus. We hold it "far the fairest of the floods that run upon the earth." How dear the border scenery was to Dr. John Brown, and how well he knew and could express its legendary magic, its charm woven of countless ancient spells, the music of old ballads, the sorcery of old stories, may be understood by readers of his essay on "Minchmoor."[3] The father of Dr. Brown was the third in a lineage of ministers of the sect called Seceders. To explain who the Seceders were, it would be necessary to explore the sinking morasses of Scotch ecclesiastical history. The minister was proud of being not only a "Seceder" but a "Burgher." He inherited, to be brief, the traditions of a most spiritually-minded and most spirited set of men, too much bent, it may appear to us, on establishing delicate distinctions of opinions, but certainly most true to themselves and to their own ideals of liberty and of faith. Dr. Brown's great-grandfather had been a shepherd boy, who taught himself Greek that he might read the New Testament; who walked twenty-four miles—leaving his folded sheep in the night—to buy the precious volume in St. Andrews, and who, finally, became a teacher of much repute among his own people. Of Dr. Brown's father, he himself wrote a most touching and beautiful account in his "Letter to John Cairns, D.D." This essay contains, perhaps, the very finest passages that the author ever penned. His sayings about his own childhood remind one of the manner of Lamb, without that curious fantastic touch which is of the essence of Lamb's style. The following lines, for example, are a revelation of childish psychology, and probably may be applied, with almost as much truth, to the childhood of our race:—

> "Children are long of seeing, or at least of looking at what is above them; they like the ground, and its flowers and stones, its 'red sodgers' and lady-birds, and all its queer things; their world is about three feet high, and they are more often stooping than gazing up. I know I was past ten before I saw, or cared to see, the ceilings of the rooms in the manse at Biggar."

I have often thought that the earliest fathers of our race, child-like in so many ways, were child-like in this, and worshipped, not

---

[3] In the third volume of his essays.

the phenomena of the heavens, but objects more on a level with their eyes—the "queer things" of their low-lying world. In this essay on his father, Dr. Brown has written lines about a child's first knowledge of death, which seem as noteworthy as Steele's famous passage about his father's death and his own half-conscious grief and anger. Dr. Brown describes a Scottish funeral—the funeral of his own mother—as he saw it with the eyes of a boy of five years old, while his younger brother, a baby of a few months—

> "leaped up and crowed with joy at the strange sight—the crowding horsemen, the coaches, and the nodding plumes of the hearse . . . Then, to my surprise and alarm, the coffin, resting on its bearers, was placed over the dark hole, and I watched with curious eye the unrolling of those neat black bunches of cords, which I have often enough seen since. My father took the one at the head, and also another much smaller, springing from the same point as his, which he had caused to be placed there, and unrolling it, put it into my hand. I twisted it firmly round my fingers, and awaited the result; the burial men with their real ropes lowered the coffin, and when it rested at the bottom it was too far down for me to see it. The grave was made very deep, as he used afterwards to tell us, that it might hold us all. My father first and abruptly let his cord drop, followed by the rest. This was too much. I now saw what was meant, and held on and fixed my fist and feet, and I believe my father had some difficulty in forcing open my small fingers; he let the little black cord drop, and I remember, in my misery and anger, seeing its open end disappearing in the gloom."[4]

The man who wrote this, and many another passage as true and tender, might surely have been famous in fiction, if he had turned his powers that way. He had imagination, humour, pathos; he was always studying and observing life; his last volume, especially, is like a collection of fragments that might have gone toward making a work, in some ways not inferior to the romances of Scott. When the third volume of Essays was published, in the spring of his last year, a reviewer, who apparently had no personal knowledge of Dr. Brown, asked why he did not write a novel. He was by that time over seventy years of age, and, though none

---

[4] "I remember I went into the room where my father's body lay, and my mother sat weeping alone by it. I had my battledore in my hand, and fell a-beating the coffin and calling 'Papa,' for I know not how, I had some slight idea that he was locked up there."—STEELE, The Tatler, June 6, 1710.

guessed it, within a few weeks of his death. What he might have done, had he given himself to literature only, it is impossible to guess. But he caused so much happiness, and did so much good, in that gentle profession of healing which he chose, and which brought him near to many who needed consolation more than physic, that we need not forget his deliberate choice. Literature had only his horae subsecivae, as he said: Subseciva quaedam tempora quae ego perire non patior, as Cicero writes, "shreds and waste ends of time, which I suffer not to be lost."

The kind of life which Dr. Brown's father and his people lived at Biggar, the austere life of work, and of thought intensely bent on the real aim of existence, on God, on the destiny of the soul, is perhaps rare now, even in rural Scotland. We are less obedient than of old to the motto of that ring found on Magus Moor, where Archbishop Shairp was murdered, Remember upon Dethe. If any reader has not yet made the acquaintance of Dr. Brown's works, one might counsel him to begin with the "Letter to John Cairns, D.D.," the fragment of biography and autobiography, the description of the fountainheads from which the genius of the author flowed. In his early boyhood, John Brown was educated by his father, a man who, from his son's affectionate description, seems to have confined a fiery and romantic genius within the channels of Seceder and Burgher theology. When the father received a call to the "Rose Street Secession Church," in Edinburgh, the son became a pupil of that ancient Scottish seminary, the High School—the school where Scott was taught not much Latin and no Greek worth mentioning. Scott was still alive and strong in those days, and Dr. Brown describes how he and his school companions would take off their hats to the Shirra as he passed in the streets.

"Though lame, he was nimble, and all rough and alive with power; had you met him anywhere else, you would say he was a Liddesdale store farmer, come of gentle blood—'a stout, blunt carle,' as he says of himself, with the swing and stride and the eye of a man of the hills—a large, sunny, out-of-door air all about him. On his broad and stooping shoulders was set that head which, with Shakespeare's and Bonaparte's, is the best known in all the world." Scott was then living in 39 Castle Street. I do not know whether the many pilgrims, whom one meets moving constantly in the direction of Melrose and Abbotsford, have thought of making pilgrimage to Castle Street, and to the grave, there, of Scott's "dear old friend,"— his dog Camp. Of Dr. Brown's schoolboy days, one knows little— days when "Bob Ainslie and I were coming up Infirmary Street from the High School, our heads together, and our arms intertwisted, as only lovers and boys know how or why." Concerning the doctor's character, he has left it on record that he liked a dog-fight. "'A dog-fight,' shouted Bob, and was off, and so was I, both of us all hot, praying that it might not be over before we were up . . . Dogs like fighting; old Isaac (Watts, not Walton) says they 'delight' in it, and for the best of all reasons; and boys are not cruel because they like to see the fight. This is a very different thing from a love of making dogs fight." And this was the most famous of all dog-fights—since the old Irish Brehons settled the laws of that sport, and gravely decided what was to be done if a child interfered, or an idiot, or a woman, or a one-eyed man—for this was the dog-fight in which Rab first was introduced to his historian.

Six years passed after this battle, and Dr. Brown was a medical student and a clerk at Minto Hospital. How he renewed his acquaintance there, and in what sad circumstances, with Rab and his friends, it is superfluous to tell, for every one who reads at all has read that story, and most readers not without tears. As a medical student in Edinburgh, Dr. Brown made the friendship of Mr. Syme, the famous surgeon—a friendship only closed by death. I only saw them once together, a very long time ago, and then from the point of view of a patient. These occasions are not agreeable, and patients, like the old cock which did not crow when plucked, are apt to be "very much absorbed"; but Dr. Brown's attitude toward the man whom he regarded with the reverence of a disciple, as well as with the affection of a friend, was very remarkable.

When his studies were over, Dr. Brown practised for a year as assistant to a surgeon in Chatham. It must have been when he was at Chatham that a curious event occurred. Many years later, Charles Dickens was in Edinburgh, reading his stories in public, and was dining with some Edinburgh people. Dickens began to speak about the panic which the cholera had caused in England: how ill some people had behaved. As a contrast, he mentioned that, at Chatham, one poor woman had died, deserted by every one except a young physician. Some one, however, ventured to open the door, and found the woman dead, and the young doctor asleep, overcome with the fatigue that mastered him on his patient's death, but quite untouched by the general panic. "Why, that was Dr. John Brown," one of the guests observed; and it seems that, thus early in his career, the doctor had been setting an example of the courage and charity of his profession. After a year spent in Chatham, he returned to Edinburgh, where he spent the rest of his life, busy partly with his art of healing, partly with literature. He lived in Rutland Street, near the railway station, by which Edinburgh is approached from the west, and close to Princes Street, the chief street of the town, separated by a green valley, once a loch, from the high Castle Rock. It was the room in which his friends were accustomed to see Dr. Brown, and a room full of interest it was. In his long life, the doctor had gathered round him many curious relics of artists and men of letters; a drawing of a dog by Turner I remember particularly, and a copy of "Don Juan," in the first edition, with Byron's manuscript notes. Dr. Brown had a great love and knowledge of art and of artists, from Turner to Leech; and he had very many friends among men of letters, such as Mr. Ruskin and Mr. Thackeray. Dr. Brown himself was a clever designer of rapid little grotesques, rough sketches of dogs and men. One or two of them are engraved in the little paper-covered booklets in which some of his essays were separately published—booklets which he was used to present to people who came to see him and who were interested in all that he did. I remember some vivacious grotesques which he drew for one of my brothers when we were schoolboys. These little things were carefully treasured by boys who knew Dr. Brown, and found him friendly, and capable of sustaining a conversation on the points of a Dandy Dinmont terrier and other mysteries important to youth. He was a bibliophile—a taste which he inherited from his father, who "began collecting books when he was twelve, and was collecting to his last hours."

The last time I ever saw Dr. Brown, a year before his death, he was kind enough to lend me one of the rarest of his treasures, "Poems," by Mr. Ruskin. Probably Mr. Ruskin had presented the book to his old friend; in no other way were it easy to procure writings which the author withdrew from publication, if, indeed, they ever were, properly speaking, published. Thus Dr. Brown was all things to all men, and to all boys. He "had a word for every one," as poor people say, and a word to the point, for he was as much at home with the shepherd on the hills, or with the angler between Hollylea and Clovenfords, as with the dusty book-hunter, or the doggy young Border yeoman, or the child who asked him to "draw her a picture," or the friend of genius famous through all the world, Thackeray, when he "spoke, as he seldom did, of divine things."

Three volumes of essays are all that Dr. Brown has left in the way of compositions: a light, but imperishable literary baggage. His studies are usually derived from personal experience, which he reproduced with singular geniality and simplicity, or they are drawn from the tradition of the elders, the reminiscences of long-lived Scotch people, who, themselves, had listened attentively to those who went before them. Since Scott, these ancient ladies with wonderful memories have had no such attentive listener or appreciative reporter as Dr. Brown. His paper called "Mystifications," a narrative of the pranks of Miss Stirling Graham,

39

is a brief, vivid record of the clever and quaint society of Scotland sixty years ago. Scotland, or at least Scottish society, is now only English society—a little narrower, a little prouder, sometimes even a little duller. But old people of position spoke the old Scotch tongue sixty years ago, and were full of wonderful genealogies, full of reminiscences of the "'45," and the adventures of the Jacobites. The very last echoes of that ancient world are dying now from memory, like the wide reverberations of that gun which Miss Nelly MacWilliam heard on the day when Prince Charles landed, and which resounded strangely all through Scotland.

The children of this generation, one fears, will hardly hear of these old raids and duels, risings and rebellions, by oral tradition handed down, unbroken, through aunts and grandmothers. Scott reaped a full, late harvest of the memories of clannish and feudal Scotland; Dr. Brown came as a later gleaner, and gathered these stirring tales of "A Jacobite Family" which are published in the last volume of his essays. When he was an observer, not a hearer only, Dr. Brown chiefly studied and best wrote of the following topics: passages and characters of humour and pathos which he encountered in his life and profession; children, dogs, Border scenery, and fellow-workers in life and science. Under one or other of these categories all his best compositions might be arranged. The most famous and most exquisite of all his works in the first class is the unrivalled "Rab and his Friends"—a study of the stoicism and tenderness of the Lowland character worthy of Scott. In a minor way the little paper on "Jeems," the door-keeper in a Dissenting house of the Lord, is interesting to Scotch people, though it must seem a rather curious revelation to all others. "Her last Half-crown" is another study of the honesty that survived in a starving and outcast Scotch girl, when all other virtues, as we commonly reckon virtue, had gone before her character to some place where, let us hope, they may rejoin her; for if we are to suffer for the vices which have abandoned us, may we not get some credit for the virtues that we have abandoned, but that once were ours, in some heaven paved with bad resolutions unfulfilled? "The Black Dwarf's Bones" is a sketch of the misshapen creature from whom Scott borrowed the character that gives a name to one of his minor Border stories. The real Black Dwarf (David Ritchie he was called among men) was fond of poetry, but hated Burns. He was polite to the fair, but classed mankind at large with his favourite aversions: ghosts, fairies, and robbers. There was this of human about the Black Dwarf, that "he hated folk that are aye gaun to dee, and never do't." The village beauties were wont to come to him for a Judgment of Paris on their charms, and he presented each with a flower, which was of a fixed value in his standard of things beautiful. One kind of rose, the prize of the most fair, he only gave thrice. Paris could not have done his dooms more courteously, and, if he had but made judicious use of rose, lily, and lotus, as prizes, he might have pleased all the three Goddesses; Troy still might be standing, and the lofty house of King Priam.

Among Dr. Brown's papers on children, that called "Pet Marjorie" holds the highest place. Perhaps certain passages are "wrote too sentimentally," as Marjorie Fleming herself remarked about the practice of many authors. But it was difficult to be perfectly composed when speaking of this wonderful fairy-like little girl, whose affection was as warm as her humour and genius were precocious. "Infant phenomena" are seldom agreeable, but Marjorie was so humorous, so quick-tempered, so kind, that we cease to regard her as an intellectual "phenomenon." Her memory remains sweet and blossoming in its dust, like that of little Penelope Boothby, the child in the mob cap whom Sir Joshua painted, and who died very soon after she was thus made Immortal.

It is superfluous to quote from the essay on Marjorie Fleming; every one knows about her and her studies: "Isabella is teaching me to make simme colings, nots of interrigations, peorids, commoes, &c." Here is a Shakespearian criticism, of which few will deny the correctness: "'Macbeth' is a pretty composition, but awful one." Again, "I never read sermons of any kind, but I read novelettes and my Bible." "'Tom Jones' and Gray's 'Elegy in a Country Churchyard' are both excellent, and much spoke of by both sex, particularly by the men." Her Calvinistic belief in "unquestionable fire and brimston" is unhesitating, but the young theologian appears to have substituted "unquestionable" for "unquenchable." There is something humorous in the alteration, as if Marjorie refused to be put off with an "excellent family substitute" for fire and brimstone, and demanded the "unquestionable" article, no other being genuine, please observe trade mark.

Among Dr. Brown's contributions to the humorous study of dogs, "Rab," of course, holds the same place as Marjorie among his sketches of children. But if his "Queen Mary's Child Garden," the description of the little garden in which Mary Stuart did not play when a child, is second to "Marjorie," so "Our Dogs" is a good second to "Rab." Perhaps Dr. Brown never wrote anything more mirthful than his description of the sudden birth of the virtue of courage in Toby, a comic but cowardly mongrel, a cur of low degree.

"Toby was in the way of hiding his culinary bones in the small gardens before his own and the neighbouring doors. Mr. Scrymgeour, two doors off, a bulky, choleric,

41

red-faced man—torvo vultu—was, by law of contrast, a great cultivator of flowers, and he had often scowled Toby into all but non-existence by a stamp of his foot and a glare of his eye. One day, his gate being open, in walks Toby with a huge bone, and making a hole where Scrymgeour had two minutes before been planting some precious slip, the name of which on paper and on a stick Toby made very light of, substituted his bone, and was engaged covering it, or thinking he was covering it up with his shovelling nose, when S. spied him through the inner glass door, and was out upon him, like the Assyrian, with a terrific gowl. I watched them. Instantly Toby made at him with a roar too, and an eye more torve than Scrymgeour's, who, retreating without reserve, fell prostrate, there is reason to believe, in his own lobby. Toby contented himself with proclaiming his victory at the door, and, returning, finished his bone-planting at his leisure; the enemy, who had scuttled behind the glass door, glared at him. From this moment Toby was an altered dog. Pluck at first sight was lord of all . . . That very evening he paid a visit to Leo, next door's dog, a big tyrannical bully and coward . . . To him Toby paid a visit that very evening, down into his den, and walked about, as much as to say, 'Come on, Macduff'; but Macduff did not come on."

This story is one of the most amazing examples of instant change of character on record, and disproves the sceptical remark that "no one was ever converted, except prize-fighters, and colonels in the army." I am sorry to say that Dr. Brown was too fond of dogs to be very much attached to cats. I never heard him say anything against cats, or, indeed, against anybody; but there are passages in his writings which tend to show that, when young and thoughtless, he was not far from regarding cats as "the higher vermin." He tells a story of a Ghazi puss, so to speak, a victorious cat, which, entrenched in a drain, defeated three dogs with severe loss, and finally escaped unharmed from her enemies. Dr. Brown's family gloried in the possession of a Dandy Dinmont named John Pym, whose cousin (Auld Pepper) belonged to one of my brothers. Dr. Brown was much interested in Pepper, a dog whose family pride was only matched by that of the mother of Candide, and, at one time, threatened to result in the extinction of this branch of the House of Pepper. Dr. Brown had remarked, and my own observations confirm it, that when a Dandy is not game, his apparent lack of courage arises "from kindness of heart."

Among Dr. Brown's landscapes, as one may call his

descriptions of scenery, and of the ancient historical associations with Scotch scenery, "Minchmoor" is the most important. He had always been a great lover of the Tweed. The walk which he commemorates in "Minchmoor" was taken, if I am not mistaken, in company with Principal Shairp, Professor of Poetry in the University of Oxford, and author of one of the most beautiful of Tweedside songs, a modern "Bush aboon Traquair:"—

> "And what saw ye there,
> At the bush aboon Traquair;
> Or what did ye hear that was worth your heed?
> I heard the cushie croon
> Thro' the gowden afternoon,
> And the Quair burn singing doon to the vale o' Tweed."

There is in the country of Scott no pleasanter walk than that which Dr. Brown took in the summer afternoon. Within a few miles, many places famous in history and ballad may be visited: the road by which Montrose's men fled from Philiphaugh fight; Traquair House, with the bears on its gates, as on the portals of the Baron of Bradwardine; Williamhope, where Scott and Mungo Park, the African explorer, parted and went their several ways. From the crest of the road you see all the Border hills, the Maiden Paps, the Eildons cloven in three, the Dunion, the Windburg, and so to the distant Cheviots, and Smailholm Tower, where Scott lay when a child, and clapped his hands at the flashes of the lightning, haud sine Dis animosus infans, like Horace.

From the crest of the hill you follow Dr. Brown into the valley of Yarrow, and the deep black pools, now called the "dowie dens," and so, "through the pomp of cultivated nature," as Wordsworth says, to the railway at Selkirk, passing the plain where Janet won back Tamlane from the queen of the fairies. All this country was familiar to Dr. Brown, and on one of the last occasions when I met him, he was living at Hollylea, on the Tweed, just above Ashestiel, Scott's home while he was happy and prosperous, before he had the unhappy thought of building Abbotsford. At the time I speak of, Dr. Brown had long ceased to write, and his health suffered from attacks of melancholy, in which the world seemed very dark to him. I have been allowed to read some letters which he wrote in one of these intervals of depression. With his habitual unselfishness, he kept his melancholy to himself, and, though he did not care for society at such times, he said nothing of his own condition that could distress his correspondent. In the last year of his life, everything around him seemed to brighten: he was unusually well, he even returned to his literary work, and saw his last volume of collected essays through the press. They were most favourably received, and the last letters which I had from him spoke of the pleasure which this success gave him. Three editions of his book ("John Leech, and Other Essays") were published in some six weeks. All seemed to go well, and one might even have hoped that, with renewed strength, he would take up his pen again. But his strength was less than we had hoped. A cold settled on his lungs, and, in spite of the most affectionate nursing, he grew rapidly weaker. He had little suffering at the end, and his mind remained unclouded. No man of letters could be more widely regretted, for he was the friend of all who read his books, as, even to people who only met him once or twice in life, he seemed to become dear and familiar.

In one of his very latest writings, "On Thackeray's Death," Dr. Brown told people (what some of them needed, and still need to be told) how good, kind, and thoughtful for others was our great writer—our greatest master of fiction, I venture to think, since Scott. Some of the lines Dr. Brown wrote of Thackerary might be applied to himself: "He looked always fresh, with that abounding silvery hair, and his young, almost infantile face"—a face very pale, and yet radiant, in his last years, and mildly lit up with eyes full of kindness, and softened by sorrow. In his last year, Mr. Swinburne wrote to Dr. Brown this sonnet, in which there seems something of the poet's prophetic gift, and a voice sounds as of a welcome home:—

"Beyond the north wind lay the land of old,
　　Where men dwelt blithe and blameless, clothed and fed
　　With joy's bright raiment, and with love's sweet bread,—
The whitest flock of earth's maternal fold,
None there might wear about his brows enrolled
　　A light of lovelier fame than rings your head,
　　Whose lovesome love of children and the dead
All men give thanks for; I, far off, behold
　　A dear dead hand that links us, and a light
　　The blithest and benignest of the night,—
　　　The night of death's sweet sleep, wherein may be
A star to show your spirit in present sight
　　Some happier isle in the Elysian sea
　　Where Rab may lick the hand of Marjorie."

CHAPTER IV

OLIVER WENDELL HOLMES

Never but once did I enjoy the privilege of meeting the author of "Elsie Venner"—Oliver Wendell Holmes. It was at a dinner given by Mr. Lowell, and of conversation with Dr. Holmes I had very little. He struck me as being wonderfully erect, active, and vivacious for his great age. He spoke (perhaps I should not chronicle this impression)—he spoke much, and freely, but rather as if he were wound up to speak, so to say—wound up, I mean, by a sense of duty to himself and kindness to strangers, who were naturally curious about so well-known a man. In his aspect there was a certain dryness, and, altogether, his vivacity, his ceaselessness, and a kind of equability of tone in his voice, reminded me of what Homer says concerning the old men around Priam, above the gate of Troy, how they "chirped like cicalas on a summer day." About the matter of his talk I remember nothing, only the manner remains with me, and mine may have been a false impression, or the manner may have been accidental, and of the moment: or, again, a manner appropriate for conversation with strangers, each coming up one after the other, to view respectfully so great a lion. Among his friends and intimates he was probably a different man, with a tone other and more reposeful.

He had a long, weary task before him, then, to talk his way, ever courteous, alert, attentive, through part of a London season. Yet, when it was all over, he seems to have enjoyed it, being a man who took pleasure in most sorts of experience. He did not affect me, for that one time, with such a sense of pleasure as Mr. Lowell did—Mr. Lowell, whom I knew so much better, and who was so big, strong, humorous, kind, learned, friendly, and delightfully natural.

Dr. Holmes, too, was a delightful companion, and I have merely tried to make a sort of photographic "snap-shot" at him, in a single casual moment, one of myriads of such moments. Turning to Dr. Holmes's popular, as distinct from his professional writings, one is reminded, as one often is, of the change which seems to come over some books as the reader grows older. Many books are to one now what they always were; some, like the Waverley novels and Shakespeare, grow better on every fresh reading. There are books which filled me, in boyhood or in youth, with a sort of admiring rapture, and a delighted wonder at their novelty, their strangeness,

45

freshness, greatness. Thus Homer, and the best novels of Thackeray, and of Fielding, the plays of Molière and Shakespeare, the poems of—well, of all the real poets, moved this astonishment of admiration, and being read again, they move it still. On a different level, one may say as much about books so unlike each other, as those of Poe and of Sir Thomas Browne, of Swift and of Charles Lamb.

There are, again, other books which caused this happy emotion of wonder, when first perused, long since, but which do so no longer. I am not much surprised to find Charles Kingsley's novels among them.

In the case of Dr. Holmes's books, I am very sensible of this disenchanting effect of time and experience. "The Professor at the Breakfast Table" and the novels came into my hands when I was very young, in "green, unknowing youth." They seemed extraordinary, new, fantasies of wisdom and wit; the reflections were such as surprised me by their depth, the illustrations dazzled by their novelty and brilliance. Probably they will still be as fortunate with young readers, and I am to be pitied, I hope, rather than blamed, if I cannot, like the wise thrush—

"Recapture
The first fine careless rapture."

By this time, of course, one understands many of the constituents of Dr. Holmes's genius, the social, historical, ancestral, and professional elements thereof. Now, it is the business of criticism to search out and illustrate these antecedents, and it seems a very odd and unlucky thing, that the results of this knowledge when acquired, should sometimes be a partial disenchantment. But we are not disenchanted at all by this kind of science, when the author whom we are examining is a great natural genius, like Shakespeare or Shelley, Keats or Scott. Such natures bring to the world far more than they receive, as far as our means of knowing what they receive are concerned. The wind of the spirit that is not of this earth, nor limited by time and space, breathes through their words, and thoughts, and deeds. They are not mere combinations, however deft and subtle, of known atoms. They must continually delight, and continually surprise; custom cannot stale them; like the heaven-born Laws in Sophocles, age can never lull them to sleep. Their works, when they are authors, never lose hold on our fancy and our interest.

46

As far as my own feelings and admiration can inform me, Dr. Holmes, though a most interesting and amiable and kindly man and writer, was not of this class. As an essayist, a delineator of men and morals, an unassuming philosopher, with a light, friendly wit, he certainly does not hold one as, for example, Addison does. The old Spectator makes me smile, pleases, tickles, diverts me now, even more than when I lay on the grass and read it by Tweedside, as a boy, when the trout were sluggish, in the early afternoon. It is only a personal fact that Dr. Holmes, read in the same old seasons, with so much pleasure and admiration and surprise, no longer affects me in the old way. Carlyle, on the other hand, in his "Frederick," which used to seem rather long, now entertains me far more than ever. But I am well aware that this is a mere subjective estimate; that Dr. Holmes may really be as great a genius as I was wont to think him, for criticism is only a part of our impressions. The opinion of mature experience, as a rule, ought to be sounder than that of youth; in this case I cannot but think that it is sounder.

Dr. Holmes was a New Englander, and born in what he calls "the Brahmin caste," the class which, in England, before the sailing of the May Flower, and ever since, had always been literary and highly educated. "I like books; I was born and bred among them," he says, "and have the easy feeling, when I get into their presence, that a stable-boy has among horses." He is fond of books, and, above all, of old books—strange, old medical works, for example—full of portents and prodigies, such as those of Wierus.

New England, owing to its famous college, Harvard, and its steady maintenance of the literary and learned tradition among the clergy, was, naturally, the home of the earliest great American school of writers. These men—Longfellow, Lowell, Ticknor, Prescott, Hawthorne, and so many others—had all received the same sort of education as Europeans of letters used to receive. They had not started as printers' devils, or newspaper reporters, or playwrights for the stage, but were academic. It does not matter much how a genius begins—as a rural butcher, or an apothecary, or a clerk of a Writer to the Signet. Still, the New Englanders were academic and classical. New England has, by this time, established a tradition of its literary origin and character. Her children are sons of the Puritans, with their independence, their narrowness, their appreciation of comfort, their hardiness in doing without it, their singular scruples of conscience, their sense of the awfulness of sin, their accessibility to superstition. We can read of the later New Englanders in the making, among the works of Cotton Mather, his father Increase Mather, and the witch-burning, periwig-hating, doctrinal Judge Sewall, who so manfully confessed and atoned for his mistake about the Salem witches. These men, or many of them, were deeply-learned Calvinists, according to the standard of their day, a day lasting from, say, the Restoration to 1730. Cotton Mather, in particular, is erudite, literary—nay, full of literary vanity—mystical, visionary, credulous to an amusing degree.

But he is really as British as Baxter, or his Scottish correspondent and counterpart, Wodrow. The sons or grandsons of these men gained the War of Independence. Of this they are naturally proud, and the circumstance is not infrequently mentioned in Dr. Holmes's works. Their democracy is not roaring modern democracy, but that of the cultivated middle classes. Their stern Calvinism slackened into many "isms," but left a kind of religiosity behind it. One of Dr. Holmes's mouthpieces sums up his whole creed in the two words Pater Noster. All these hereditary influences are consciously made conspicuous in Dr. Holmes's writings, as in Hawthorne's. In Hawthorne you see the old horror of sin, the old terror of conscience, the old dread of witchcraft, the old concern about conduct, converted into æsthetic sources of literary pleasure, of literary effects.

As a physician and a man of science, Dr. Holmes added abundant knowledge of the new sort; and apt, unexpected bits of science made popular, analogies and illustrations afforded by science are frequent in his works. Thus, in "Elsie Venner," and in "The Guardian Angel," "heredity" is his theme. He is always brooding over the thought that each of us is so much made up of earlier people, our ancestors, who bequeath to us so many disagreeable things—vice, madness, disease, emotions, tricks of gesture. No doubt these things are bequeathed, but all in such new proportions and relations, that each of us is himself and nobody else, and therefore had better make up his mind to be himself, and for himself responsible.

All this doctrine of heredity, still so dimly understood, Dr. Holmes derives from science. But, in passing through his mind, that of a New Englander conscious of New England's past, science takes a stain of romance and superstition. Elsie Venner, through an experience of her mother's, inherits the nature of the serpent, so the novel is as far from common life as the tale of "Mélusine," or any other echidna. The fantasy has its setting in a commonplace New England environment, and thus recalls a Hawthorne less subtle and concentrated, but much more humorous. The heroine of the "Guardian Angel," again, exposes a character in layers, as it were, each stratum of consciousness being inherited from a different ancestor—among others, a red Indian. She has many personalities, like the queer women we read about in French treatises on hysterics and nervous diseases. These stories are "fairy tales of science," by a man of science, who is also a humourist, and has a touch of the poet, and of the old fathers who were afraid of witches. The "blend" is singular enough, and not without its originality of fascination.

Though a man of science Dr. Holmes apparently took an imaginative pleasure in all shapes of superstition that he could muster. I must quote a passage from "The Professor at the Breakfast Table," as peculiarly illustrative of his method, and his ways of half accepting the abnormally romantic—accepting just enough for pleasure, like Sir Walter Scott. Connected with the extract is a curious anecdote.

"I think I am a little superstitious. There were two things, when I was a boy, that diabolised my imagination,—I mean, that gave me a distinct apprehension of a formidable bodily shape which prowled round the neighbourhood where I was born and bred. The first was a series of marks called the 'Devil's footsteps.' These were patches of sand in the pastures, where no grass grew, where even the low-bush blackberry, the 'dewberry,' as our Southern neighbours call it, in prettier and more Shakespearian language, did not spread its clinging creepers, where even the pale, dry, sadly-sweet 'everlasting' could not grow, but all was bare and blasted. The second was a mark in one of the public buildings near my home,—the college dormitory named after a Colonial Governor. I do not think many persons are aware of the existence of this mark,—little having been said about the story in print, as it was considered very desirable, for the sake of the Institution, to hush it up. In the north-west corner, and on the level of the third or fourth storey, there are signs of a breach in the walls, mended pretty well, but not to be mistaken. A considerable portion of that corner must have been carried away, from within outward. It was an unpleasant affair, and I do not care to repeat the particulars; but some young men had been using sacred things in a profane and unlawful way, when the occurrence, which was variously explained, took place. The story of the Appearance in the chamber was, I suppose, invented afterwards; but of the injury to the building there could be no question; and the zigzag line, where the mortar is a little thicker than before, is still distinctly visible.

"The queer burnt spots, called the 'Devil's footsteps,' had never attracted attention before this time, though there is no evidence that they had not existed previously, except that of the late Miss M., a 'Goody,' so called, who was positive on the subject, but had a strange horror of referring to an affair of which she was thought to know something . . . I tell you it was not so pleasant for a little boy of impressible nature to go up to bed in an old gambrel-roofed house, with untenanted locked upper chambers, and a most ghostly garret,—with 'Devil's footsteps' in the fields behind the house, and in front of it the patched dormitory, where the unexplained occurrence had taken place which startled those godless youths at their mock devotions, so that one of them was epileptic from that day forward, and another, after a dreadful season of mental conflict, took to religion, and became renowned for his ascetic sanctity."

It is a pity that Dr. Holmes does not give the whole story, instead of hinting at it, for a similar tale is told at Brazenose College, and elsewhere. Now take, along with Dr. Holmes's confession to a grain of superstition, this remark on, and explanation of, the curious coincidences which thrust themselves on the notice of most people.

"Excuse me,—I return to my story of the Commonstable. Young fellows being always hungry, and tea and dry toast being the meagre fare of the evening meal, it was a trick of some of the boys to impale a slice of meat upon a fork, at dinner-time, and stick the fork, holding it, beneath the table, so that they could get it at tea-time. The dragons that guarded this table of the Hesperides found out the trick at last, and kept a sharp look-out for missing forks;— they knew where to find one, if it was not in its place. Now the odd thing was, that, after waiting so many years to hear of this College trick, I should hear it mentioned a second time within the same twenty-four hours by a College youth of the present generation. Strange, but true. And so it has happened to me and to every person, often and often, to be hit in rapid succession by these twinned facts or thoughts, as if they were linked like chain-shot.

"I was going to leave the simple reader to wonder over this, taking it as an unexplained marvel. I think, however, I will turn over a furrow of subsoil in it. The explanation is, of course, that in a great many thoughts there must be a few coincidences, and these instantly arrest our attention. Now we shall probably never have the least idea of the enormous number of impressions which pass through our consciousness, until in some future life we see the photographic record of our thoughts and the stereoscopic picture of our actions.

"Now, my dear friends, who are putting your hands to your foreheads, and saying to yourselves that you feel a little confused, as if you had been waltzing until things began to whirl slightly round

50

you, is it possible that you do not clearly apprehend the exact connection of all I have been saying, and its bearing on what is now to come? Listen, then. The number of these living elements in our bodies illustrates the incalculable multitude of our thoughts; the number of our thoughts accounts for those frequent coincidences spoken of; these coincidences in the world of thought illustrate those which we constantly observe in the world of outward events."

Now for the anecdote—one of Mark Twain's.

Some years ago, Mark Twain published in Harper's Magazine an article on "Mental Telegraphy." He illustrated his meaning by a story of how he once wrote a long letter on a complicated subject, which had popped into his head between asleep and awake, to a friend on the other side of America. He did not send the letter, but, by return of post, received one from his friend. "Now, I'll tell you what he is going to say," said Mark Twain, read his own unsent epistle aloud, and then, opening his friend's despatch, proved that they were essentially identical. This is what he calls "Mental Telegraphy"; others call it "Telepathy," and the term is merely descriptive.

Now, on his own showing, in our second extract, Dr. Holmes should have explained coincidences like this as purely the work of chance, and I rather incline to think that he would have been right. But Mark Twain, in his article on "Mental Telegraphy," cites Dr. Holmes for a story of how he once, after dinner, as his letters came in, felt constrained to tell, à propos des bottes, the story of the last challenge to judicial combat in England (1817). He then opened a newspaper directed to him from England, the Sporting Times, and therein his eyes lighted on an account of this very affair—Abraham Thornton's challenge to battle when he was accused of murder, in 1817. According to Mark Twain, Dr. Holmes was disposed to accept "Mental Telegraphy" rather than mere chance as the cause of this coincidence. Yet the anecdote of the challenge seems to have been a favourite of his. It occurs in, "The Professor," in the fifth section. Perhaps he told it pretty frequently; probably that is why the printed version was sent to him; still, he was a little staggered by the coincidence. There was enough of Cotton Mather in the man of science to give him pause.

The form of Dr. Holmes's best known books, the set concerned with the breakfast-table and "Over the Teacups," is not very fortunate. Much conversation at breakfast is a weariness of the flesh. We want to eat what is necessary, and then to go about our work or play. If American citizens in a boarding-house could endure these long palavers, they must have been very unlike the hasty feeders caricatured in "Martin Chuzzlewit." Macaulay may have monologuised thus at his breakfast parties in the Albany; but breakfast parties are obsolete—an unregrettable parcel of things lost. The monologues, or dialogues, were published serially in the Atlantic Monthly, but they have had a vitality and a vogue far beyond those of the magazine causerie. Some of their popularity they may owe to the description of the other boarders, and to the kind of novel which connects the fortunes of these personages. But it is impossible for an Englishman to know whether these American types are exactly drawn or not. Their fortunes do not strongly interest one, though the "Sculpin"—the patriotic, deformed Bostonian, with his great-great-grandmother's ring (she was hanged for a witch)—is a very original and singular creation. The real interest lies in the wit, wisdom, and learning. The wit, now and then, seems to-day rather in the nature of a "goak." One might give examples, but to do so seems ill-natured and ungrateful.

There are some very perishable puns. The learning is not so recherché as it appeared when we knew nothing of Cotton Mather and Robert Calef, the author of a book against the persecution of witches. Calef, of course, was in the right, but I cannot forgive him for refusing to see a lady, known to Mr. Mather, who floated about in the air. That she did so was no good reason for hanging or burning a number of parishioners; but, did she float, and, if so, how? Mr. Calef said it would be a miracle, so he declined to view the performance. His logic was thin, though of a familiar description. Of all old things, at all events, Dr. Holmes was fond. He found America scarcely aired, new and raw, devoid of history and of associations. "The Tiber has a voice for me, as it whispers to the piers of the Pons Ælius, even more full of meaning than my well-beloved Charles, eddying round the piles of West Boston Bridge." No doubt this is a common sentiment among Americans.

Occasionally, like Hawthorne, they sigh for an historical atmosphere, and then, when they come to Europe and get it, they do not like it, and think Schenectady, New York, "a better place." It is not easy to understand what ailed Hawthorne with Europe; he was extremely caustic in his writings about that continent, and discontented. Our matrons were so stout and placid that they irritated him. Indeed, they are a little heavy in hand, still there are examples of agreeable slimness, even in this poor old country. Fond as he was of the historical past, Mr. Holmes remained loyal to the historical present. He was not one of those Americans who are always censuring England, and always hankering after her. He had none of that irritable feeling, which made a great contemporary of his angrily declare that he could endure to hear "Ye Mariners of England" sung, because of his own country's successes, some time ago. They were gallant and conspicuous victories of the American frigates; we do not grudge them. A fair fight should leave no rancour, above all in the victors, and Dr. Holmes's withers would have been unwrung by Campbell's ditty.

He visited England in youth, and fifty years later. On the anniversary of the American defeat at Bunker's Hill (June 17), Dr. Holmes got his degree in the old Cambridge. He received degrees at Edinburgh and at Oxford, in his "Hundred Days in Europe" he says very little about these historic cities. The men at Oxford asked, "Did he come in the 'One Hoss Shay'?" the name of his most familiar poem in the lighter vein. The whole visit to England pleased and wearied him. He likened it to the shass caffy of Mr. Henry Foker— the fillip at the end of the long banquet of life. He went to see the Derby, for he was fond of horses, of racing, and, in a sportsmanlike way, of boxing. He had the great boldness once, audax juventa, to write a song in praise of that comfortable creature—wine. The prudery of many Americans about the juice of the grape is a thing very astonishing to a temperate Briton. An admirable author, who wrote an account of the old convivial days of an American city, found that reputable magazines could not accept such a degrading historical record. There was no nonsense about Dr. Holmes. His poems were mainly "occasional" verses for friendly meetings; or humorous, like the celebrated "One Horse Shay." Of his serious verses, the "Nautilus" is probably too familiar to need quotation; a noble fancy is nobly and tunefully "moralised." Pleasing, cultivated, and so forth, are adjectives not dear to poets. To say "sublime," or "magical," or "strenuous," of Dr. Holmes's muse, would be to exaggerate. How far he maintained his scholarship, I am not certain; but it is odd that, in his preface to "The Guardian Angel," he should quote from "Jonathan Edwards the younger," a story for which he might have cited Aristotle.

Were I to choose one character out of Dr. Holmes's creations as my favourite, it would be "a frequent correspondent of his," and of mine—the immortal Gifted Hopkins. Never was minor poet more kindly and genially portrayed. And if one had to pick out three of his books, as the best worth reading, they would be "The Professor," "Elsie Venner," and "The Guardian Angel." They have not the impeccable art and distinction of "The House of the Seven Gables" and "The Scarlet Letter," but they combine fantasy with living human interest, and with humour. With Sir Thomas Browne, and Dr. John Brown, and—may we not add Dr. Weir Mitchell?—Dr.

Holmes excellently represents the physician in humane letters. He has left a blameless and most amiable memory, unspotted by the world. His works are full of the savour of his native soil, naturally, without straining after "Americanism;" and they are national, not local or provincial. He crossed the great gulf of years, between the central age of American literary production—the time of Hawthorne and Poe—to our own time, and, like Nestor, he reigned among the third generation. As far as the world knows, the shadow of a literary quarrel never fell on him; he was without envy or jealousy, incurious of his own place, never vain, petulant, or severe. He was even too good-humoured, and the worst thing I have heard of him is that he could never say "no" to an autograph hunter.

CHAPTER V

MR. MORRIS'S POEMS

"Enough," said the pupil of the wise Imlac, "you have convinced me that no man can be a poet." The study of Mr. William Morris's poems, in the new collected edition,[5] has convinced me that no man, or, at least, no middle-aged man, can be a critic. I read Mr. Morris's poems (thanks to the knightly honours conferred on the Bard of Penrhyn, there is now no ambiguity as to 'Mr. Morris'), but it is not the book only that I read. The scroll of my youth is unfolded. I see the dear place where first I perused "The Blue Closet"; the old faces of old friends flock around me; old chaff, old laughter, old happiness re-echo and revive. St. Andrews, Oxford, come before the mind's eye, with

> "Many a place
> That's in sad case
> Where joy was wont afore, oh!"

as Minstrel Burne sings. These voices, faces, landscapes mingle with the music and blur the pictures of the poet who enchanted for us certain hours passed in the paradise of youth. A reviewer who finds himself in this case may as well frankly confess that he can no more criticise Mr. Morris dispassionately than he could criticise his old self and the friends whom he shall never see again, till he meets them

> "Beyond the sphere of time,
>   And sin, and grief's control,
> Serene in changeless prime
>   Of body and of soul."

To write of one's own "adventures among books" may be to provide anecdotage more or less trivial, more or less futile, but, at least, it is to write historically. We know how books have affected, and do affect ourselves, our bundle of prejudices and tastes, of old impressions and revived sensations. To judge books dispassionately and impersonally, is much more difficult—indeed, it is practically impossible, for our own tastes and experiences must, more or less,

---

[5] Longmans.

55

modify our verdicts, do what we will. However, the effort must be made, for to say that, at a certain age, in certain circumstances, an individual took much pleasure in "The Life and Death of Jason," the present of a college friend, is certainly not to criticise "The Life and Death of Jason."

There have been three blossoming times in the English poetry of the nineteenth century. The first dates from Wordsworth, Coleridge, Scott, and, later, from Shelley, Byron, Keats. By 1822 the blossoming time was over, and the second blossoming time began in 1830-1833, with young Mr. Tennyson and Mr. Browning. It broke forth again, in 1842 and did not practically cease till England's greatest laureate sang of the "Crossing of the Bar." But while Tennyson put out his full strength in 1842, and Mr. Browning rather later, in "Bells and Pomegranates" ("Men and Women"), the third spring came in 1858, with Mr. Morris's "Defence of Guenevere," and flowered till Mr. Swinburne's "Atalanta in Calydon" appeared in 1865, followed by his poems of 1866. Mr. Rossetti's book of 1870 belonged, in date of composition, mainly to this period.

In 1858, when "The Defence of Guenevere" came out, Mr. Morris must have been but a year or two from his undergraduateship. Every one has heard enough about his companions, Mr. Burne Jones, Mr. Rossetti, Canon Dixon, and the others of the old Oxford and Cambridge Magazine, where Mr. Morris's wonderful prose fantasies are buried. Why should they not be revived, these strangely coloured and magical dreams? As literature, I prefer them vastly above Mr. Morris's later romances in prose—"The Hollow Land" above "News from Nowhere!" Mr. Morris and his friends were active in the fresh dawn of a new romanticism, a mediæval and Catholic revival, with very little Catholicism in it for the most part. This revival is more "innerly," as the Scotch say, more intimate, more "earnest" than the larger and more genial, if more superficial, restoration by Scott. The painful doubt, the scepticism of the Ages of Faith, the dark hours of that epoch, its fantasy, cruelty, luxury, no less than its colour and passion, inform Mr. Morris's first poems. The fourteenth and the early fifteenth century is his "period." In "The Defence of Guenevere" he is not under the influence of Chaucer, whose narrative manner, without one grain of his humour, inspires "The Life and Death of Jason" and "The Earthly Paradise." In the early book the rugged style of Mr. Browning has left a mark. There are cockney rhymes, too, such as "short" rhyming to "thought." But, on the whole, Mr. Morris's early manner was all his own, nor has he ever returned to it. In the first poem, "The Queen's Apology," is this passage:—

"Listen: suppose your time were come to die,
And you were quite alone and very weak;
Yea, laid a-dying, while very mightily

"The wind was ruffling up the narrow streak
Of river through your broad lands running well:
Suppose a hush should come, then some one speak:

"'One of these cloths is heaven, and one is hell,
Now choose one cloth for ever, which they be,
I will not tell you, you must somehow tell

"'Of your own strength and mightiness; here, see!'
Yea, yea, my lord, and you to ope your eyes,
At foot of your familiar bed to see

"A great God's angel standing, with such dyes,
Not known on earth, on his great wings, and hands,
Held out two ways, light from the inner skies

"Showing him well, and making his commands
Seem to be God's commands, moreover, too,
Holding within his hands the cloths on wands;

"And one of these strange choosing-cloths was blue,
Wavy and long, and one cut short and red;
No man could tell the better of the two.

"After a shivering half-hour you said,
'God help! heaven's colour, the blue;' and he said, 'Hell.'
Perhaps you then would roll upon your bed,

"And cry to all good men that loved you well,
'Ah, Christ! if only I had known, known, known.'"

There was nothing like that before in English poetry; it has the
bizarrerie of a new thing in beauty. How far it is really beautiful
how can I tell? How can I discount the "personal bias"? Only I
know that it is unforgettable. Again (Galahad speaks):—

"I saw
One sitting on the altar as a throne,
   Whose face no man could say he did not know,
And, though the bell still rang, he sat alone,

57

With raiment half blood-red, half white as snow."

Such things made their own special ineffaceable impact.

Leaving the Arthurian cycle, Mr. Morris entered on his especially sympathetic period—the gloom and sad sunset glory of the late fourteenth century, the age of Froissart and wicked, wasteful wars. To Froissart it all seemed one magnificent pageant of knightly and kingly fortunes; he only murmurs a "great pity" for the death of a knight or the massacre of a town. It is rather the pity of it that Mr. Morris sees: the hearts broken in a corner, as in "Sir Peter Harpedon's End," or beside "The Haystack in the Floods." Here is a picture like life of what befell a hundred times. Lady Alice de la Barde hears of the death of her knight:—

"ALICE

"Can you talk faster, sir?
Get over all this quicker? fix your eyes
On mine, I pray you, and whate'er you see
Still go on talking fast, unless I fall,
Or bid you stop.

"SQUIRE

"I pray your pardon then,
And looking in your eyes, fair lady, say
I am unhappy that your knight is dead.
Take heart, and listen! let me tell you all.
We were five thousand goodly men-at-arms,
And scant five hundred had he in that hold;
His rotten sandstone walls were wet with rain,
And fell in lumps wherever a stone hit;
Yet for three days about the barriers there
The deadly glaives were gather'd, laid across,
And push'd and pull'd; the fourth our engines came;
But still amid the crash of falling walls,
And roar of bombards, rattle of hard bolts,
The steady bow-strings flash'd, and still stream'd out
St. George's banner, and the seven swords,
And still they cried, 'St. George Guienne,' until
Their walls were flat as Jericho's of old,
And our rush came, and cut them from the keep."

The astonishing vividness, again, of the tragedy told in

58

"Geffray Teste Noire" is like that of a vision in a magic mirror or a crystal ball, rather than like a picture suggested by printed words. "Shameful Death" has the same enchanted kind of presentment. We look through a "magic casement opening on the foam" of the old waves of war. Poems of a pure fantasy, unequalled out of Coleridge and Poe, are "The Wind" and "The Blue Closet." Each only lives in fantasy. Motives, and facts, and "story" are unimportant and out of view. The pictures arise distinct, unsummoned, spontaneous, like the faces and places which are flashed on our eyes between sleeping and waking. Fantastic, too, but with more of a recognisable human setting, is "Golden Wings," which to a slight degree reminds one of Théophile Gautier's Château de Souvenir.

"The apples now grow green and sour
Upon the mouldering castle wall,
Before they ripen there they fall:
There are no banners on the tower,

The draggled swans most eagerly eat
The green weeds trailing in the moat;
Inside the rotting leaky boat
You see a slain man's stiffen'd feet."

These, with "The Sailing of the Sword," are my own old favourites. There was nothing like them before, nor will be again, for Mr. Morris, after several years of silence, abandoned his early manner. No doubt it was not a manner to persevere in, but happily, in a mood and a moment never to be re-born or return, Mr. Morris did fill a fresh page in English poetry with these imperishable fantasies. They were absolutely neglected by "the reading public," but they found a few staunch friends. Indeed, I think of "Guenevere" as FitzGerald did of Tennyson's poems before 1842. But this, of course, is a purely personal, probably a purely capricious, estimate. Criticism may aver that the influence of Mr. Rossetti was strong on Mr. Morris before 1858. Perhaps so, but we read Mr. Morris first (as the world read the "Lay" before "Christabel"), and my own preference is for Mr. Morris.

It was after eight or nine years of silence that Mr. Morris produced, in 1866 or 1867, "The Life and Death of Jason." Young men who had read "Guenevere" hastened to purchase it, and, of course, found themselves in contact with something very unlike their old favourite. Mr. Morris had told a classical tale in decasyllabic couplets of the Chaucerian sort, and he regarded the heroic age from a mediæval point of view; at all events, not from an historical and archæological point of view. It was natural in Mr. Morris to "envisage" the Greek heroic age in this way, but it would not be natural in most other writers. The poem is not much shorter than the "Odyssey," and long narrative poems had been out of fashion since "The Lord of the Isles" (1814).

All this was a little disconcerting. We read "Jason," and read it with pleasure, but without much of the more essential pleasure which comes from magic and distinction of style. The peculiar qualities of Keats, and Tennyson, and Virgil are not among the gifts of Mr. Morris. As people say of Scott in his long poems, so it may be said of Mr. Morris—that he does not furnish many quotations, does not glitter in "jewels five words long."

In "Jason" he entered on his long career as a narrator; a poet retelling the immortal primeval stories of the human race. In one guise or another the legend of Jason is the most widely distributed of romances; the North American Indians have it, and the Samoans and the Samoyeds, as well as all Indo-European peoples. This tale, told briefly by Pindar, and at greater length by Apollonius Rhodius, and in the "Orphica," Mr. Morris took up and handled in a single and objective way. His art was always pictorial, but, in "Jason" and later, he described more, and was less apt, as it were, to flash a picture on the reader, in some incommunicable way.

In the covers of the first edition were announcements of the "Earthly Paradise": that vast collection of the world's old tales retold. One might almost conjecture that "Jason" had originally been intended for a part of the "Earthly Paradise," and had outgrown its limits. The tone is much the same, though the "criticism of life" is less formally and explicitly stated.

For Mr. Morris came at last to a "criticism of life." It would not have satisfied Mr. Matthew Arnold, and it did not satisfy Mr. Morris! The burden of these long narrative poems is vanitas vanitatum: the fleeting, perishable, unsatisfying nature of human existence, the dream "rounded by a sleep." The lesson drawn is to make life as full and as beautiful as may be, by love, and adventure, and art. The hideousness of modern industrialism was oppressing to Mr. Morris; that hideousness he was doing his best to relieve and redeem, by poetry, and by all the many arts and crafts in which he was a master. His narrative poems are, indeed, part of his industry in this field. He was not born to slay monsters, he says, "the idle singer of an empty day." Later, he set about slaying monsters, like Jason, or unlike Jason, scattering dragon's teeth to raise forces which he could not lay, and could not direct.

I shall go no further into politics or agitation, and I say this much only to prove that Mr. Morris's "criticism of life," and prolonged, wistful dwelling on the thought of death, ceased to satisfy himself. His own later part, as a poet and an ally of Socialism, proved this to be true. It seems to follow that the peculiarly level, lifeless, decorative effect of his narratives, which remind us rather of glorious tapestries than of pictures, was no longer wholly satisfactory to himself. There is plenty of charmed and delightful reading—"Jason" and the "Earthly Paradise" are literature for The Castle of Indolence, but we do miss a strenuous rendering of action and passion. These Mr. Morris had rendered in "The Defence of Guinevere": now he gave us something different, something beautiful, but something deficient in dramatic vigour. Apollonius Rhodius is, no doubt, much of a pedant, a literary writer of epic, in an age of Criticism. He dealt with the tale of "Jason," and conceivably he may have borrowed from older minstrels. But the Medea of Apollonius Rhodius, in her love, her tenderness, her regret for home, in all her maiden words and ways, is undeniably a character more living, more human, more passionate, and more sympathetic, than the Medea of Mr. Morris. I could almost wish that he had closely followed that classical original, the first true love story in literature. In the same way I prefer Apollonius's spell for soothing the dragon, as much terser and more somniferous than the spell put by Mr. Morris into the lips of Medea. Scholars will find it pleasant to compare these passages of the Alexandrine and of the London poets. As a brick out of the vast palace of "Jason" we may select the song of the Nereid to Hylas—Mr. Morris is always happy with his Nymphs and Nereids:—

> "I know a little garden-close
> Set thick with lily and with rose,
> Where I would wander if I might
> From dewy dawn to dewy night,
> And have one with me wandering.
> And though within it no birds sing,
> And though no pillared house is there,
> And though the apple boughs are bare
> Of fruit and blossom, would to God,
> Her feet upon the green grass trod,
> And I beheld them as before.
> There comes a murmur from the shore,
> And in the place two fair streams are,
> Drawn from the purple hills afar,
> Drawn down unto the restless sea;
> The hills whose flowers ne'er fed the bee,
> The shore no ship has ever seen,

Still beaten by the billows green,
Whose murmur comes unceasingly
Unto the place for which I cry.
  For which I cry both day and night,
For which I let slip all delight,
That maketh me both deaf and blind,
Careless to win, unskilled to find,
And quick to lose what all men seek.
  Yet tottering as I am, and weak,
Still have I left a little breath
To seek within the jaws of death
An entrance to that happy place,
To seek the unforgotten face
Once seen, once kissed, once rest from me
Anigh the murmuring of the sea."

"Jason" is, practically, a very long tale from the "Earthly Paradise," as the "Earthly Paradise" is an immense treasure of shorter tales in the manner of "Jason." Mr. Morris reverted for an hour to his fourteenth century, a period when London was "clean." This is a poetic license; many a plague found mediæval London abominably dirty! A Celt himself, no doubt, with the Celt's proverbial way of being impossibilium cupitor, Mr. Morris was in full sympathy with his Breton Squire, who, in the reign of Edward III., sets forth to seek the Earthly Paradise, and the land where Death never comes. Much more dramatic, I venture to think, than any passage of "Jason," is that where the dreamy seekers of dreamland, Breton and Northman, encounter the stout King Edward III., whose kingdom is of this world. Action and fantasy are met, and the wanderers explain the nature of their quest. One of them speaks of death in many a form, and of the flight from death:—

"His words nigh made me weep, but while he spoke
I noted how a mocking smile just broke
The thin line of the Prince's lips, and he
Who carried the afore-named armoury
Puffed out his wind-beat cheeks and whistled low:
But the King smiled, and said, 'Can it be so?
I know not, and ye twain are such as find
The things whereto old kings must needs be blind.
For you the world is wide—but not for me,
Who once had dreams of one great victory
Wherein that world lay vanquished by my throne,

And now, the victor in so many an one,
Find that in Asia Alexander died
And will not live again; the world is wide
For you I say,—for me a narrow space
Betwixt the four walls of a fighting place.
  Poor man, why should I stay thee? live thy fill
Of that fair life, wherein thou seest no ill
But fear of that fair rest I hope to win
One day, when I have purged me of my sin.
  Farewell, it yet may hap that I a king
Shall be remembered but by this one thing,
That on the morn before ye crossed the sea
Ye gave and took in common talk with me;
But with this ring keep memory with the morn,
O Breton, and thou Northman, by this horn
Remember me, who am of Odin's blood.'"

All this encounter is a passage of high invention. The adventures in Anahuac are such as Bishop Erie may have achieved when he set out to find Vinland the Good, and came back no more, whether he was or was not remembered by the Aztecs as Quetzalcoatl. The tale of the wanderers was Mr. Morris's own; all the rest are of the dateless heritage of our race, fairy tales coming to us, now "softly breathed through the flutes of the Grecians," now told by Sagamen of Iceland. The whole performance is astonishingly equable; we move on a high tableland, where no tall peaks of Parnassus are to be climbed. Once more literature has a narrator, on the whole much more akin to Spenser than to Chaucer, Homer, or Sir Walter. Humour and action are not so prominent as contemplation of a pageant reflected in a fairy mirror. But Mr. Morris has said himself, about his poem, what I am trying to say:—

"Death have we hated, knowing not what it meant;
Life have we loved, through green leaf and through sere,
Though still the less we knew of its intent;
The Earth and Heaven through countless year on year,
Slow changing, were to us but curtains fair,
Hung round about a little room, where play
Weeping and laughter of man's empty day."

Mr. Morris had shown, in various ways, the strength of his sympathy with the heroic sagas of Iceland. He had rendered one into verse, in "The Earthly Paradise," above all, "Grettir the Strong" and "The Volsunga" he had done into English prose. His next great

63

poem was "The Story of Sigurd," a poetic rendering of the theme which is, to the North, what the Tale of Troy is to Greece, and to all the world. Mr. Morris took the form of the story which is most archaic, and bears most birthmarks of its savage origin—the version of the "Volsunga," not the German shape of the "Nibelungenlied." He showed extraordinary skill, especially in making human and intelligible the story of Regin, Otter, Fafnir, and the Dwarf Andvari's Hoard.

"It was Reidmar the Ancient begat me; and now was he waxen old,
And a covetous man and a king; and he bade, and I built him a hall,
And a golden glorious house; and thereto his sons did he call,
And he bade them be evil and wise, that his will through them might be wrought.
Then he gave unto Fafnir my brother the soul that feareth nought,
And the brow of the hardened iron, and the hand that may never fail,
And the greedy heart of a king, and the ear that hears no wail.

"But next unto Otter my brother he gave the snare and the net,
And the longing to wend through the wild-wood, and wade the highways wet;
And the foot that never resteth, while aught be left alive
That hath cunning to match man's cunning or might with his might to strive.

"And to me, the least and the youngest, what gift for the slaying of ease?
Save the grief that remembers the past, and the fear that the future sees;
And the hammer and fashioning-iron, and the living coal of fire;
And the craft that createth a semblance, and fails of the heart's desire;
And the toil that each dawning quickens, and the task that is never done;
And the heart that longeth ever, nor will look to the deed that is won.

"Thus gave my father the gifts that might never be taken again;
Far worse were we now than the Gods, and but little better than men.
But yet of our ancient might one thing had we left us still:
We had craft to change our semblance, and could shift us at our will
Into bodies of the beast-kind, or fowl, or fishes cold;
For belike no fixèd semblance we had in the days of old,
Till the Gods were waxen busy, and all things their form must take
That knew of good and evil, and longed to gather and make."

But when we turn to the passage of the éclaircissement between Sigurd and Brynhild, that most dramatic and most modern moment in the ancient tragedy, the moment where the clouds of savage fancy scatter in the light of a hopeless human love, then, I must confess, I prefer the simple, brief prose of Mr. Morris's translation of the "Volsunga" to his rather periphrastic paraphrase.

Every student of poetry may make the comparison for himself, and decide for himself whether the old or the new is better. Again, in the final fight and massacre in the hall of Atli, I cannot but prefer the Slaying of the Wooers, at the close of the "Odyssey," or the last fight of Roland at Roncesvaux, or the prose version of the "Volsunga." All these are the work of men who were war-smiths as well as song-smiths. Here is a passage from the "murder grim and great":—

"So he saith in the midst of the foemen with his war-flame reared on high,
But all about and around him goes up a bitter cry
From the iron men of Atli, and the bickering of the steel
Sends a roar up to the roof-ridge, and the Niblung war-ranks reel
Behind the steadfast Gunnar: but lo, have ye seen the corn,
While yet men grind the sickle, by the wind streak overborne
When the sudden rain sweeps downward, and summer groweth black,
And the smitten wood-side roareth 'neath the driving thunder-wrack?
So before the wise-heart Hogni shrank the champions of the East
As his great voice shook the timbers in the hall of Atli's feast,
There he smote and beheld not the smitten, and by nought were his edges stopped;
He smote and the dead were thrust from him; a hand with its shield he lopped;
There met him Atli's marshal, and his arm at the shoulder he shred;
Three swords were upreared against him of the best of the kin of the dead;
And he struck off a head to the rightward, and his sword through a throat he thrust,
But the third stroke fell on his helm-crest, and he stooped to the ruddy dust,
And uprose as the ancient Giant, and both his hands were wet:
Red then was the world to his eyen, as his hand to the labour he set;
Swords shook and fell in his pathway, huge bodies leapt and fell;
Harsh grided shield and war-helm like the tempest-smitten bell,
And the war-cries ran together, and no man his brother knew,
And the dead men loaded the living, as he went the war-wood through;
And man 'gainst man was huddled, till no sword rose to smite,
And clear stood the glorious Hogni in an island of the fight,
And there ran a river of death 'twixt the Niblung and his foes,
And therefrom the terror of men and the wrath of the Gods arose."

I admit that this does not affect me as does the figure of Odysseus raining his darts of doom, or the courtesy of Roland when the blinded Oliver smites him by mischance, and, indeed, the Keeping of the Stair by Umslopogaas appeals to me more vigorously as a strenuous picture of war. To be just to Mr. Morris, let us give his rendering of part of the Slaying of the Wooers, from his translation of the "Odyssey":—

"And e'en as the word he uttered, he drew his keen sword out
Brazen, on each side shearing, and with a fearful shout
Rushed on him; but Odysseus that very while let fly
And smote him with the arrow in the breast, the pap hard by,
And drove the swift shaft to the liver, and adown to the ground fell the sword
From out of his hand, and doubled he hung above the board,
And staggered; and whirling he fell, and the meat was scattered around,
And the double cup moreover, and his forehead smote the ground;
And his heart was wrung with torment, and with both feet spurning he smote
The high-seat; and over his eyen did the cloud of darkness float.

"And then it was Amphinomus, who drew his whetted sword
And fell on, making his onrush 'gainst Odysseus the glorious lord,
If perchance he might get him out-doors: but Telemachus him forewent,
And a cast of the brazen war-spear from behind him therewith sent
Amidmost of his shoulders, that drave through his breast and out,
And clattering he fell, and the earth all the breadth of his forehead smote."

There is no need to say more of Mr. Morris's "Odysseus." Close to the letter of the Greek he usually keeps, but where are the surge and thunder of Homer? Apparently we must accent the penultimate in "Amphinomus" if the line is to scan. I select a passage of peaceful beauty from Book V:—

"But all about that cavern there grew a blossoming wood,
Of alder and of poplar and of cypress savouring good;
And fowl therein wing-spreading were wont to roost and be,
For owls were there and falcons, and long-tongued crows of the sea,
And deeds of the sea they deal with and thereof they have a care
But round the hollow cavern there spread and flourished fair
A vine of garden breeding, and in its grapes was glad;
And four wells of the white water their heads together had,
And flowing on in order four ways they thence did get;
And soft were the meadows blooming with parsley and violet.
Yea, if thither indeed had come e'en one of the Deathless, e'en he
Had wondered and gladdened his heart with all that was there to see.
And there in sooth stood wondering the Flitter, the Argus-bane.
But when o'er all these matters in his soul he had marvelled amain,
Then into the wide cave went he, and Calypso, Godhead's Grace,
Failed nowise there to know him as she looked upon his face;
For never unknown to each other are the Deathless Gods, though they

Apart from one another may be dwelling far away.
But Odysseus the mighty-hearted within he met not there,
Who on the beach sat weeping, as oft he was wont to wear
His soul with grief and groaning, and weeping; yea, and he
As the tears he was pouring downward yet gazed o'er the untilled sea."

This is close enough to the Greek, but

"And flowing on in order four ways they thence did get"

is not precisely musical. Why is Hermes "The Flitter"? But I have often ventured to remonstrate against these archaistic peculiarities, which to some extent mar our pleasure in Mr. Morris's translations. In his version of the rich Virgilian measure they are especially out of place. The "Æneid" is rendered with a roughness which might better befit a translation of Ennius. Thus the reader of Mr. Morris's poetical translations has in his hands versions of almost literal closeness, and (what is extremely rare) versions of poetry by a poet. But his acquaintance with Early English and Icelandic has added to the poet a strain of the philologist, and his English in the "Odyssey," still more in the "Æneid," is occasionally more archaic than the Greek of 900 B.C. So at least it seems to a reader not unversed in attempts to fit the classical poets with an English rendering. But the true test is in the appreciation of the lovers of poetry in general.

To them, as to all who desire the restoration of beauty in modern life, Mr. Morris has been a benefactor almost without example. Indeed, were adequate knowledge mine, Mr. Morris's poetry should have been criticised as only a part of the vast industry of his life in many crafts and many arts. His place in English life and literature is unique as it is honourable. He did what he desired to do—he made vast additions to simple and stainless pleasures.

CHAPTER VI

MRS. RADCLIFFE'S NOVELS

Does any one now read Mrs. Radcliffe, or am I the only wanderer in her windy corridors, listening timidly to groans and hollow voices, and shielding the flame of a lamp, which, I fear, will presently flicker out, and leave me in darkness? People know the name of "The Mysteries of Udolpho;" they know that boys would say to Thackeray, at school, "Old fellow, draw us Vivaldi in the Inquisition." But have they penetrated into the chill galleries of the Castle of Udolpho? Have they shuddered for Vivaldi in face of the sable-clad and masked Inquisition? Certainly Mrs. Radcliffe, within the memory of man, has been extremely popular. The thick double-columned volume in which I peruse the works of the Enchantress belongs to a public library. It is quite the dirtiest, greasiest, most dog's-eared, and most bescribbled tome in the collection. Many of the books have remained, during the last hundred years, uncut, even to this day, and I have had to apply the paper knife to many an author, from Alciphron (1790) to Mr. Max Müller, and Dr. Birkbeck Hill's edition of Bozzy's "Life of Dr. Johnson." But Mrs. Radcliffe has been read diligently, and copiously annotated.

This lady was, in a literary sense, and though, like the sire of Evelina, he cast her off, the daughter of Horace Walpole. Just when King Romance seemed as dead as Queen Anne, Walpole produced that Gothic tale, "The Castle of Otranto," in 1764. In that very year was born Anne Ward, who, in 1787, married William Radcliffe, Esq., M.A., Oxon. In 1789 she published "The Castles of Athlin and Dunbayne." The scene, she tells us, is laid in "the most romantic part of the Highlands, the north-east coast of Scotland." On castles, anywhere, she doted. Walpole, not Smollett or Miss Burney, inspired her with a passion for these homes of old romance. But the north-east coast of Scotland is hardly part of the Highlands at all, and is far from being very romantic. The period is "the dark ages" in general. Yet the captive Earl, when "the sweet tranquillity of evening threw an air of tender melancholy over his mind . . . composed the following sonnet, which (having committed it to paper) he the next evening dropped upon the terrace. He had the pleasure to observe that the paper was taken up by the ladies, who immediately retired into the castle." These were not the manners of the local Mackays, of the Sinclairs, and of "the small but fierce clan of Gunn," in the dark ages.

But this was Mrs. Radcliffe's way. She delighted in descriptions of scenery, the more romantic the better, and usually drawn entirely from her inner consciousness. Her heroines write sonnets (which never but once are sonnets) and other lyrics, on every occasion. With his usual generosity Scott praised her landscape and her lyrics, but, indeed, they are, as Sir Walter said of Mrs. Hemans, "too poetical," and probably they were skipped, even by her contemporary devotees. "The Castles of Athlin and Dunbayne" frankly do not permit themselves to be read, and it was not till 1790, with "A Sicilian Romance," that Mrs. Radcliffe "found herself," and her public. After reading, with breathless haste, through, "A Sicilian Romance," and "The Romance of the Forest," in a single day, it would ill become me to speak lightly of Mrs. Radcliffe. Like Catherine Morland, I love this lady's tender yet terrific fancy.

Mrs. Radcliffe does not always keep on her highest level, but we must remember that her last romance, "The Italian," is by far her best. She had been feeling her way to this pitch of excellence, and, when she had attained to it, she published no more. The reason is uncertain. She became a Woman's Rights woman, and wrote "The Female Advocate," not a novel! Scott thinks that she may have been annoyed by her imitators, or by her critics, against whom he defends her in an admirable passage, to be cited later. Meanwhile let us follow Mrs. Radcliffe in her upward course.

The "Sicilian Romance" appeared in 1790, when the author's age was twenty-six. The book has a treble attraction, for it contains the germ of "Northanger Abbey," and the germ of "Jane Eyre," and—the germ of Byron! Like "Joseph Andrews," "Northanger Abbey" began as a parody (of Mrs. Radcliffe) and developed into a real novel of character. So too Byron's gloomy scowling adventurers, with their darkling past, are mere repetitions in rhyme of Mrs. Radcliffe's Schedoni. This is so obvious that, when discussing Mrs. Radcliffe's Schedoni, Scott adds, in a note, parallel passages from Byron's "Giaour." Sir Walter did not mean to mock, he merely compared two kindred spirits. "The noble poet" "kept on the business still," and broke into octosyllabics, borrowed from Scott, his descriptions of miscreants borrowed from Mrs. Radcliffe.

"A Sicilian Romance" has its scene in the palace of Ferdinand, fifth Marquis of Mazzini, on the northern coast of Sicily. The time is about 1580, but there is nothing in the manners or costume to indicate that, or any other period. Such "local colour" was unknown to Mrs. Radcliffe, as to Clara Reeve. In Horace Walpole, however, a character goes so far in the mediæval way as to say "by my halidome."

The Marquis Mazzini had one son and two daughters by his first amiable consort, supposed to be long dead when the story opens. The son is the original of Henry Tilney in "Northanger Abbey," and in General Tilney does Catherine Morland recognise a modern Marquis of Mazzini. But the Marquis's wife, to be sure, is not dead; like the first Mrs. Rochester she is concealed about the back premises, and, as in "Jane Eyre," it is her movements, and those of her gaolers, that produce mystery, and make the reader suppose that "the place is haunted." It is, of course, only the mystery and the "machinery" of Mrs. Radcliffe that Miss Brontë adapted. These passages in "Jane Eyre" have been censured, but it is not easy to see how the novel could do without them. Mrs. Radcliffe's tale entirely depends on its machinery. Her wicked Marquis, having secretly immured Number One, has now a new and beautiful Number Two, whose character does not bear inspection. This domestic position, as Number Two, we know, was declined by the austere virtue of Jane Eyre.

"Phenomena" begin in the first chapter of "A Sicilian Romance," mysterious lights wander about uninhabited parts of the castle, and are vainly investigated by young Ferdinand, son of the Marquis. This Hippolytus the Chaste, loved all in vain by the reigning Marchioness, is adored by, and adores, her stepdaughter, Julia. Jealousy and revenge are clearly indicated. But, in chasing mysterious lights and figures through mouldering towers, Ferdinand gets into the very undesirable position of David Balfour, when he climbs, in the dark, the broken turret stair in his uncle's house of Shaws (in "Kidnapped"). Here is a fourth author indebted to Mrs. Radcliffe: her disciples are Miss Austen, Byron, Miss Brontë, and Mr. Louis Stevenson! Ferdinand "began the ascent. He had not proceeded very far, when the stones of a step which his foot had just quitted gave way, and, dragging with them those adjoining, formed a chasm in the staircase that terrified even Ferdinand, who was left tottering on the suspended half of the steps, in momentary expectation of falling to the bottom with the stone on which he rested. In the terror which this occasioned, he attempted to save himself by catching at a kind of beam which suspended over the stairs, when the lamp dropped from his hand, and he was left in total darkness."

Can anything be more "amazing horrid," above all as there are mysterious figures in and about the tower? Mrs. Radcliffe's lamps always fall, or are blown out, in the nick of time, an expedient already used by Clara Reeve in that very mild but once popular ghost story, "The Old English Baron" (1777). All authors have such favourite devices, and I wonder how many fights Mr. Stanley

70

Weyman's heroes have fought, from the cellar to their favourite tilting ground, the roof of a strange house!

Ferdinand hung on to the beam for an hour, when the ladies came with a light, and he scrambled back to solid earth. In his next nocturnal research, "a sullen groan arose from beneath where he stood," and when he tried to force a door (there are scores of such weird doors in Mrs. Radcliffe) "a groan was repeated, more hollow and dreadful than the first. His courage forsook him"—and no wonder! Of course he could not know that the author of the groans was, in fact, his long-lost mother, immured by his father, the wicked Marquis. We need not follow the narrative through the darkling crimes and crumbling galleries of this terrible castle on the north coast of Sicily. Everybody is always "gazing in silent terror," and all the locks are rusty. "A savage and dexterous banditti" play a prominent part, and the imprisoned Ferdinand "did not hesitate to believe that the moans he heard came from the restless spirit of the murdered della Campo." No working hypothesis could seem more plausible, but it was erroneous. Mrs. Radcliffe does not deal in a single avowed ghost. She finally explains away, by normal causes, everything that she does not forget to explain. At the most, she indulges herself in a premonitory dream. On this point she is true to common sense, without quite adopting the philosophy of David Hume. "I do not say that spirits have appeared," she remarks, "but if several discreet unprejudiced persons were to assure me that they had seen one—I should not be bold or proud enough to reply, it is impossible!" But Hume was bold and proud enough: he went further than Mrs. Radcliffe.

Scott censures Mrs. Radcliffe's employment of explanations. He is in favour of "boldly avowing the use of supernatural machinery," or of leaving the matter in the vague, as in the appearance of the wraith of the dying Alice to Ravenswood. But, in Mrs. Radcliffe's day, common sense was so tyrannical, that the poor lady's romances would have been excluded from families, if she had not provided normal explanations of her groans, moans, voices, lights, and wandering figures. The ghost-hunt in the castle finally brings Julia to a door, whose bolts, "strengthened by desperation, she forced back." There was a middle-aged lady in the room, who, after steadily gazing on Julia, "suddenly exclaimed, 'My daughter!' and fainted away." Julia being about seventeen, and Madame Mazzini, her mamma, having been immured for fifteen years, we observe, in this recognition, the force of the maternal instinct.

The wicked Marquis was poisoned by the partner of his iniquities, who anon stabbed herself with a poniard. The virtuous Julia marries the chaste Hippolytus, and, says the author, "in reviewing this story, we perceive a singular and striking instance of moral retribution."

We also remark the futility of locking up an inconvenient wife, fabled to be defunct, in one's own country house. Had Mr. Rochester, in "Jane Eyre," studied the "Sicilian Romance," he would have shunned an obsolete system, inconvenient at best, and apt, in the long run, to be disastrous.

In the "Romance of the Forest" (1791), Mrs. Radcliffe remained true to Mr. Stanley Weyman's favourite period, the end of the sixteenth century. But there are no historical characters or costumes in the story, and all the persons, as far as language and dress go, might have been alive in 1791.

The story runs thus: one de la Motte, who appears to have fallen from dissipation to swindling, is, on the first page, discovered flying from Paris and the law, with his wife, in a carriage. Lost in the dark on a moor, he follows a light, and enters an old lonely house. He is seized by ruffians, locked in, and expects to be murdered, which he knows that he cannot stand, for he is timid by nature. In fact, a ruffian puts a pistol to La Motte's breast with one hand, while with the other he drags along a beautiful girl of eighteen. "Swear that you will convey this girl where I may never see her more," exclaims the bully, and La Motte, with the young lady, is taken back to his carriage. "If you return within an hour you will be welcomed with a brace of bullets," is the ruffian's parting threat.

So La Motte, Madame La Motte, and the beautiful girl drive away, La Motte's one desire being to find a retreat safe from the police of an offended justice.

Is this not a very original, striking, and affecting situation; provocative, too, of the utmost curiosity? A fugitive from justice, in a strange, small, dark, ancient house, is seized, threatened, and presented with a young and lovely female stranger. In this opening we recognise the hand of a master genius. There must be an explanation of proceedings so highly unconventional, and what can the reason be? The reader is empoigné in the first page, and eagerly follows the flight of La Motte, also of Peter, his coachman, an attached, comic, and familiar domestic. After a few days, the party observe, in the recesses of a gloomy forest, the remains of a Gothic abbey. They enter; by the light of a flickering lamp they penetrate "horrible recesses," discover a room handsomely provided with a trapdoor, and determine to reside in a dwelling so congenial, though, as La Motte judiciously remarks, "not in all respects strictly Gothic." After a few days, La Motte finds that somebody is inquiring for him in the nearest town. He seeks for a hiding-place, and explores the chambers under the trapdoor. Here he finds, in a large chest—what do you suppose he finds? It was a human skeleton! Yet in this awful vicinity he and his wife, with Adeline (the fair stranger) conceal themselves. The brave Adeline, when footsteps are heard, and a figure is beheld in the upper rooms, accosts the stranger. His keen eye presently detects the practicable trapdoor, he raises it, and the cowering La Motte recognises in the dreaded visitor—his own son, who had sought him out of filial affection.

Already Madame La Motte has become jealous of Adeline, especially as her husband is oddly melancholy, and apt to withdraw into a glade, where he mysteriously disappears into the recesses of a genuine Gothic sepulchre. This, to the watchful eyes of a wife, is proof of faithlessness on the part of a husband. As the son, Louis, really falls in love with Adeline, Madame La Motte becomes doubly unkind to her, and Adeline now composes quantities of poems to Night, to Sunset, to the Nocturnal Gale, and so on.

In this uncomfortable situation, two strangers arrive in a terrific thunderstorm. One is young, the other is a Marquis. On seeing this nobleman, "La Motte's limbs trembled, and a ghastly paleness overspread his countenance. The Marquis was little less agitated," and was, at first, decidedly hostile. La Motte implored forgiveness—for what?—and the Marquis (who, in fact, owned the Abbey, and had a shooting lodge not far off) was mollified. They all became rather friendly, and Adeline asked La Motte about the stories of hauntings, and a murder said to have been, at some time, committed in the Abbey. La Motte said that the Marquis could have no connection with such fables; still, there was the skeleton.

Meanwhile, Adeline had conceived a flame for Theodore, the young officer who accompanied his colonel, the Marquis, on their first visit to the family. Theodore, who returned her passion, had vaguely warned her of an impending danger, and then had failed to keep tryst with her, one evening, and had mysteriously disappeared. Then unhappy Adeline dreamed about a prisoner, a dying man, a coffin, a voice from the coffin, and the appearance within it of the dying man, amidst torrents of blood. The chamber in which she saw these visions was most vividly represented. Next day the Marquis came to dinner, and, though reluctantly, consented to pass the night: Adeline, therefore, was put in a new bedroom. Disturbed by the wind shaking the mouldering tapestry, she found a concealed door behind the arras and a suite of rooms, one of which was the chamber of her dream! On the floor lay a rusty dagger! The bedstead, being touched, crumbled, and disclosed a small roll of manuscripts. They were not washing bills, like those discovered by

73

Catherine Morland in "Northanger Abbey." Returning to her own chamber, Adeline heard the Marquis professing to La Motte a passion for herself. Conceive her horror! Silence then reigned, till all was sudden noise and confusion; the Marquis flying in terror from his room, and insisting on instant departure. His emotion was powerfully displayed.

What had occurred? Mrs. Radcliffe does not say, but horror, whether caused by a conscience ill at ease, or by events of a terrific and supernatural kind, is plainly indicated. In daylight, the Marquis audaciously pressed his unholy suit, and even offered marriage, a hollow mockery, for he was well known to be already a married man. The scenes of Adeline's flight, capture, retention in an elegant villa of the licentious noble, renewed flight, rescue by Theodore, with Theodore's arrest, and wounding of the tyrannical Marquis, are all of breathless interest. Mrs. Radcliffe excels in narratives of romantic escapes, a topic always thrilling when well handled. Adeline herself is carried back to the Abbey, but La Motte, who had rather not be a villain if he could avoid it, enables her again to secure her freedom. He is clearly in the power of the Marquis, and his life has been unscrupulous, but he retains traces of better things. Adeline is now secretly conveyed to a peaceful valley in Savoy, the home of the honest Peter (the coachman), who accompanies her. Here she learns to know and value the family of La Luc, the kindred of her Theodore (by a romantic coincidence), and, in the adorable scenery of Savoy, she throws many a ballad to the Moon.

La Motte, on the discovery of Adeline's flight, was cast into prison by the revengeful Marquis, for, in fact, soon after settling in the Abbey, it had occurred to La Motte to commence highwayman. His very first victim had been the Marquis, and, during his mysterious retreats to a tomb in a glade in the forest, he had, in short, been contemplating his booty, jewels which he could not convert into ready money. Consequently, when the Marquis first entered the Abbey, La Motte had every reason for alarm, and only pacified the vindictive aristocrat by yielding to his cruel schemes against the virtue of Adeline.

Happily for La Motte, a witness appeared at his trial, who cast a lurid light on the character of the Marquis. That villain, to be plain, had murdered his elder brother (the skeleton of the Abbey), and had been anxious to murder, it was added, his own natural daughter—that is, Adeline! His hired felons, however, placed her in a convent, and, later (rather than kill her, on which the Marquis insisted), simply thrust her into the hands of La Motte, who happened to pass by that way, as we saw in the opening of this romance. Thus, in making love to Adeline, his daughter, the

Marquis was, unconsciously, in an awkward position. On further examination of evidence, however, things proved otherwise. Adeline was not the natural daughter of the Marquis, but his niece, the legitimate daughter and heiress of his brother (the skeleton of the Abbey). The MS. found by Adeline in the room of the rusty dagger added documentary evidence, for it was a narrative of the sufferings of her father (later the skeleton), written by him in the Abbey where he was imprisoned and stabbed, and where his bones were discovered by La Motte. The hasty nocturnal flight of the Marquis from the Abbey is thus accounted for: he had probably been the victim of a terrific hallucination representing his murdered brother; whether it was veridical or merely subjective Mrs. Radcliffe does not decide. Rather than face the outraged justice of his country, the Marquis, after these revelations, took poison. La Motte was banished; and Adeline, now mistress of the Abbey, removed the paternal skeleton to "the vault of his ancestors." Theodore and Adeline were united, and virtuously resided in a villa on the beautiful banks of the Lake of Geneva.

Such is the "Romance of the Forest," a fiction in which character is subordinate to plot and incident. There is an attempt at character drawing in La Motte, and in his wife; the hero and heroine are not distinguishable from Julia and Hippolytus. But Mrs. Radcliffe does not aim at psychological niceties, and we must not blame her for withholding what it was no part of her purpose to give. "The Romance of the Forest" was, so far, infinitely the most thrilling of modern English works of fiction. "Every reader felt the force," says Scott, "from the sage in his study, to the family group in middle life," and nobody felt it more than Scott himself, then a young gentleman of nineteen, who, when asked how his time was employed, answered, "I read no Civil Law." He did read Mrs. Radcliffe, and, in "The Betrothed," followed her example in the story of the haunted chamber where the heroine faces the spectre attached to her ancient family.

"The Mysteries of Udolpho," Mrs. Radcliffe's next and most celebrated work, is not (in the judgment of this reader, at least) her masterpiece. The booksellers paid her what Scott, erroneously, calls "the unprecedented sum of £500" for the romance, and they must have made a profitable bargain. "The public," says Scott, "rushed upon it with all the eagerness of curiosity, and rose from it with unsated appetite." I arise with a thoroughly sated appetite from the "Mysteries of Udolpho." The book, as Sir Walter saw, is "The Romance of the Forest" raised to a higher power. We have a similar and similarly situated heroine, cruelly detached from her young man, and immured in a howling wilderness of a brigand castle in the Apennines. In place of the Marquis is a miscreant on a larger and more ferocious scale. The usual mysteries of voices, lights, secret passages, and innumerable doors are provided regardless of economy. The great question, which I shall not answer, is, what did the Black Veil conceal? Not "the bones of Laurentina," as Catherine Morland supposed.

Here is Emily's adventure with the veil. "She paused again, and then, with a timid hand, lifted the veil; but instantly let it fall—perceiving that what it had concealed was no picture, and before she could leave the chamber she dropped senseless on the floor. When she recovered her recollection, . . . horror occupied her mind." Countless mysteries coagulate around this veil, and the reader is apt to be disappointed when the awful curtain is withdrawn. But he has enjoyed, for several hundred pages, the pleasures of anticipation. A pedantic censor may remark that, while the date of the story is 1580, all the virtuous people live in an idyllic fashion, like creatures of Rousseau, existing solely for landscape and the affections, writing poetry on Nature, animate and inanimate, including the common Bat, and drawing in water colours. In those elegant avocations began, and in these, after an interval of adventures "amazing horrid," concluded the career of Emily.

Mrs. Radcliffe keeps the many entangled threads of her complex web well in hand, and incidents which puzzle you at the beginning fall naturally into place before the end. The character of the heroine's silly, vain, unkind, and unreasonable aunt is vividly designed (that Emily should mistake the corse of a moustached bandit for that of her aunt is an incident hard to defend). Valancourt is not an ordinary spotless hero, but sows his wild oats, and reaps the usual harvest; and Annette is a good sample of the usual soubrette. When one has said that the landscapes and bandits of this romance are worthy of Poussin and Salvator Rosa, from whom they were probably translated into words, not much remains to be added. Sir Walter, after repeated perusals, considered "Udolpho" "a step beyond Mrs. Radcliffe's former work, high as that had justly advanced her." But he admits that "persons of no mean judgment" preferred "The Romance of the Forest." With these amateurs I would be ranked. The ingenuity and originality of the "Romance" are greater: our friend the skeleton is better than that Thing which was behind the Black Veil, the escapes of Adeline are more thrilling than the escape of Emily, and the "Romance" is not nearly so long, not nearly so prolix as "Udolpho."

The roof and crown of Mrs. Radcliffe's work is "The Italian" (1797), for which she received £800.[6] The scene is Naples, the date

---

[6] I like to know what the author got.

about 1764; the topic is the thwarted loves of Vivaldi and Ellena; the villain is the admirable Schedoni, the prototype of Byron's lurid characters.

"The Italian" is an excellent novel. The Prelude, "the dark and vaulted gateway," is not unworthy of Hawthorne, who, I suspect, had studied Mrs. Radcliffe. The theme is more like a theme of this world than usual. The parents of a young noble might well try to prevent him from marrying an unknown and penniless girl. The Marchese Vivaldi only adopts the ordinary paternal measures; the Marchesa, and her confessor the dark-souled Schedoni, go farther— as far as assassination. The casuistry by which Schedoni brings the lady to this pass, while representing her as the originator of the scheme, is really subtle, and the scenes between the pair show an extraordinary advance on Mrs. Radcliffe's earlier art. The mysterious Monk who counteracts Schedoni remains an unsolved mystery to me, but of that I do not complain. He is as good as the Dweller in the Catacombs who haunts Miriam in Hawthorne's "Marble Faun." The Inquisition, its cells, and its tribunals are coloured

> "As when some great painter dips
> His pencil in the gloom of earthquake and eclipse."

The comic valet, Paulo, who insists on being locked up in the dungeons of the Inquisition merely because his master is there, reminds one of Samuel Weller, he is a Neapolitan Samivel. The escapes are Mrs. Radcliffe's most exciting escapes, and to say that is to say a good deal. Poetry is not written, or not often, by the heroine. The scene in which Schedoni has his dagger raised to murder Ellena, when he discovers that she is his daughter, "is of a new, grand, and powerful character" (Scott), while it is even more satisfactory to learn later that Ellena was not Schedoni's daughter after all.

Why Mrs. Radcliffe, having reached such a pitch of success, never again published a novel, remains more mysterious than any of her Mysteries. Scott justly remarks that her censors attacked her "by showing that she does not possess the excellences proper to a style of composition totally different from that which she has attempted." This is the usual way of reviewers. Tales that fascinated Scott, Fox, and Sheridan, "which possess charms for the learned and unlearned, the grave and gay, the gentleman and clown," do not deserve to be dismissed with a sneer by people who have never read them. Following Horace Walpole in some degree, Mrs. Radcliffe paved the way for Scott, Byron, Maturin, Lewis, and

Charlotte Brontë, just as Miss Burney filled the gap between Smollett and Miss Austen. Mrs. Radcliffe, in short, kept the Lamp of Romance burning much more steadily than the lamps which, in her novels, are always blown out, in the moment of excited apprehension, by the night wind walking in the dank corridors of haunted abbeys. But mark the cruelty of an intellectual parent! Horace Walpole was Mrs. Radcliffe's father in the spirit. Yet, on September 4, 1794, he wrote to Lady Ossory: "I have read some of the descriptive verbose tales, of which your Ladyship says I was the patriarch by several mothers" (Miss Reeve and Mrs. Radcliffe?). "All I can say for myself is that I do not think my concubines have produced issue more natural for excluding the aid of anything marvellous."

CHAPTER VII

A SCOTTISH ROMANTICIST OF 1830

The finding of a rare book that you have wanted long is one of the happier moments in life. Whatever we may think of life when we contemplate it as a whole, it is a delight to discover what one has sought for years, especially if the book be a book which you really want to read, and not a thing whose value is given by the fashion of collecting. Perhaps nobody ever collected before

THE
DEATH-WAKE, OR LUNACY
A NECROMAUNT

In Three Chimeras

BY THOMAS T. STODDART.

"Is't like that lead contains her?—
It were too gross
To rib her cerecloth in the obscure grave."—
Shakespeare.

EDINBURGH:

Printed for HENRY CONSTABLE, Edinburgh,
And HURST, CHANCE, & CO., London.

MDCCCXXXI.

This is my rare book, and it is rare for an excellent good reason, as will be shown. But first of the author. Mr. Thomas Tod Stoddart was born in 1810. He died in 1880. Through all his pilgrimage of three-score years and ten, his "rod and staff did comfort him," as the Scottish version of the Psalms has it; nay, his staff was his rod. He "was an angler," as he remarked when a friend asked: "Well, Tom, what are you doing now." He was the patriarch, the Father Izaak, of Scottish fishers, and he sleeps, according to his desire, like Scott, within hearing of the Tweed. His memoir, published by his daughter, in "Stoddart's Angling Songs" (Blackwood), is an admirable biography, quo fit ut omnis Votiva pateat veluti descripta tabella Vita senis.

But it is with the "young Tom Stoddart," the poet of twenty, not with the old angling sage, that we have to do. Miss Stoddart has discreetly republished only the Angling Songs of her father, the pick of them being classical in their way. Now, as Mr. Arnold writes:—

> "Two desires toss about
> The poet's feverish blood,
> One drives him to the world without,
> And one to solitude."

The young Stoddart's two desires were poetry and fishing. He began with poetry. "At the age of ten his whole desire was to produce an immortal tragedy . . . Blood and battle were the powers with which he worked, and with no meaner tool. Every other dramatic form he despised." It is curious to think of the schoolboy, the born Romanticist, labouring at these things, while Gérard de Nerval, and Victor Hugo, and Théophile Gautier, and Pétrus Borel were boys also—boys of the same ambitions, and with much the same romantic tastes. Stoddart had, luckily, another love besides the Muse. "With the spring and the May fly, the dagger dipped in gore paled before the supple rod, and the dainty midge." Finally, the rod and midge prevailed.

> "Wee dour-looking hooks are the thing,
> Mouse body and laverock wing."

But before he quite abandoned all poetry save fishing ditties, he wrote and published the volume whose title-page we have printed, "The Death Wake." The lad who drove home from an angling expedition in a hearse had an odd way of combining his amusements. He lived among poets and critics who were anglers— Hogg, the Ettrick Shepherd (who cast but a heavy line, they say, in Yarrow), Aytoun, Christopher North, De Quincey—

> "No fisher
> But a well-wisher
> To the game,"

as Scott has it—these were his companions, older or younger. None of these, certainly not Wilson, nor Hogg, nor Aytoun, were friends of the Romantic school, as illustrated by Keats and Shelley. None of them probably knew much of Gautier, De Nerval, Borel, le lycanthrope, and the other boys in that boyish movement of 1830. It was only Stoddart, unconsciously in sympathy with Paris, and censured by his literary friends, who produced the one British Romantic work of 1830. The title itself shows that he was partly

80

laughing at his own performance; he has the mockery of Les Jeunes France in him, as well as the wormy and obituary joys of La Comédie de la Mort. The little book came out, inspired by "all the poetasters." Christopher North wrote, four years later, in Blackwood's Magazine, a tardy review. He styled it "an ingeniously absurd poem, with an ingeniously absurd title, written in a strange, namby-pamby sort of style, between the weakest of Shelley and the strongest of Barry Cornwall." The book "fell dead from the Press," far more dead than "Omar Khayyam." Nay, misfortune pursued it, Miss Stoddart kindly informs me, and it was doomed to the flames. The "remainder," the bulk of the edition, was returned to the poet in sheets, and by him was deposited in a garret. The family had a cook, one Betty, a descendant, perhaps, of "that unhappy Betty or Elizabeth Barnes, cook of Mr. Warburton, Somerset Herald," who burned, among other quartos, Shakespeare's "Henry I.," "Henry II.," and "King Stephen." True to her inherited instincts, Mr. Stoddart's Betty, slowly, relentlessly, through forty years, used "The Death Wake" for the needs and processes of her art. The whole of the edition, except probably a few "presentation copies," perished in the kitchen. As for that fell cook, let us hope that

> "The Biblioclastic Dead
> Have diverse pains to brook,
> They break Affliction's bread
> With Betty Barnes, the Cook,"

as the author of "The Bird Bride" sings.

Miss Stoddart had just informed me of this disaster, which left one almost hopeless of ever owning a copy of "The Death Wake," when I found a brown paper parcel among many that contained to-day's minor poetry "with the author's compliments," and lo, in this unpromising parcel was the long-sought volume! Ever since one was a small boy, reading Stoddart's "Scottish Angler," and old Blackwood's, one had pined for a sight of "The Necromaunt," and here, clean in its "pure purple mantle" of smooth cloth, lay the desired one!

> "Like Dian's kiss, unasked, unsought,
> It gave itself, and was not bought,"

being, indeed, the discovery and gift of a friend who fishes and studies the Lacustrine Muses.

The copy has a peculiar interest; it once belonged to Aytoun, the writer of "The Scottish Cavaliers," of "The Bon Gaultier Ballads," and of "Firmilian," the scourge of the Spasmodic School. Mr. Aytoun has adorned the margins with notes and with caricatures of skulls and cross-bones, while the fly-leaves bear a sonnet to the author, and a lyric in doggerel. Surely this is, indeed, a literary curiosity. The sonnet runs thus:—

"O wormy Thomas Stoddart, who inheritest
Rich thoughts and loathsome, nauseous words and rare,
Tell me, my friend, why is it that thou ferretest
And gropest in each death-corrupted lair?
Seek'st thou for maggots such as have affinity
With those in thine own brain, or dost thou think
That all is sweet which hath a horrid stink?
Why dost thou make Haut-gout thy sole divinity?
Here is enough of genius to convert
Vile dung to precious diamonds and to spare,
Then why transform the diamond into dirt,
And change thy mind, which should be rich and fair,
Into a medley of creations foul,
As if a Seraph would become a Ghoul?"

No doubt Mr. Stoddart's other passion for angling, in which he used a Scottish latitude concerning bait,[7] impelled him to search for "worms and maggots":—

"Fire and faggots,
Worms and maggots,"

as Aytoun writes on the other fly-leaf, are indeed the matter of "The Death Wake."

Then, why, some one may ask, write about "The Death Wake" at all? Why rouse again the nightmare of a boy of twenty? Certainly I am not to say that "The Death Wake" is a pearl of great price, but it does contain passages of poetry—of poetry very curious because it is full of the new note, the new melody which young Mr. Tennyson was beginning to waken. It anticipates Beddoes, it coincides with Gautier and Les Chimères of Gérard, it answers the accents, then unheard in England, of Poe. Some American who read out of the way things, and was not too scrupulous, recognised, and robbed, a brother in Tom Stoddart. Eleven years after "The Death Wake" appeared in England, it was published in Graham's Magazine, as "Agatha, a Necromaunt in Three Chimeras," by Louis Fitzgerald

---

[7] Salmon roe, I am sorry to say.

Tasistro. Now Poe was closely connected with Graham's Magazine, and after "Arthur Gordon Pym," "Louis Fitzgerald Tasistro" does suggest Edgar Allen Poe. But Poe was not Tasistro.

So much for the literary history of the Lunacy.

The poem begins—Chimera I. begins:—

> "An anthem of a sister choristry!
> And, like a windward murmur of the sea,
> O'er silver shells, so solemnly it falls!"

The anthem accompanies a procession of holy fathers towards a bier;

> "Agathè
> Was on the lid—a name. And who? No more!
> 'Twas only Agathè."

A solitary monk is prowling around in the moonlit cathedral; he has a brow of stony marble, he has raven hair, and he falters out the name of Agathè. He has said adieu to that fair one, and to her sister Peace, that lieth in her grave. He has loved, and loves, the silent Agathè. He was the son of a Crusader,

> "And Julio had fain
> Have been a warrior, but his very brain
> Grew fevered at the sickly thought of death,
> And to be stricken with a want of breath."

On the whole he did well not to enter the service. Mr. Aytoun has here written—"A rum Cove for a hussar."

> "And he would say
> A curse be on their laurels.
> And anon
> Was Julio forgotten and his line—
> No wonder for this frenzied tale of mine."

How? asks Aytoun, nor has the grammatical enigma yet been unriddled.

> "Oh! he was wearied of this passing scene!
> But loved not Death; his purpose was between
> Life and the grave; and it would vibrate there
> Like a wild bird that floated far and fair
> Betwixt the sun and sea!"

So "he became monk," and was sorry he had done so, especially when he met a pretty maid,

> "And this was Agathè, young Agathè,
> A motherless fair girl,"

whose father was a kind of Dombey, for

> "When she smiled
> He bade no father's welcome to the child,
> But even told his wish, and will'd it done,
> For her to be sad-hearted, and a nun!"
> So she "took the dreary veil."

They met like a blighted Isabella and Lorenzo:

> "They met many a time
> In the lone chapels after vesper chime,
> They met in love and fear."

Then, one day,

> "He heard it said:
> Poor Julio, thy Agathè is dead."

She died

> "Like to a star within the twilight hours
> Of morning, and she was not! Some have thought
> The Lady Abbess gave her a mad draught."

Here Mr. Aytoun, with sympathy, writes "Damn her!" (the Lady Abbess, that is) and suggests that thought must be read "thaft."

Through "the arras of the gloom" (arras is good), the pale breezes are moaning, and Julio is wan as stars unseen for paleness. However, he lifts the tombstone "as it were lightsome as a summer gladness." "A summer gladness," remarks Mr. Aytoun, "may possibly weigh about half-an-ounce." Julio came on a skull, a haggard one, in the grave, and Mr. Aytoun kindly designs a skeleton, ringing a bell, and crying "Dust ho!"

Now go, and give your poems to your friends!

Finally Julio unburies Agathè:—

"Thou must go,
My sweet betrothed, with me, but not below,
Where there is darkness, dream, and solitude,
But where is light, and life, and one to brood
Above thee, till thou wakest. Ha, I fear
Thou wilt not wake for ever, sleeping here,
Where there are none but the winds to visit thee.
And Convent fathers, and a choristry
Of sisters saying Hush! But I will sing
Rare songs to thy pure spirit, wandering
Down on the dews to hear me; I will tune
The instrument of the ethereal moon,
And all the choir of stars, to rise and fall
In harmony and beauty musical."

Is this not melodious madness, and is this picture of the distraught priest, setting forth to sail the seas with his dead lady, not an invention that Nanteuil might have illustrated, and the clan of Bousingots approved?

The Second Chimera opens nobly:—

"A curse! a curse![8] the beautiful pale wing
Of a sea-bird was worn with wandering,
And, on a sunny rock beside the shore,
It stood, the golden waters gazing o'er;
And they were nearing a brown amber flow
Of weeds, that glittered gloriously below!"

Julio appears with Agathè in his arms, and what ensues is excellent of its kind:—

"He dropt upon a rock, and by him placed,
Over a bed of sea-pinks growing waste,
The silent ladye, and he mutter'd wild,
Strange words about a mother and no child.
"And I shall wed thee, Agathè! although
Ours be no God-blest bridal—even so!"
And from the sand he took a silver shell,
That had been wasted by the fall and swell
Of many a moon-borne tide into a ring—
A rude, rude ring; it was a snow-white thing,
Where a lone hermit limpet slept and died

---

[8] "Why and Wherefore," Aytoun.

85

In ages far away. 'Thou art a bride,
Sweet Agathè! Wake up; we must not linger!'
He press'd the ring upon her chilly finger,
And to the sea-bird on its sunny stone
Shouted, 'Pale priest that liest all alone
Upon thy ocean altar, rise, away
To our glad bridal!' and its wings of gray
All lazily it spread, and hover'd by
With a wild shriek—a melancholy cry!
Then, swooping slowly o'er the heaving breast
Of the blue ocean, vanished in the west."

Julio sang a mad song of a mad priest to a dead maid:—
. . .
"A rosary of stars, love! a prayer as we glide,
And a whisper on the wind, and a murmur on the tide,
And we'll say a fair adieu to the flowers that are seen,
With shells of silver sown in radiancy between.

"A rosary of stars, love! the purest they shall be,
Like spirits of pale pearls in the bosom of the sea;
Now help thee,[9] Virgin Mother, with a blessing as we go,
Upon the laughing waters that are wandering below."

One can readily believe that Poe admired this musical sad
song, if, indeed, he ever saw the poem.
One may give too many extracts, and there is scant room for
the extraordinary witchery of the midnight sea and sky, where the
dead and the distraught drift wandering,

"And the great ocean, like the holy hall,
Where slept a Seraph host maritimal,
Was gorgeous with wings of diamond"—

it was a sea

"Of radiant and moon-breasted emerald."

There follows another song—

"'Tis light to love thee living, girl, when hope is full and fair,

---

[9] Fersitan legendum, "Help Thou."

In the springtide of thy beauty, when there is no sorrow
there
No sorrow on thy brow, and no shadow on thy heart,
When, like a floating sea-bird, bright and beautiful thou art

. . .

"But when the brow is blighted, like a star at morning tide
And faded is the crimson blush upon the cheek beside,
It is to love as seldom love the brightest and the best,
When our love lies like a dew upon the one that is at rest."

We ought to distrust our own admiration of what is rare, odd, novel to us, found by us in a sense, and especially one must distrust one's liking for the verses of a Tweedside angler, of a poet whose forebears lie in the green kirkyard of Yarrow. But, allowing for all this, I cannot but think these very musical, accomplished, and, in their place, appropriate verses, to have been written by a boy of twenty. Nor is it a common imagination, though busy in this vulgar field of horrors, that lifts the pallid bride to look upon the mirror of the sea—

"And bids her gaze into the startled sea,
And says, 'Thine image, from eternity,
Hath come to meet thee, ladye!' and anon
He bade the cold corse kiss the shadowy one
That shook amid the waters."

The picture of the madness of thirst, allied to the disease of the brain, is extremely powerful, the delirious monk tells the salt sea waves

"That ye have power, and passion, and a sound
As of the flying of an angel round
The mighty world; that ye are one with time!"

Here, I can't but think, is imagination.

Mr. Aytoun, however, noted none of those passages, nor that where, in tempest and thunder, a shipwrecked sailor swims to the strange boat, sees the Living Love and the Dead, and falls back into the trough of the wave. But even the friendly pencil of Bon Gaultier approves the passage where an isle rises above the sea, and the boat is lightly stranded on the shore of pure and silver shells. The horrors of corruption, in the Third Chimera, may be left unquoted, Aytoun parodies—

87

"The chalk, the chalk, the cheese, the cheese, the cheeses,
And straightway dropped he down upon his kneeses."

Julio comes back to reason, hates the dreadful bride, and feeds on limpets, "by the mass, he feasteth well!"
There was a holy hermit on the isle,

"I ween like other hermits, so was he."

He is Agathè's father, and he has retired to an eligible island where he may repent his cruelty to his daughter. Julio tells his tale, and goes mad again. The apostrophe to Lunacy which follows is marked "Beautiful" by Aytoun, and is in the spirit of Charles Lamb's remark that madness has pleasures unknown to the sane.

"Thou art, thou art alone,
A pure, pure being, but the God on high
Is with thee ever as thou goest by."

Julio watches again beside the Dead, till morning comes, bringing

"A murmur far and far, of those that stirred
Within the great encampment of the sea."

The tide sweeps the mad and the dead down the shores. "He perished in a dream." As for the Hermit, he buried them, not knowing who they were, but on a later day found and recognised the golden cross of Agathè,

"For long ago he gave that blessed cross
To his fair girl, and knew the relic still."

So the Hermit died of remorse, and one cannot say, with Walton, "and I hope the reader is sorry."
The "other poems" are vague memories of Shelley, or anticipations of Poe. One of them is curiously styled "Her, a Statue," and contains a passage that reminds us of a rubaiyat of Omar's,

"She might see
A love-wing'd Seraph glide in glory by,
Striking the tent of its mortality.

"But that is but a tent wherein may rest
A Sultan to the realm of Death addrest;

88

The Sultan rises, and the dark Ferrásh
Strikes, and prepares it for another guest."

Most akin to Poe is the "Hymn to Orion,"

"Dost thou, in thy vigil, hail
Arcturus on his chariot pale,
Leading him with a fiery flight—
Over the hollow hill of night?"

This, then, is a hasty sketch, and incomplete, of a book which, perhaps, is only a curiosity, but which, I venture to think, gave promise of a poet. Where is the lad of twenty who has written as well to-day—nay, where is the mature person of forty? There was a wind of poetry abroad in 1830, blowing over the barricades of Paris, breathing by the sedges of Cam, stirring the heather on the hills of Yarrow. Hugo, Mr. Browning, Lord Tennyson, caught the breeze in their sails, and were borne adown the Tigris of romance. But the breath that stirred the loch where Tom Stoddart lay and mused in his boat, soon became to him merely the curl on the waters of lone St. Mary's or Loch Skene, and he began casting over the great uneducated trout of a happier time, forgetful of the Muse. He wrote another piece, with a sonorous and delightful title, "Ajalon of the Winds." Where is "Ajalon of the Winds"? Miss Stoddart knows nothing of it, but I fancy that the thrice-loathed Betty could have told a tale.

MALIM CONVIVIS QVAM PLACVISSE COQVIS

We need not, perhaps, regret that Mr. Stoddart withdrew from the struggles and competitions of poetic literature. No very high place, no very glorious crown, one fancies, would have been his. His would have been anxiety, doubt of self, disappointment, or, if he succeeded, the hatred, and envyings, and lies which even then dogged the steps of the victor. It was better to be quiet and go a-fishing.

"Sorrow, sorrow speed away
To our angler's quiet mound,
With the old pilgrim, twilight gray,
Enter through the holy ground;
There he sleeps whose heart is twined
With wild stream and wandering burn,
Wooer of the western wind
Watcher of the April morn!"

89

CHAPTER VIII

THE CONFESSIONS OF SAINT AUGUSTINE

My copy of the Confessions is a dark little book, "a size uncumbersome to the nicest hand," in the format of an Elzevir, bound in black morocco, and adorned with "blind-tooled," that is ungilt, skulls and crossbones. It has lost the title-page with the date, but retains the frontispiece, engraved by Huret. Saint Augustine, in his mitre and other episcopal array, with a quill in his hand, sits under a flood of inspiring sunshine. The dumpy book has been much read, was at some time the property of Mr. John Philips, and bears one touching manuscript note, of which more hereafter. It is, I presume, a copy of the translation by Sir Toby Matthew. The author of the Preface declares, with truth, that the translator "hath consulted so closely and earnestly with the saint that he seemeth to have lighted his torch att his fire, and to speak in the best and most significant English, what and how he would have done had he understood our language."

There can be no better English version of this famous book, in which Saint Augustine tells the story of his eager and passionate youth—a youth tossed about by the contending tides of Love, human and divine. Reading it to-day, with a mundane curiosity, we may half regret the space which he gives to theological metaphysics, and his brief tantalising glimpses of what most interests us now— the common life of men when the Church was becoming mistress of the world, when the old Religions were dying of allegory and moral interpretations and occult dreams. But, even so, Saint Augustine's interest in himself, in the very obscure origins of each human existence, in the psychology of infancy and youth, in school disputes, and magical pretensions; his ardent affections, his exultations, and his faults, make his memoirs immortal among the unveilings of the spirit. He has studied babies, that he may know his dark beginnings, and the seeds of grace and of evil. "Then, by degrees, I began to find where I was; and I had certain desires to declare my will to those by whom it might be executed. But I could not do it, ... therefore would I be tossing my arms, and sending out certain cryes, ... and when they obeyed me not ... I would fall into a rage, and that not against such as were my subjects or servants, but against my Elders and my betters, and I would revenge myself upon them by crying." He has observed that infants "begin to laugh, first sleeping, and then shortly waking;" a curious note, but he does not ask wherefore the sense of humour, or the expression of it, comes to children first in their slumber. Of what do babies dream? And what do the nested swallows chirrup to each other in their sleep?

"Such have I understood that such infants are as I could know, and such have I been told that I was by them who brought me up, though even they may rather be accounted not to know, than to know these things." One thing he knows, "that even infancy is subject to sin." From the womb we are touched with evil. "Myselfe have seene and observed some little child, who could not speake; and yet he was all in an envious kind of wrath, looking pale with a bitter countenance upon his foster-brother." In an envious kind of wrath! Is it not the motive of half our politics, and too much of our criticism? Such is man's inborn nature, not to be cured by laws or reforms, not to be washed out of his veins, though "blood be shed like rain, and tears like a mist." For "an infant cannot endure a companion to feed with him in a fountain of milk which is richly abounding and overflowing, although that companion be wholly destitute, and can take no other food but that." This is the Original Sin, inherited, innate, unacquired; for this are "babes span-long" to suffer, as the famous or infamous preacher declared. "Where, or at what time, was I ever innocent?" he cries, and hears no answer from "the dark backward and abysm" of the pre-natal life.

Then the Saint describes a child's learning to speak; how he amasses verbal tokens of things, "having tamed, and, as it were, broken my mouth to the pronouncing of them." "And so I began to launch out more deeply into the tempestuous traffique and society of mankind." Tempestuous enough he found or made it—this child of a Pagan father and a Christian saint, Monica, the saint of Motherhood. The past generations had "chalked out certain laborious ways of learning," and, perhaps, Saint Augustine never forgave the flogging pedagogue—the plagosus Orbilius of his boyhood. Long before his day he had found out that the sorrows of children, and their joys, are no less serious than the sorrows of mature age. "Is there, Lord, any man of so great a mind that he can think lightly of those racks, and hooks, and other torments, for the avoiding whereof men pray unto Thee with great fear from one end of the world to the other, as that he can make sport at such as doe most sharply inflict these things upon them, as our parents laughed at the torments which we children susteyned at our master's hands?" Can we suppose that Monica laughed, or was it only the heathen father who approved of "roughing it?" "Being yet a childe, I began to beg Thy ayde and succour; and I did loosen the knots of my tongue in praying Thee; and I begged, being yet a little one, with no little devotion, that I might not be beaten at the schoole." One is reminded of Tom Tulliver, who gave up even praying that he might learn one part of his work: "Please make Mr. --- say that I am not to do mathematics."

The Saint admits that he lacked neither memory nor wit, "but he took delight in playing." "The plays and toys of men are called business, yet, when children fall unto them, the same men punish them." Yet the schoolmaster was "more fed upon by rage," if beaten in any little question of learning, than the boy; "if in any match at Ball I had been maistered by one of my playfellows." He "aspired proudly to be victorious in the matches which he made," and I seriously regret to say that he would buy a match, and pay his opponent to lose when he could not win fairly. He liked romances also, "to have myne eares scratched with lying fables"—a "lazy, idle boy," like him who dallied with Rebecca and Rowena in the holidays of Charter House.

Saint Augustine, like Sir Walter Scott at the University of Edinburgh, was "The Greek Dunce." Both of these great men, to their sorrow and loss, absolutely and totally declined to learn Greek. "But what the reason was why I hated the Greeke language, while I was taught it, being a child, I do not yet understand." The Saint was far from being alone in that distaste, and he who writes loathed Greek like poison—till he came to Homer. Latin the Saint loved, except "when reading, writing, and casting of accounts was taught in Latin, which I held not for lesse paynefull or penal than the very Greeke. I wept for Dido's death, who made herselfe away with the sword," he declares, "and even so, the saying that two and two makes foure was an ungrateful song in mine ears; whereas the wooden horse full of armed men, the burning of Troy, and the very Ghost of Creusa, was a most delightful spectacle of vanity."

In short, the Saint was a regular Boy—a high-spirited, clever, sportive, and wilful creature. He was as fond as most boys of the mythical tales, "and for that I was accounted to be a towardly boy." Meanwhile he does not record that Monica disliked his learning the foolish dear old heathen fables—"that flood of hell!"

Boyhood gave place to youth, and, allowing for the vanity of self-accusation, there can be little doubt that the youth of Saint Augustine was une jeunesse orageuse. "And what was that wherein I took delight but to love and to be beloved." There was ever much sentiment and affection in his amours, but his soul "could not distinguish the beauty of chast love from the muddy darkness of lust. Streams of them did confusedly boyl in me"—in his African veins. "With a restless kind of weariness" he pursued that Other Self of the Platonic dream, neglecting the Love of God:

"Oh, how late art thou come, O my Joy!"

The course of his education—for the Bar, as we should say—carried him from home to Carthage, where he rapidly forgot the pure counsels of his mother "as old wife's consailes." "And we delighted in doing ill, not only for the pleasure of the fact, but even for the affection of prayse." Even Monica, it seems, justified the saying:

"Every woman is at heart a Rake."

Marriage would have been his making, Saint Augustine says, "but she desired not even that so very much, lest the cloggs of a wife might have hindered her hopes of me . . . In the meantime the reins were loosed to me beyond reason." Yet the sin which he regrets most bitterly was nothing more dreadful than the robbery of an orchard! Pears he had in plenty, none the less he went, with a band of roisterers, and pillaged another man's pear tree. "I loved the sin, not that which I obtained by the same, but I loved the sin itself." There lay the sting of it! They were not even unusually excellent pears. "A Peare tree ther was, neere our vineyard, heavy loaden with fruite, which tempted not greatly either the sight or tast. To the shaking and robbing thereof, certaine most wicked youthes (whereof I was one) went late at night. We carried away huge burthens of fruit from thence, not for our owne eating, but to be cast before the hoggs."

Oh, moonlit night of Africa, and orchard by these wild seabanks where once Dido stood; oh, laughter of boys among the shaken leaves, and sound of falling fruit; how do you live alone out of so many nights that no man remembers? For Carthage is destroyed, indeed, and forsaken of the sea, yet that one hour of summer is to be unforgotten while man has memory of the story of his past.

Nothing of this, to be sure, is in the mind of the Saint, but a long remorse for this great sin, which he earnestly analyses. Nor is he so penitent but that he is clear-sighted, and finds the spring of his mis-doing in the Sense of Humour! "It was a delight and laughter which tickled us, even at the very hart, to find that we were upon the point of deceiving them who feared no such thing from us, and who, if they had known it, would earnestly have procured the contrary."

Saint Augustine admits that he lived with a fast set, as people say now—"the Depravers" or "Destroyers"; though he loved them little, "whose actions I ever did abhor, that is, their Destruction of others, amongst whom I yet lived with a kind of shameless

93

bashfulness." In short, the "Hell-Fire Club" of that day numbered a reluctant Saint among its members! It was no Christian gospel, but the Hortensius of Cicero which won him from this perilous society. "It altered my affection, and made me address my prayers to Thee, O Lord, and gave me other desires and purposes than I had before. All vain hopes did instantly grow base in myne eyes, and I did, with an incredible heat of hart, aspire towards the Immortality of Wisdom." Thus it was really "Saint Tully," and not the mystic call of Tolle! Lege! that "converted" Augustine, diverting the current of his life into the channel of Righteousness. "How was I kindled then, oh, my God, with a desire to fly from earthly things towards Thee."

There now remained only the choice of a Road. Saint Augustine dates his own conversion from the day of his turning to the strait Christian orthodoxy. Even the Platonic writings, had he known Greek, would not have satisfied his desire. "For where was that Charity that buildeth upon the foundation of Humility, which is Christ Jesus? . . . These pages" (of the Platonists) "carried not in them this countenance of piety—the tears of confession, and that sacrifice of Thine which is an afflicted spirit, a contrite and humbled heart, the salvation of Thy people, the Spouse, the City, the pledge of Thy Holy Spirit, the Cup of our Redemption. No man doth there thus express himself. Shall not my soul be subject to God, for of Him is my salvation? For He is my God, and my salvation, my protectour; I shall never be moved. No man doth there once call and say to him: 'Come unto me all you that labour.'"

The heathen doctors had not the grace which Saint Augustine instinctively knew he lacked—the grace of Humility, nor the Comfort that is not from within but from without. To these he aspired; let us follow him on the path by which he came within their influence; but let us not forget that the guide on the way to the City was kind, clever, wordy, vain old Marcus Tullius Cicero. It is to the City that all our faces should be set, if we knew what belongs to our peace; thither we cast fond, hopeless, backward glances, even if we be of those whom Tertullian calls "Saint Satan's Penitents." Here, in Augustine, we meet a man who found the path—one of the few who have found it, of the few who have won that Love which is our only rest. It may be worth while to follow him to the journey's end.

The treatise of Cicero, then, inflamed Augustine "to the loving and seeking and finding and holding and inseparably embracing of wisdom itself, wheresoever it was." Yet, when he looked for wisdom in the Christian Scriptures, all the literary man, the rhetorician in him, was repelled by the simplicity of the style. Without going further than Mr. Pater's book, "Marius, the Epicurean," and his account of Apuleius, an English reader may learn what kind of style a learned African of that date found not too simple. But Cicero, rather than Apuleius, was Augustine's ideal; that verbose and sonorous eloquence captivated him, as it did the early scholars when learning revived. Augustine had dallied a little with the sect of the Manichees, which appears to have grieved his mother more than his wild life.

But she was comforted by a vision, when she found herself in a wood, and met "a glorious young man," who informed her that "where she was there should her son be also." Curious it is to think that this very semblance of a glorious young man haunts the magical dreams of heathen Red Indians, advising them where they shall find game, and was beheld in such ecstasies by John Tanner, a white man who lived with the Indians, and adopted their religion. The Greeks would have called this appearance Hermes, even in this guise Odysseus met him in the oak wood of Circe's Isle. But Augustine was not yet in his mother's faith; he still taught and studied rhetoric, contending for its prizes, but declining to be aided by a certain wizard of his acquaintance. He had entered as a competitor for a "Tragicall poeme," but was too sportsmanlike to seek victory by art necromantic. Yet he followed after Astrologers, because they used no sacrifices, and did not pretend to consult spirits. Even the derision of his dear friend Nebridius could not then move him from those absurd speculations. His friend died, and "his whole heart was darkened;" "mine eyes would be looking for him in all places, but they found him not, and I hated all things because they told me no news of him." He fell into an extreme weariness of life, and no less fear of death. He lived but by halves; having lost dimidium animae suae, and yet dreaded death, "Lest he might chance to have wholy dyed whome I extremely loved." So he returned to Carthage for change, and sought pleasure in other friendships; but "Blessed is the man that loves Thee and his friend in Thee and his enemy for Thee. For he only never loseth a dear friend to whom all men are dear, for His sake, who is never lost."

Here, on the margin of the old book, beside these thoughts, so beautiful if so helpless, like all words, to console, some reader long dead has written:—

"Pray for your poor servant, J. M."

And again,

"Pray for your poor friend."

Doubtless, some Catholic reader, himself bereaved, is imploring the prayers of a dear friend dead; and sure we need their petitions more than they need ours, who have left this world of temptation, and are at peace.

After this loss Saint Augustine went to Rome, his ambition urging him, perhaps, but more his disgust with the violent and riotous life of students in Carthage. To leave his mother was difficult, but "I lyed to my mother, yea, such a mother, and so escaped from her." And now he had a dangerous sickness, and afterwards betook himself to converse with the orthodox, for example at Milan with Saint Ambrose. In Milan his mother would willingly have continued in the African ritual—a Pagan survival—carrying wine and food to the graves of the dead; but this Saint Ambrose forbade, and she obeyed him for him "she did extremely affect for the regard of my spirituall good."

From Milan his friend Alipius preceded him to Rome, and there "was damnably delighted" with the gladiatorial combats, being "made drunk with a delight in blood." Augustine followed him to Rome, and there lost the girl of his heart, "so that my heart was wounded, as that the very blood did follow." The lady had made a vow of eternal chastity, "having left me with a son by her." But he fell to a new love as the old one was departed, and yet the ancient wound pained him still "after a more desperate and dogged manner."

Haeret letalis arundo!

By these passions his conversion was delayed, the carnal and spiritual wills fighting against each other within him. "Give me chastity and continency, O Lord," he would pray, "but do not give it yet," and perhaps this is the frankest of the confessions of Saint Augustine. In the midst of this war of the spirit and the flesh, "Behold I heard a voyce, as if it had been of some boy or girl from some house not farre off, uttering and often repeating these words in a kind of singing voice,

"Tolle, Lege; Tolle, Lege,
Take up and read, take up and read."

So he took up a Testament, and, opening it at random, after the manner of his Virgilian lots, read:—

"Not in surfeiting and wantonness, not in causality and uncleanness," with what follows. "Neither would I read any further, neither was there any cause why I should." Saint Augustine does not, perhaps, mean us to understand (as his translator does), that he was "miraculously called." He knew what was right perfectly well before; the text only clinched a resolve which he has found it very hard to make. Perhaps there was a trifle of superstition in the matter. We never know how superstitious we are. At all events, henceforth "I neither desired a wife, nor had I any ambitious care of

96

any worldly thing." He told his mother, and Monica rejoiced, believing that now her prayers were answered.

Such is the story of the conversion of Saint Augustine. It was the maturing of an old purpose, and long deferred. Much stranger stories are told of Bunyan and Colonel Gardiner. He gave up rhetoric; another man was engaged "to sell words" to the students of Milan. Being now converted, the Saint becomes less interesting, except for his account of his mother's death, and of that ecstatic converse they held "she and I alone, leaning against a window, which had a prospect upon the garden of our lodging at Ostia." They

> "Came on that which is, and heard
> The vast pulsations of the world."

"And whilest we thus spake, and panted towards the divine, we grew able to take a little taste thereof, with the whole strife of our hearts, and we sighed profoundly, and left there, confined, the very top and flower of our souls and spirits; and we returned to the noyse of language again, where words are begun and ended."

Then Monica fell sick to death, and though she had ever wished to lie beside her husband in Africa, she said: "Lay this Body where you will. Let not any care of it disquiet you; only this I entreat, that you will remember me at the altar of the Lord, wheresoever you be." "But upon the ninth day of her sickness, in the six-and-fiftieth year of her age, and the three-and-thirtieth of mine, that religious and pious soul was discharged from the prison of her body."

The grief of Augustine was not less keen, it seems, than it had been at the death of his friend. But he could remember how "she related with great dearness of affection, how she never heard any harsh or unkind word to be darted out of my mouth against her." And to this consolation was added who knows what of confidence and tenderness of certain hope, or a kind of deadness, perhaps, that may lighten the pain of a heart very often tried and inured to every pain. For it is certain that "this green wound" was green and grievous for a briefer time than the agony of his earlier sorrows. He himself, so earnest in analysing his own emotions, is perplexed by the short date of his tears, and his sharpest grief: "Let him read it who will, and interpret it as it pleaseth him."

So, with the death of Monica, we may leave Saint Augustine. The most human of books, the "Confessions," now strays into theology. Of all books that which it most oddly resembles, to my fancy at least, is the poems of Catullus. The passion and the tender heart they have in common, and in common the war of flesh and spirit; the shameful inappeasable love of Lesbia, or of the worldly life; so delightful and dear to the poet and to the saint, so despised in other moods conquered and victorious again, among the battles of the war in our members. The very words in which the Veronese and the Bishop of Hippo described the pleasure and gaiety of an early friendship are almost the same, and we feel that, born four hundred years later, the lover of Lesbia, the singer of Sirmio might actually have found peace in religion, and exchanged the earthly for the heavenly love.

CHAPTER IX

SMOLLETT

The great English novelists of the eighteenth century turned the course of English Literature out of its older channel. Her streams had descended from the double peaks of Parnassus to irrigate the enamelled fields and elegant parterres of poetry and the drama, as the critics of the period might have said. But Richardson, Fielding, Smollett, and Sterne, diverted the waters, from poetry and plays, into the region of the novel, whither they have brought down a copious alluvial deposit. Modern authors do little but till this fertile Delta: the drama is now in the desert, poetry is a drug, and fiction is literature. Among the writers who made this revolution, Smollett is, personally, the least well known to the world, despite the great part which autobiography and confessions play in his work. He is always talking about himself, and introducing his own experiences. But there is little evidence from without; his extant correspondence is scanty; he was not in Dr. Johnson's circle, much less was he in that of Horace Walpole. He was not a popular man, and probably he has long ceased to be a popular author. About 1780 the vendors of children's books issued abridgments of "Tom Jones" and "Pamela," "Clarissa" and "Joseph Andrews," adapted to the needs of infant minds. It was a curious enterprise, certainly, but the booksellers do not seem to have produced "Every Boy's Roderick Random," or "Peregrine Pickle for the Young." Smollett, in short, is less known than Fielding and Sterne, even Thackeray says but a word about him, in the "English Humorists," and he has no place in the series of "English Men of Letters."

What we know of Smollett reveals a thoroughly typical Scot of his period; a Scot of the species absolutely opposed to Sir Pertinax Macsycophant, and rather akin to the species of Robert Burns. "Rather akin," we may say, for Smollett, like Burns, was a humorist, and in his humour far from dainty; he was a personal satirist, and a satirist far from chivalrous. Like Burns, too, he was a poet of independence; like Burns, and even more than Burns, in a time of patronage he was recalcitrant against patrons. But, unlike Burns, he was farouche to an extreme degree; and, unlike Burns, he carried very far his prejudices about his "gentrice," his gentle birth. Herein he is at the opposite pole from the great peasant poet.

Two potent characteristics of his country were at war within him. There was, first, the belief in "gentrice," in a natural difference of kind between men of coat armour and men without it. Thus Roderick Random, the starving cadet of a line of small lairds, accepts the almost incredible self-denial and devotion of Strap as merely his due. Prince Charles could not have taken the devotion of Henry Goring, or of Neil MacEachain, more entirely as a matter of course, involving no consideration in return, than Roderick took the unparalleled self-sacrifice of his barber friend and school-mate. Scott has remarked on this contemptuous and ungrateful selfishness, and has contrasted it with the relations of Tom Jones and Partridge. Of course, it is not to be assumed that Smollett would have behaved like Roderick, when, "finding the fire in my apartment almost extinguished, I vented my fury upon poor Strap, whose ear I pinched with such violence that he roared hideously with pain..." To be sure Roderick presently "felt unspeakable remorse . . . foamed at the mouth, and kicked the chairs about the room." Now Strap had rescued Roderick from starvation, had bestowed on him hundreds of pounds, and had carried his baggage, and dined on his leavings. But Strap was not gently born! Smollett would not, probably, have acted thus, but he did not consider such conduct a thing out of nature.

On the other side was Smollett's Scottish spirit of independence. As early as 1515, James Ingles, chaplain of Margaret Tudor, wrote to Adam Williamson, "You know the use of this country. . . . The man hath more words than the master, and will not be content except he know the master's counsel. There is no order among us." Strap had the instinct of feudal loyalty to a descendant of a laird. But Smollett boasts that, being at the time about twenty, and having burdened a nobleman with his impossible play, "The Regicide," "resolved to punish his barbarous indifference, and actually discarded my Patron." He was not given to "booing" (in the sense of bowing), but had, of all known Scots, the most "canty conceit o' himsel'." These qualities, with a violence of temper which took the form of beating people when on his travels, cannot have made Smollett a popular character. He knew his faults, as he shows in the dedication of "Ferdinand, Count Fathom," to himself. "I have known you trifling, superficial, and obstinate in dispute; meanly jealous and awkwardly reserved; rash and haughty in your resentment; and coarse and lowly in your connections."

He could, it is true, on occasion, forgive (even where he had not been wronged), and could compensate, in milder moods, for the fierce attacks made in hours when he was "meanly jealous." Yet, in early life at least, he regarded his own Roderick Random as "modest and meritorious," struggling nobly with the difficulties which beset a "friendless orphan," especially from the "selfishness, envy, malice,

100

and base indifference of mankind." Roderick himself is, in fact, the incarnation of the basest selfishness. In one of his adventures he is guilty of that extreme infamy which the d'Artagnan of "The Three Musketeers" and of the "Memoirs" committed, and for which the d'Artagnan of Le Vicomte de Bragelonne took shame to himself. While engaged in a virtuous passion, Roderick not only behaves like a vulgar debauchee, but pursues the meanest arts of the fortune-hunter who is ready to marry any woman for her money. Such is the modest and meritorious orphan, and mankind now carries its "base indifference" so far, that Smollett's biographer, Mr. Hannay, says, "if Roderick had been hanged, I, for my part, should have heard the tidings unmoved . . . Smollett obviously died without realising how nearly the hero, who was in some sort a portrait of himself, came to being a ruffian."

Dr. Carlyle, in 1758, being in London, found Smollett "much of a humorist, and not to be put out of his way." A "humorist," here, means an overbearingly eccentric person, such as Smollett, who lived much in a society of literary dependants, was apt to become. But Dr. Carlyle also found that, though Smollett "described so well the characters of ruffians and profligates," he did not resemble them. Dr. Robertson, the historian, "expressed great surprise at his polished and agreeable manners, and the great urbanity of his conversation." He was handsome in person, as his portrait shows, but his "nervous system was exceedingly irritable and subject to passion," as he says in the Latin account of his health which, in 1763, he drew up for the physician at Montpellier. Though, when he chose, he could behave like a man of breeding, and though he undeniably had a warm heart for his wife and daughter, he did not always choose to behave well. Except Dr. Moore, his biographer, he seems to have had few real friends during most of his career.

As to persons whom he chose to regard as his enemies, he was beyond measure rancorous and dangerous. From his first patron, Lord Lyttelton, to his last, he pursued them with unscrupulous animosity. If he did not mean actually to draw portraits of his grandfather, his cousins, his school-master, and the apothecary whose gallipots he attended—in "Roderick Random,"—yet he left the originals who suggested his characters in a very awkward situation. For assuredly he did entertain a spite against his grandfather: and as many of the incidents in "Roderick Random" were autobiographical, the public readily inferred that others were founded on fact.

The outlines of Smollett's career are familiar, though gaps in our knowledge occur. Perhaps they may partly be filled up by the aid of passages in his novels, plays, and poems: in these, at all events, he describes conditions and situations through which he himself may, or must, have passed.

Born in 1721, he was a younger son of Archibald, a younger son of Sir James Smollett of Bonhill, a house on the now polluted Leven, between Loch Lomond and the estuary of the Clyde. Smollett's father made an imprudent marriage: the grandfather provided a small, but competent provision for him and his family, during his own life. The father, Archibald, died; the grandfather left nothing to the mother of Tobias and her children, but they were assisted with scrimp decency by the heirs. Hence the attacks on the grandfather and cousins of Roderick Random: but, later, Smollett returned to kinder feelings.

In some ways Tobias resembled his old grandsire. About 1710 that gentleman wrote a Memoir of his own life. Hence we learn that he, in childhood, like Roderick Random, was regarded as "a clog and burden," and was neglected by his father, ill-used by his stepmother. Thus Tobias had not only his own early poverty to resent, but had a hereditary grudge against fortune, and "the base indifference of mankind." The old gentleman was lodged "with very hard and penurious people," at Glasgow University. He rose in the world, and was a good Presbyterian Whig, but "had no liberty" to help to forfeit James II. "The puir child, his son" (James III. and VIII.), "if he was really such, was innocent, and it were hard to do anything that would touch the son for the father's fault." The old gentleman, therefore, though a Member of Parliament, evaded attending the first Parliament after the Union: "I had no freedom to do it, because I understood that the great business to be agitated therein was to make laws for abjuring the Pretender . . . which I could not go in with, being always of opinion that it was hard to impose oaths on people who had not freedom to take them."

This was uncommonly liberal conduct, in a Whig, and our Smollett, though no Jacobite, was in distinct and courageous sympathy with Jacobite Scotland. Indeed, he was as patriotic as Burns, or as his own Lismahago. These were times, we must remember, in which Scottish patriotism was more than a mere historical sentiment. Scotland was inconceivably poor, and Scots, in England, were therefore ridiculous. The country had, so far, gained very little by the Union, and the Union was detested even by Scottish Whig Earls. It is recorded by Moore that, while at the Dumbarton Grammar School, Smollett wrote "verses to the memory of Wallace, of whom he became an early admirer," having read "Blind Harry's translation of the Latin poems of John Blair," chaplain to that hero. There probably never were any such Latin poems, but Smollett began with the same hero-worship as Burns.

He had the attachment of a Scot to his native stream, the Leven, which later he was to celebrate. Now if Smollett had credited Roderick Random with these rural, poetical, and patriotic tastes, his hero would have been much more human and amiable. There was much good in Smollett which is absent in Random. But for some reason, probably because Scotland was unpopular after the Forty-Five, Smollett merely describes the woes, ill usage, and retaliations of Roderick. That he suffered as Random did is to the last degree improbable. He had a fair knowledge of Latin, and was not destitute of Greek, while his master, a Mr. Love, bore a good character both for humanity and scholarship. He must have studied the classics at Glasgow University, where he was apprenticed to Mr. Gordon, a surgeon. Gordon, again, was an excellent man, appreciated by Smollett himself in after days, and the odious Potion of "Roderick Random" must, like his rival, Crab, have been merely a fancy sketch of meanness, hypocrisy, and profligacy. Perhaps the good surgeon became the victim of that "one continued string of epigrammatic sarcasms," such as Mr. Colquhoun told Ramsay of Ochtertyre, Smollett used to play off on his companions, "for which no talents could compensate." Judging by Dr. Carlyle's Memoirs this intolerable kind of display was not unusual in Caledonian conversation: but it was not likely to make Tobias popular in England.

Thither he went in 1739, with very little money, "and a very large assortment of letters of recommendation: whether his relatives intended to compensate for the scantiness of the one by their profusion in the other is uncertain; but he has often been heard to declare that their liberality in the last article was prodigious." The Smolletts were not "kinless loons"; they had connections: but who, in Scotland, had money? Tobias had passed his medical examinations, but he rather trusted in his MS. tragedy, "The Regicide." Tragical were its results for the author. Inspired by George Buchanan's Latin history of Scotland, Smollett had produced a play, in blank verse, on the murder of James I. That a boy, even a Scottish boy, should have an overweening passion for this unlucky piece, that he should expect by such a work to climb a step on fortune's ladder, is nowadays amazing. For ten years he clung to it, modified it, polished it, improved it, and then published it in 1749, after the success of "Roderick Random." Twice he told the story of his theatrical mishaps and disappointments, which were such as occur to every writer for the stage. He wailed over them in "Roderick Random," in the story of Mr. Melopoyn; he prolonged his cry, in the preface to "The Regicide," and probably the noble whom he "lashed" (very indecently) in his two satires ("Advice," 1746,

"Reproof," 1747, and in "Roderick Random") was the patron who could not get the tragedy acted. First, in 1739, he had a patron whom he "discarded." Then he went to the West Indies, and, returning in 1744, he lugged out his tragedy again, and fell foul again of patrons, actors, and managers. What befell him was the common fate. People did not, probably, hasten to read his play: managers and "supercilious peers" postponed that entertainment, or, at least, the noblemen could not make the managers accept it if they did not want it. Our taste differs so much from that of the time which admired Home's "Douglas," and "The Regicide" was so often altered to meet objections, that we can scarcely criticise it. Of course it is absolutely unhistorical; of course it is empty of character, and replete with fustian, and ineffably tedious; but perhaps it is not much worse than other luckier tragedies of the age. Naturally a lover calls his wounded lady "the bleeding fair." Naturally she exclaims—

> "Celestial powers
> Protect my father, shower upon his—oh!" (Dies).

Naturally her adorer answers with—

> "So may our mingling souls
> To bliss supernal wing our happy—oh!" (Dies).

We are reminded of—

> "Alas, my Bom!" (Dies).
> "'Bastes' he would have said!"

The piece, if presented, must have been damned. But Smollett was so angry with one patron, Lord Lyttelton, that he burlesqued the poor man's dirge on the death of his wife. He was so angry with Garrick that he dragged him into "Roderick Random" as Marmozet. Later, obliged by Garrick, and forgiving Lyttelton, he wrote respectfully about both. But, in 1746 (in "Advice"), he had assailed the "proud lord, who smiles a gracious lie," and "the varnished ruffians of the State." Because Tobias's play was unacted, people who tried to aid him were liars and ruffians, and a great deal worse, for in his satire, as in his first novel, Smollett charges men of high rank with the worst of unnamable crimes. Pollio and Lord Strutwell, whoever they may have been, were probably recognisable then, and were undeniably libelled, though they did not appeal to a jury. It is improbable that Sir John Cope had ever tried to oblige

Smollett. His ignoble attack on Cope, after that unfortunate General had been fairly and honourably acquitted of incompetence and cowardice, was, then, wholly disinterested. Cope is "a courtier Ape, appointed General."

> "Then Pug, aghast, fled faster than the wind,
> Nor deign'd, in three-score miles, to look behind;
> While every band for orders bleat in vain,
> And fall in slaughtered heaps upon the plain,"—

of Preston Pans.

Nothing could be more remote from the truth, or more unjustly cruel. Smollett had not here even the excuse of patriotism. Sir John Cope was no Butcher Cumberland. In fact the poet's friend is not wrong, when, in "Reproof," he calls Smollett "a flagrant misanthrope." The world was out of joint for the cadet of Bonhill: both before and after his very trying experiences as a ship surgeon the managers would not accept "The Regicide." This was reason good why Smollett should try to make a little money and notoriety by penning satires. They are fierce, foul-mouthed, and pointless. But Smollett was poor, and he was angry; he had the examples of Pope and Swift before him; which, as far as truculence went, he could imitate. Above all, it was then the fixed belief of men of letters that some peer or other ought to aid and support them; and, as no peer did support Smollett, obviously they were "varnished ruffians." He erred as he would not err now, for times, and ways of going wrong, are changed. But, at best, how different are his angry couplets from the lofty melancholy of Johnson's satires!

Smollett's "small sum of money" did not permit him long to push the fortunes of his tragedy, in 1739; and as for his "very large assortment of letters of recommendation," they only procured for him the post of surgeon's mate in the Cumberland of the line. Here he saw enough of the horrors of naval life, enough of misery, brutality, and mismanagement, at Carthagena (1741), to supply materials for the salutary and sickening pages on that theme in "Roderick Random." He also saw and appreciated the sterling qualities of courage, simplicity, and generosity, which he has made immortal in his Bowlings and Trunnions.

It is part of a novelist's business to make one half of the world know how the other half lives; and in this province Smollett anticipated Dickens. He left the service as soon as he could, when the beaten fleet was refitting at Jamaica. In that isle he seems to have practised as a doctor; and he married, or was betrothed to, a Miss Lascelles, who had a small and far from valuable property.

105

The real date of his marriage is obscure: more obscure are Smollett's resources on his return to London, in 1744. Houses in Downing Street can never have been cheap, but we find "Mr. Smollett, surgeon in Downing Street, Westminster," and, in 1746, he was living in May Fair, not a region for slender purses. His tragedy was now bringing in nothing but trouble, to himself and others. His satires cannot have been lucrative. As a dweller in May Fair he could not support himself, like his Mr. Melopoyn, by writing ballads for street singers. Probably he practised in his profession. In "Count Fathom" he makes his adventurer "purchase an old chariot, which was new painted for the occasion, and likewise hire a footman . . . This equipage, though much more expensive than his finances could bear, he found absolutely necessary to give him a chance of employment . . . A walking physician was considered as an obscure pedlar." A chariot, Smollett insists, was necessary to "every raw surgeon"; while Bob Sawyer's expedient of "being called from church" was already vieux jeu, in the way of advertisement. Such things had been "injudiciously hackneyed." In this passage of Fathom's adventures, Smollett proclaims his insight into methods of getting practice. A physician must ingratiate himself with apothecaries and ladies' maids, or "acquire interest enough" to have an infirmary erected "by the voluntary subscriptions of his friends." Here Smollett denounces hospitals, which "encourage the vulgar to be idle and dissolute, by opening an asylum to them and their families, from the diseases of poverty and intemperance." This is odd morality for one who suffered from "the base indifference of mankind." He ought to have known that poverty is not a vice for which the poor are to be blamed; and that intemperance is not the only other cause of their diseases. Perhaps the unfeeling passage is a mere paradox in the style of his own Lismahago.

With or without a chariot, it is probable that Tobias had not an insinuating style, or "a good bedside manner"; friends to support a hospital for his renown he had none; but, somehow, he could live in May Fair, and, in 1746, could meet Dr. Carlyle and Stewart, son of the Provost of Edinburgh, and other Scots, at the Golden Ball in Cockspur Street. There they were enjoying "a frugal supper and a little punch," when the news of Culloden arrived. Carlyle had been a Whig volunteer: he, probably, was happy enough; but Stewart, whose father was in prison, grew pale, and left the room. Smollett and Carlyle then walked home through secluded streets, and were silent, lest their speech should bewray them for Scots. "John Bull," quoth Smollett, "is as haughty and valiant to-day, as he was abject and cowardly on the Black Wednesday when the Highlanders were at Derby."

"Weep, Caledonia, weep!" he had written in his tragedy. Now he wrote "Mourn, hapless Caledonia, mourn." Scott has quoted, from Graham of Gartmore, the story of Smollett's writing verses, while Gartmore and others were playing cards. He read them what he had written, "The Tears of Scotland," and added the last verse on the spot, when warned that his opinions might give offence.

> "Yes, spite of thine insulting foe,
> My sympathising verse shall flow."

The "Tears" are better than the "Ode to Blue-Eyed Ann," probably Mrs. Smollett. But the courageous author of "The Tears of Scotland," had manifestly broken with patrons. He also broke with Rich, the manager at Covent Garden, for whom he had written an opera libretto. He had failed as doctor, and as dramatist; nor, as satirist, had he succeeded. Yet he managed to wear wig and sword, and to be seen in good men's company. Perhaps his wife's little fortune supported him, till, in 1748, he produced "Roderick Random." It is certain that we never find Smollett in the deep distresses of Dr. Johnson and Goldsmith. Novels were now in vogue; "Pamela" was recent, "Joseph Andrews" was yet more recent, "Clarissa Harlowe" had just appeared, and Fielding was publishing "Tom Jones." Smollett, too, tried his hand, and, at last, he succeeded.

His ideas of the novel are offered in his preface. The Novel, for him, is a department of Satire; "the most entertaining and universally improving." To Smollett, "Roderick Random" seemed an "improving" work! Où le didacticisme va t'il se nicher? Romance, he declares, "arose in ignorance, vanity, and superstition," and declined into "the ludicrous and unnatural." Then Cervantes "converted romance to purposes far more useful and entertaining, by making it assume the sock, and point out the follies of ordinary life." Romance was to revive again some twenty years after its funeral oration was thus delivered. As for Smollett himself, he professedly "follows the plan" of Le Sage, in "Gil Blas" (a plan as old as Petronius Arbiter, and the "Golden Ass" of Apuleius); but he gives more place to "compassion," so as not to interfere with "generous indignation, which ought to animate the reader against the sordid and vicious disposition of the world." As a contrast to sordid vice, we are to admire "modest merit" in that exemplary orphan, Mr. Random. This gentleman is a North Briton, because only in North Britain can a poor orphan get such an education as Roderick's "birth and character require," and for other reasons. Now, as for Roderick, the schoolmaster "gave himself no concern about the progress I made," but, "should endeavour, with God's help, to prevent my future improvement." It must have been at Glasgow University, then, that Roderick learned "Greek very well, and was pretty far advanced in the mathematics," and here he must have used his genius for the belles lettres, in the interest of his "amorous complexion," by "lampooning the rivals" of the young ladies who admired him.

Such are the happy beginnings, accompanied by practical jokes, of this interesting model. Smollett's heroes, one conceives, were intended to be fine, though not faultless young fellows; men, not plaster images; brave, generous, free-living, but, as Roderick finds once, when examining his conscience, pure from serious stains on that important faculty. To us these heroes often appear no better than ruffians; Peregrine Pickle, for example, rather excels the infamy of Ferdinand, Count Fathom, in certain respects; though Ferdinand is professedly "often the object of our detestation and abhorrence," and is left in a very bad, but, as "Humphrey Clinker" shows, in by no means a hopeless way. Yet, throughout, Smollett regarded himself as a moralist, a writer of improving tendencies; one who "lashed the vices of the age." He was by no means wholly mistaken, but we should probably wrong the eighteenth century if we accepted all Smollett's censures as entirely deserved. The vices which he lashed are those which he detected, or fancied that he detected, in people who regarded a modest and meritorious Scottish orphan with base indifference. Unluckily the greater part of mankind was guilty of this crime, and consequently was capable of everything.

Enough has probably been said about the utterly distasteful figure of Smollett's hero. In Chapter LX. we find him living on the resources of Strap, then losing all Strap's money at play, and then "I bilk my taylor." That is, Roderick orders several suits of new clothes, and sells them for what they will fetch. Meanwhile Strap can live honestly anywhere, while he has his ten fingers. Roderick rescues himself from poverty by engaging, with his uncle, in the slave trade. We are apt to consider this commerce infamous. But, in 1763, the Evangelical director who helped to make Cowper "a castaway," wrote, as to the slaver's profession: "It is, indeed, accounted a genteel employment, and is usually very profitable, though to me it did not prove so, the Lord seeing that a large increase of wealth could not be good for me." The reverend gentleman had, doubtless, often sung—

> *"Time for us to go,*
> *Time for us to go,*

And when we'd got the hatches down,
'Twas time for us to go!"

Roderick, apart from "black ivory," is aided by his uncle and his long lost father. The base world, in the persons of Strap, Thompson, the uncle, Mr. Sagely, and other people, treats him infinitely better than he deserves. His very love (as always in Smollett) is only an animal appetite, vigorously insisted upon by the author. By a natural reaction, Scott, much as he admired Smollett, introduced his own blameless heroes, and even Thackeray could only hint at the defects of youth, in "Esmond." Thackeray is accused of making his good people stupid, or too simple, or eccentric, and otherwise contemptible. Smollett went further: Strap, a model of benevolence, is ludicrous and a coward; even Bowling has the stage eccentricities of the sailor. Mankind was certain, in the long run, to demand heroes more amiable and worthy of respect. Our inclinations, as Scott says, are with "the open-hearted, good-humoured, and noble-minded Tom Jones, whose libertinism (one particular omitted) is perhaps rendered but too amiable by his good qualities." To be sure Roderick does befriend "a reclaimed street-walker" in her worst need, but why make her the confidante of the virginal Narcissa? Why reward Strap with her hand? Fielding decidedly, as Scott insists, "places before us heroes, and especially heroines, of a much higher as well as more pleasing character, than Smollett was able to present."

"But the deep and fertile genius of Smollett afforded resources sufficient to make up for these deficiencies . . . If Fielding had superior taste, the palm of more brilliancy of genius, more inexhaustible richness of invention, must in justice be awarded to Smollett. In comparison with his sphere, that in which Fielding walked was limited . . . " The second part of Scott's parallel between the men whom he considered the greatest of our novelists, qualifies the first. Smollett's invention was not richer than Fielding's, but the sphere in which he walked, the circle of his experience, was much wider. One division of life they knew about equally well, the category of rakes, adventurers, card-sharpers, unhappy authors, people of the stage, and ladies without reputations, in every degree. There were conditions of higher society, of English rural society, and of clerical society, which Fielding, by birth and education, knew much better than Smollett. But Smollett had the advantage of his early years in Scotland, then as little known as Japan; with the "nautical multitude," from captain to loblolly boy, he was intimately familiar; with the West Indies he was acquainted; and he later resided in Paris, and travelled in Flanders, so that he had more experience, certainly, if not more invention, than Fielding.

In "Roderick Random" he used Scottish "local colour" very little, but his life had furnished him with a surprising wealth of "strange experiences." Inns were, we must believe, the favourite home of adventures, and Smollett could ring endless changes on mistakes about bedrooms. None of them is so innocently diverting as the affair of Mr. Pickwick and the lady in yellow curl-papers; but the absence of that innocence which heightens Mr. Pickwick's distresses was welcome to admirers of what Lady Mary Wortley Montagu calls "gay reading."

She wrote from abroad, in 1752, "There is something humorous in R. Random, that makes me believe that the author is H. Fielding"—her kinsman. Her ladyship did her cousin little justice. She did not complain of the morals of "R. Random," but thought "Pamela" and "Clarissa" "likely to do more general mischief than the works of Lord Rochester." Probably "R. Random" did little harm. His career is too obviously ideal. Too many ups and downs occur to him, and few orphans of merit could set before themselves the ideal of bilking their tailors, gambling by way of a profession, dealing in the slave trade, and wheedling heiresses.

The variety of character in the book is vast; in Morgan we have an excellent, fiery, Welshman, of the stage type; the different minor miscreants are all vividly designed; the eccentric lady author may have had a real original; Miss Snapper has much vivacity as a wit; the French adventures in the army are, in their rude barbaric way, a forecast of Barry Lyndon's; and, generally, both Scott and Thackeray owe a good deal to Smollett in the way of suggestions. Smollett's extraordinary love of dilating on noisome smells and noisome sights, that intense affection for the physically nauseous, which he shared with Swift, is rather less marked in "Roderick" than in "Humphrey Clinker," and "The Adventures of an Atom." The scenes in the Marshalsea must have been familiar to Dickens. The terrible history of Miss Williams is Hogarth's Harlot's Progress done into unsparing prose. Smollett guides us at a brisk pace through the shady and brutal side of the eighteenth century; his vivacity is as unflagging as that of his disagreeable rattle of a hero. The passion usually understood as love is, to be sure, one of which he seems to have no conception; he regards a woman much as a greedy person might regard a sirloin of beef, or, at least, a plate of ortolans. At her marriage a bride is "dished up;" that is all.

Thus this "gay writing" no longer makes us gay. In reading "Peregrine Pickle" and "Humphrey Clinker," a man may find himself laughing aloud, but hardly in reading "Roderick Random." The fun is of the cruel primitive sort, arising merely from the contemplation of somebody's painful discomfiture. Bowling and

110

Rattlin may be regarded with affectionate respect; but Roderick has only physical courage and vivacity to recommend him. Whether Smollett, in Flaubert's deliberate way, purposely abstained from moralising on the many scenes of physical distress which he painted; or whether he merely regarded them without emotion, has been debated. It seems more probable that he thought they carried their own moral. It is the most sympathetic touch in Roderick's character, that he writes thus of his miserable crew of slaves: "Our ship being freed from the disagreeable lading of negroes, to whom indeed I had been a miserable slave since our leaving the coast of Guinea, I began to enjoy myself." Smollett was a physician, and had the pitifulness of his profession; though we see how casually he makes Random touch on his own unwonted benevolence.

People had not begun to know the extent of their own brutality in the slave trade, but Smollett probably did know it. If a curious prophetic letter attributed to him, and published more than twenty years after his death, be genuine; he had the strongest opinions about this form of commercial enterprise. But he did not wear his heart on his sleeve, where he wore his irritable nervous system. It is probable enough that he felt for the victims of poverty, neglect, and oppression (despite his remarks on hospitals) as keenly as Dickens. We might regard his offensively ungrateful Roderick as a purely dramatic exhibition of a young man, if his other heroes were not as bad, or worse; if their few redeeming qualities were not stuck on in patches; and if he had omitted his remark about Roderick's "modest merit." On the other hand, the good side of Matthew Bramble seems to be drawn from Smollett's own character, and, if that be the case, he can have had little sympathy with his own humorous Barry Lyndons. Scott and Thackeray leaned to the favourable view: Smollett, his nervous system apart, was manly and kindly.

As regards plot, "Roderick Random" is a mere string of picturesque adventures. It is at the opposite pole from "Tom Jones" in the matter of construction. There is no reason why it should ever stop except the convenience of printers and binders. Perhaps we lay too much stress on the somewhat mechanical art of plot-building. Fielding was then setting the first and best English example of a craft in which the very greatest authors have been weak, or of which they were careless. Smollett was always rather more incapable, or rather more indifferent, in plot-weaving, than greater men.

In our day of royalties, and gossip about the gains of authors, it would be interesting to know what manner and size of a cheque Smollett received from his publisher, the celebrated Mr. Osborne. We do not know, but Smollett published his next novel "on commission," "printed for the Author"; so probably he was not well satisfied with the pecuniary result of "Roderick Random." Thereby, says Dr. Moore, he "acquired much more reputation than money." So he now published "The Regicide" "by subscription, that method of publication being then more reputable than it has been thought since" (1797). Of "The Regicide," and its unlucky preface, enough, or more, has been said. The public sided with the managers, not with the meritorious orphan.

For the sake of pleasure, or of new experiences, or of economy, Smollett went to Paris in 1750, where he met Dr. Moore, later his biographer, the poetical Dr. Akenside, and an affected painter. He introduced the poet and painter into "Peregrine Pickle"; and makes slight use of a group of exiled Jacobites, including Mr. Hunter of Burnside. In 1750, there were Jacobites enough in the French capital, all wondering very much where Prince Charles might be, and quite unconscious that he was their neighbour in a convent in the Rue St. Dominique. Though Moore does not say so (he is provokingly economical of detail), we may presume that Smollett went wandering in Flanders, as does Peregrine Pickle. It is curious that he should introduce a Capucin, a Jew, and a black-eyed damsel, all in the Ghent diligence, when we know that Prince Charles did live in Ghent, with the black-eyed Miss Walkenshaw, did go about disguised as a Capucin, and was tracked by a Jewish spy, while the other spy, Young Glengarry, styled himself "Pickle." But all those events occurred about a year after the novel was published in 1751.

Before that date Smollett had got an M.D. degree from Aberdeen University, and, after returning from France, he practised for a year or two at Bath. But he could not expect to be successful among fashionable invalids, and, in "Humphrey Clinker," he make Matthew Bramble give such an account of the Bath waters as M. Zola might envy. He was still trying to gain ground in his profession, when, in March 1751, Mr. D. Wilson published the first edition of "Peregrine Pickle" "for the Author," unnamed. I have never seen this first edition, which was "very curious and disgusting." Smollett, in his preface to the second edition, talks of "the art and industry that were used to stifle him in the birth, by certain booksellers and others." He now "reformed the manners, and corrected the expressions," removed or modified some passages of personal satire, and held himself exempt from "the numerous shafts of envy, rancour, and revenge, that have lately, both in private and public, been levelled at his reputation." Who were these base and pitiless dastards? Probably every one who did not write favourably about the book. Perhaps Smollett suspected Fielding, whom he attacks in several parts of his works, treating him as a kind of Jonathan Wild, a thief-taker, and an associate with thieves. Why Smollett thus misconducted himself is a problem, unless he was either "meanly jealous," or had taken offence at some remarks in Fielding's newspaper. Smollett certainly began the war, in the first edition of "Peregrine Pickle." He made a kind of palinode to the "trading justice" later, as other people of his kind have done.

A point in "Peregrine Pickle" easily assailed was the long episode about a Lady of Quality: the beautiful Lady Vane, whose memoirs Smollett introduced into his tale. Horace Walpole found that she had omitted the only feature in her career of which she had just reason to be proud: the number of her lovers. Nobody doubted that Smollett was paid for casting his mantle over Lady Vane: moreover, he might expect a success of scandal. The roman à clef is always popular with scandal-mongers, but its authors can hardly hope to escape rebuke.

It was not till 1752 that Lady Mary Wortley Montagu, in Italy, received "Peregrine," with other fashionable romances—"Pompey the Little," "The Parish Girl," "Eleanora's Adventures," "The Life of Mrs. Theresa Constantia Phipps," "The Adventures of Mrs. Loveil," and so on. Most of them contained portraits of real people, and, no doubt, most of them were therefore successful. But where are they now? Lady Mary thought Lady Vane's part of "Peregrine" "more instructive to young women than any sermon that I know." She regarded Fielding as with Congreve, the only "original" of her age, but Fielding had to write for bread, and that is "the most contemptible way of getting bread." She did not, at this time, even know Smollett's name, but she admired him, and, later, calls him "my dear Smollett." This lady thought that Fielding did not know what sorry fellows his Tom Jones and Captain Booth were. Not near so sorry as Peregine Pickle were they, for this gentleman is a far more atrocious ruffian than Roderick Random.

None the less "Peregrine" is Smollett's greatest work. Nothing is so rich in variety of character, scene, and adventure. We are carried along by the swift and copious volume of the current, carried into very queer places, and into the oddest miscellaneous company, but we cannot escape from Smollett's vigorous grasp. Sir Walter thought that "Roderick" excelled its successor in "ease and simplicity," and that Smollett's sailors, in "Pickle," "border on caricature." No doubt they do: the eccentricities of Hawser Trunnion, Esq., are exaggerated, and Pipes is less subdued than Rattlin, though always delightful. But Trunnion absolutely makes one laugh out aloud: whether he is criticising the sister of Mr. Gamaliel Pickle in that gentleman's presence, at a pot-house; or riding to the altar with his squadron of sailors, tacking in an unfavourable gale; or being run away into a pack of hounds, and clearing a hollow road over a waggoner, who views him with "unspeakable terror and amazement." Mr. Winkle as an equestrian is not more entirely acceptable to the mind than Trunnion. We may speak of "caricature," but if an author can make us sob with laughter, to criticise him solemnly is ungrateful.

Except Fielding occasionally, and Smollett, and Swift, and Sheridan, and the authors of "The Rovers," one does not remember any writers of the eighteenth century who quite upset the gravity of the reader. The scene of the pedant's dinner after the manner of the ancients, does not seem to myself so comic as the adventures of Trunnion, while the bride is at the altar, and the bridegroom is tacking and veering with his convoy about the fields. One sees how the dinner is done: with a knowledge of Athenæus, Juvenal, Petronius, and Horace, many men could have written this set piece. But Trunnion is quite inimitable: he is a child of humour and of the highest spirits, like Mr. Weller the elder. Till Scott created Mause Headrig, no Caledonian had ever produced anything except "Tam o' Shanter," that could be a pendant to Trunnion. His pathos is possibly just a trifle overdone, though that is not my own opinion. Dear Trunnion! he makes me overlook the gambols of his detestable protégé, the hero.

That scoundrel is not an impossible caricature of an obstinate, vain, cruel libertine. Peregrine was precisely the man to fall in love with Emilia pour le bon motif, and then attempt to ruin her, though she was the sister of his friend, by devices worthy of Lovelace at his last and lowest stage. Peregrine's overwhelming vanity, swollen by facile conquests, would inevitably have degraded him to this abyss. The intrigue was only the worst of those infamous practical jokes of his, in which Smollett takes a cruel and unholy delight. Peregrine, in fact, is a hero of naturalisme, except that his fits of generosity are mere patches daubed on, and that his reformation is a farce, in which a modern naturaliste would have disdained to indulge. Emilia, in her scene with Peregrine in the bouge to which he has carried her, rises much above Smollett's heroines, and we could like her, if she had never forgiven behaviour which was beneath pardon.

Peregrine's education at Winchester bears out Lord Elcho's description of that academy in his lately published Memoirs. It was apt to develop Peregrines; and Lord Elcho himself might have furnished Smollett with suitable adventures. There can be no doubt that Cadwallader Crabtree suggested Sir Malachi Malagrowther to Scott, and that Hatchway and Pipes, taking up their abode with Peregrine in the Fleet, gave a hint to Dickens for Sam Weller and

Mr. Pickwick in the same abode. That "Peregrine" "does far excel 'Joseph Andrews' and 'Amelia'," as Scott declares, few modern readers will admit. The world could do much better without "Peregrine" than without "Joseph"; while Amelia herself alone is a study greatly preferable to the whole works of Smollett: such, at least, is the opinion of a declared worshipper of that peerless lady. Yet "Peregrine" is a kind of Odyssey of the eighteenth century: an epic of humour and of adventure.

In February 1753, Smollett "obliged the town" with his "Adventures of Ferdinand, Count Fathom," a cosmopolitan swindler and adventurer. The book is Smollett's "Barry Lyndon," yet as his hero does not tell his own story, but is perpetually held up as a "dreadful example," there is none of Thackeray's irony, none of his subtlety. "Here is a really bad man, a foreigner too," Smollett seems to say, "do not be misled, oh maidens, by the wiles of such a Count! Impetuous youth, play not with him at billiards, basset, or gleek. Fathers, on such a rogue shut your doors: collectors, handle not his nefarious antiques. Let all avoid the path and shun the example of Ferdinand, Count Fathom!"

Such is Smollett's sermon, but, after all, Ferdinand is hardly worse than Roderick or Peregrine. The son of a terrible old sutler and camp-follower, a robber and slayer of wounded men, Ferdinand had to live by his wits, and he was hardly less scrupulous, after all, than Peregrine and Roderick. The daubs of casual generosity were not laid on, and that is all the difference. As Sophia Western was mistaken for Miss Jenny Cameron, so Ferdinand was arrested as Prince Charles, who, in fact, caused much inconvenience to harmless travellers. People were often arrested as "The Pretender's son" abroad as well as in England.

The life and death of Ferdinand's mother, shot by a wounded hussar in her moment of victory, make perhaps the most original and interesting part of this hero's adventures. The rest is much akin to his earlier novels, but the history of Rinaldo and Monimia has a passage not quite alien to the vein of Mrs. Radcliffe. Some remarks in the first chapter show that Smollett felt the censures on his brutality and "lowness," and he promises to seek "that goal of perfection where nature is castigated almost even to still life . . . where decency, divested of all substance, hovers about like a fantastic shadow."

Smollett never reached that goal, and even the shadow of decency never haunted him so as to make him afraid with any amazement. Smollett avers that he "has had the courage to call in question the talents of a pseudo-patron," and so is charged with "insolence, rancour, and scurrility." Of all these things, and of worse, he had been guilty; his offence had never been limited to "calling in question the talents" of persons who had been unsuccessful in getting his play represented. Remonstrance merely irritated Tobias. His new novel was but a fainter echo of his old novels, a panorama of scoundrelism, with the melodramatic fortunes of the virtuous Monimia for a foil. If read to-day, it is read as a sketch of manners, or want of manners. The scene in which the bumpkin squire rooks the accomplished Fathom at hazard, in Paris, is prettily conceived, and Smollett's indignation at the British system of pews in church is edifying. But when Monimia appears to her lover as he weeps at her tomb, and proves to be no phantom, but a "warm and substantial" Monimia, capable of being "dished up," like any other Smollettian heroine, the reader is sensibly annoyed. Tobias as un romantique is absolutely too absurd; "not here, oh Tobias, are haunts meet for thee."

Smollett's next novel, "Sir Launcelot Greaves," was not published till 1761, after it had appeared in numbers, in The British Magazine. This was a sixpenny serial, published by Newbery. The years between 1753 and 1760 had been occupied by Smollett in quarrelling, getting imprisoned for libel, editing the Critical Review, writing his "History of England," translating (or adapting old translations of) "Don Quixote," and driving a team of literary hacks, whose labours he superintended, and to whom he gave a weekly dinner. These exploits are described by Dr. Carlyle, and by Smollett himself, in "Humphrey Clinker." He did not treat his vassals with much courtesy or consideration; but then they expected no such treatment. We have no right to talk of his doings as "a blood-sucking method, literary sweating," like a recent biographer of Smollett. Not to speak of the oddly mixed metaphor, we do not know what Smollett's relations to his retainers really were. As an editor he had to see his contributors. The work of others he may have recommended, as "reader" to publishers. Others may have made transcripts for him, or translations. That Smollett "sweated" men, or sucked their blood, or both, seems a crude way of saying that he found them employment. Nobody says that Johnson "sweated" the persons who helped him in compiling his Dictionary; or that Mr. Jowett "sweated" the friends and pupils who aided him in his translation of Plato. Authors have a perfect right to procure literary assistance, especially in learned books, if they pay for it, and acknowledge their debt to their allies. On the second point, Smollett was probably not in advance of his age.

"Sir Launcelot Greaves" is, according to Chambers, "a sorry specimen of the genius of the author," and Mr. Oliphant Smeaton calls it "decidedly the least popular" of his novels, while Scott

116

astonishes us by preferring it to "Jonathan Wild." Certainly it is inferior to "Roderick Random" and to "Peregrine Pickle," but it cannot be so utterly unreal as "The Adventures of an Atom." I, for one, venture to prefer "Sir Launcelot" to "Ferdinand, Count Fathom." Smollett was really trying an experiment in the fantastic. Just as Mr. Anstey Guthrie transfers the mediæval myth of Venus and the Ring, or the Arabian tale of the bottled-up geni (or djinn) into modern life, so Smollett transferred Don Quixote. His hero, a young baronet of wealth, and of a benevolent and generous temper, is crossed in love. Though not mad, he is eccentric, and commences knight-errant. Scott, and others, object to his armour, and say that, in his ordinary clothes, and with his well-filled purse, he would have been more successful in righting wrongs. Certainly, but then the comic fantasy of the armed knight arriving at the ale-house, and jangling about the rose-hung lanes among the astonished folk of town and country, would have been lost. Smollett is certainly less unsuccessful in wild fantasy, than in the ridiculous romantic scenes where the substantial phantom of Monimia disports itself. The imitation of the knight by the nautical Captain Crowe (an excellent Smollettian mariner) is entertaining, and Sir Launcelot's crusty Sancho is a pleasant variety in squires. The various forms of oppression which the knight resists are of historical interest, as also is the contested election between a rustic Tory and a smooth Ministerialist: "sincerely attached to the Protestant succession, in detestation of a popish, an abjured, and an outlawed Pretender." The heroine, Aurelia Darrel, is more of a lady, and less of a luxury, than perhaps any other of Smollett's women. But how Smollett makes love! "Tea was called. The lovers were seated; he looked and languished; she flushed and faltered; all was doubt and delirium, fondness and flutter."

"All was gas and gaiters," said the insane lover of Mrs. Nickleby, with equal delicacy and point.

Scott says that Smollett, when on a visit to Scotland, used to write his chapter of "copy" in the half-hour before the post went out. Scott was very capable of having the same thing happen to himself. "Sir Launcelot" is hurriedly, but vigorously written: the fantasy was not understood as Smollett intended it to be, and the book is blotted, as usual, with loathsome medical details. But people in Madame du Deffand's circle used openly to discuss the same topics, to the confusion of Horace Walpole. As the hero of this book is a generous gentleman, as the most of it is kind and manly, and the humour provocative of an honest laugh, it is by no means to be despised, while the manners, if caricatured, are based on fact.

It is curious to note that in "Sir Launcelot Greaves," we find a character, Ferret, who frankly poses as a strugforlifeur. M. Daudet's strugforlifeur had heard of Darwin. Mr. Ferret had read Hobbes, learned that man was in a state of nature, and inferred that we ought to prey upon each other, as a pike eats trout. Miss Burney, too, at Bath, about 1780, met a perfectly emancipated young "New Woman." She had read Bolingbroke and Hume, believed in nothing, and was ready to be a "Woman who Did." Our ancestors could be just as advanced as we are.

Smollett went on compiling, and supporting himself by his compilations, and those of his vassals. In 1762 he unluckily edited a paper called The Briton in the interests of Lord Bute. The Briton was silenced by Wilkes's North Briton. Smollett lost his last patron; he fell ill; his daughter died; he travelled angrily in France and Italy. His "Travels" show the choleric nature of the man, and he was especially blamed for not admiring the Venus de Medici. Modern taste, enlightened by the works of a better period of Greek art, has come round to Smollett's opinions. But, in his own day, he was regarded as a Vandal and a heretic.

In 1764, he visited Scotland, and was warmly welcomed by his kinsman, the laird of Bonhill. In 1769, he published "The Adventures of an Atom," a stupid, foul, and scurrilous political satire, in which Lord Bute, having been his patron, was "lashed" in Smollett's usual style. In 1768, Smollett left England for ever. He desired a consulship, but no consulship was found for him, which is not surprising. He died at Monte Nova, near Leghorn, in September (others say October) 1771. He had finished "Humphrey Clinker," which appeared a day or two before his death.

Thackeray thought "Humphrey Clinker" the most laughable book that ever was written. Certainly nobody is to be envied who does not laugh over the epistles of Winifred Jenkins. The book is too well known for analysis. The family of Matthew Bramble, Esq., are on their travels, with his nephew and niece, young Melford and Lydia Melford, with Miss Jenkins, and the squire's tart, greedy, and amorous old maid of a sister, Tabitha Bramble. This lady's persistent amours and mean avarice scarcely strike modern readers as amusing. Smollett gave aspects of his own character in the choleric, kind, benevolent Matthew Bramble, and in the patriotic and paradoxical Lieutenant Lismahago. Bramble, a gouty invalid, is as full of medical abominations as Smollett himself, as ready to fight, and as generous and open-handed. Probably the author shared Lismahago's contempt of trade, his dislike of the Union (1707), his fiery independence (yet he does marry Tabitha!), and those opinions in which Lismahago heralds some of the social notions of Mr. Ruskin.

118

Melford is an honourable kind of "walking gentleman"; Lydia, though enamoured, is modest and dignified; Clinker is a worthy son of Bramble, with abundant good humour, and a pleasing vein of Wesleyan Methodism. But the grotesque spelling, rural vanity, and naïveté of Winifred Jenkins, with her affection for her kitten, make her the most delightful of this wandering company. After beholding the humours and partaking of the waters of Bath, they follow Smollett's own Scottish tour, and each character gives his picture of the country which Smollett had left at its lowest ebb of industry and comfort, and found so much more prosperous. The book is a mine for the historian of manners and customs: the novel-reader finds Count Fathom metamorphosed into Mr. Grieve, an exemplary apothecary, "a sincere convert to virtue," and "unaffectedly pious."

Apparently a wave of good-nature came over Smollett: he forgave everybody, his own relations even, and he reclaimed his villain. A patron might have played with him. He mellowed in Scotland: Matthew there became less tart, and more tolerant; an actual English Matthew would have behaved quite otherwise. "Humphrey Clinker" is an astonishing book, as the work of an exiled, poor, and dying man. None of his works leaves so admirable an impression of Smollett's virtues: none has so few of his less amiable qualities.

With the cadet of Bonhill, outworn with living, and with labour, died the burly, brawling, picturesque old English novel of humour and of the road. We have nothing notable in this manner, before the arrival of Mr. Pickwick. An exception will scarcely be made in the interest of Richard Cumberland, who, as Scott says, "has occasionally . . . become disgusting, when he meant to be humorous." Already Walpole had begun the new "Gothic romance," and the "Castle of Otranto," with Miss Burney's novels, was to lead up to Mrs. Radcliffe and Scott, to Miss Edgeworth and Miss Austen.

CHAPTER X

NATHANIEL HAWTHORNE

Sainte-Beuve says somewhere that it is impossible to speak of "The German Classics." Perhaps he would not have allowed us to talk of the American classics. American literature is too nearly contemporary. Time has not tried it. But, if America possesses a classic author (and I am not denying that she may have several), that author is decidedly Hawthorne. His renown is unimpeached: his greatness is probably permanent, because he is at once such an original and personal genius, and such a judicious and determined artist.

Hawthorne did not set himself to "compete with life." He did not make the effort—the proverbially tedious effort—to say everything. To his mind, fiction was not a mirror of commonplace persons, and he was not the analyst of the minutest among their ordinary emotions. Nor did he make a moral, or social, or political purpose the end and aim of his art. Moral as many of his pieces naturally are, we cannot call them didactic. He did not expect, nor intend, to better people by them. He drew the Rev. Arthur Dimmesdale without hoping that his Awful Example would persuade readers to "make a clean breast" of their iniquities and their secrets. It was the moral situation that interested him, not the edifying effect of his picture of that situation upon the minds of novel-readers.

He set himself to write Romance, with a definite idea of what Romance-writing should be; "to dream strange things, and make them look like truth." Nothing can be more remote from the modern system of reporting commonplace things, in the hope that they will read like truth. As all painters must do, according to good traditions, he selected a subject, and then placed it in a deliberately arranged light—not in the full glare of the noonday sun, and in the disturbances of wind, and weather, and cloud. Moonshine filling a familiar chamber, and making it unfamiliar, moonshine mixed with the "faint ruddiness on walls and ceiling" of fire, was the light, or a clear brown twilight was the light by which he chose to work. So he tells us in the preface to "The Scarlet Letter." The room could be filled with the ghosts of old dwellers in it; faint, yet distinct, all the life that had passed through it came back, and spoke with him, and inspired him. He kept his eyes on these figures, tangled in some rare knot of Fate, and of Desire: these he painted, not attending much to the bustle of existence that surrounded them, not

120

permitting superfluous elements to mingle with them, and to distract him.

The method of Hawthorne can be more easily traced than that of most artists as great as himself. Pope's brilliant passages and disconnected trains of thought are explained when we remember that "paper-sparing," as he says, he wrote two, or four, or six couplets on odd, stray bits of casual writing material. These he had to join together, somehow, and between his "Orient Pearls at Random Strung" there is occasionally "too much string," as Dickens once said on another opportunity. Hawthorne's method is revealed in his published note-books. In these he jotted the germ of an idea, the first notion of a singular, perhaps supernatural moral situation. Many of these he never used at all, on others he would dream, and dream, till the persons in the situations became characters, and the thing was evolved into a story. Thus he may have invented such a problem as this: "The effect of a great, sudden sin on a simple and joyous nature," and thence came all the substance of "The Marble Faun" ("Transformation"). The original and germinal idea would naturally divide itself into another, as the protozoa reproduce themselves. Another idea was the effect of nearness to the great crime on a pure and spotless nature: hence the character of Hilda. In the preface to "The Scarlet Letter," Hawthorne shows us how he tried, by reflection and dream, to warm the vague persons of the first mere notion or hint into such life as characters in romance inherit. While he was in the Civil Service of his country, in the Custom House at Salem, he could not do this; he needed freedom. He was dismissed by political opponents from office, and instantly he was himself again, and wrote his most popular and, perhaps, his best book. The evolution of his work was from the prime notion (which he confessed that he loved best when "strange") to the short story, and thence to the full and rounded novel. All his work was leisurely. All his language was picked, though not with affectation. He did not strive to make a style out of the use of odd words, or of familiar words in odd places. Almost always he looked for "a kind of spiritual medium, seen through which" his romances, like the Old Manse in which he dwelt, "had not quite the aspect of belonging to the material world."

The spiritual medium which he liked, he was partly born into, and partly he created it. The child of a race which came from England, robust and Puritanic, he had in his veins the blood of judges—of those judges who burned witches and persecuted Quakers. His fancy is as much influenced by the old fanciful traditions of Providence, of Witchcraft, of haunting Indian magic, as Scott's is influenced by legends of foray and feud, by ballad, and song, and old wives' tales, and records of conspiracies, fire-raisings, tragic love-adventures, and border wars. Like Scott, Hawthorne lived in phantasy—in phantasy which returned to the romantic past, wherein his ancestors had been notable men. It is a commonplace, but an inevitable commonplace, to add that he was filled with the idea of Heredity, with the belief that we are all only new combinations of our fathers that were before us. This has been made into a kind of pseudo-scientific doctrine by M. Zola, in the long series of his Rougon-Macquart novels. Hawthorne treated it with a more delicate and a serener art in "The House of the Seven Gables."

It is curious to mark Hawthorne's attempts to break away from himself—from the man that heredity, and circumstance, and the divine gift of genius had made him. He naturally "haunts the mouldering lodges of the past"; but when he came to England (where such lodges are abundant), he was ill-pleased and cross-grained. He knew that a long past, with mysteries, dark places, malisons, curses, historic wrongs, was the proper atmosphere of his art. But a kind of conscientious desire to be something other than himself—something more ordinary and popular—make him thank Heaven that his chosen atmosphere was rare in his native land. He grumbled at it, when he was in the midst of it; he grumbled in England; and how he grumbled in Rome! He permitted the American Eagle to make her nest in his bosom, "with the customary infirmity of temper that characterises this unhappy fowl," as he says in his essay "The Custom House." "The general truculency of her attitude" seems to "threaten mischief to the inoffensive community" of Europe, and especially of England and Italy.

Perhaps Hawthorne travelled too late, when his habits were too much fixed. It does not become Englishmen to be angry because a voyager is annoyed at not finding everything familiar and customary in lands which he only visits because they are strange. This is an inconsistency to which English travellers are particularly prone. But it is, in Hawthorne's case, perhaps, another instance of his conscientious attempts to be, what he was not, very much like other people. His unexpected explosions of Puritanism, perhaps, are caused by the sense of being too much himself. He speaks of "the Squeamish love of the Beautiful" as if the love of the Beautiful were something unworthy of an able-bodied citizen. In some arts, as in painting and sculpture, his taste was very far from being at home, as his Italian journals especially prove. In short, he was an artist in a community for long most inartistic. He could not do what many of us find very difficult—he could not take Beauty with gladness as it comes, neither shrinking from it as immoral, nor getting girlishly drunk upon it, in the æsthetic fashion, and screaming over it in an intoxication of surprise. His tendency was to be rather shy and afraid of Beauty, as a pleasant but not immaculately respectable acquaintance. Or, perhaps, he was merely deferring to Anglo-Saxon public opinion.

Possibly he was trying to wean himself from himself, and from his own genius, when he consorted with odd amateur socialists in farm-work, and when he mixed, at Concord, with the "queer, strangely-dressed, oddly-behaved mortals, most of whom took upon themselves to be important agents of the world's destiny, yet were simple bores of a very intense water." They haunted Mr. Emerson as they haunted Shelley, and Hawthorne had to see much of them. But they neither made a convert of him, nor irritated him into resentment. His long-enduring kindness to the unfortunate Miss Delia Bacon, an early believer in the nonsense about Bacon and Shakespeare, was a model of manly and generous conduct. He was, indeed, an admirable character, and his goodness had the bloom on it of a courteous and kindly nature that loved the Muses. But, as one has ventured to hint, the development of his genius and taste was hampered now and then, apparently, by a desire to put himself on the level of the general public, and of their ideas. This, at least, is how one explains to oneself various remarks in his prefaces, journals, and note-books. This may account for the moral allegories which too weirdly haunt some of his short, early pieces. Edgar Poe, in a passage full of very honest and well-chosen praise, found fault with the allegorical business.

Mr. Hutton, from whose "Literary Essays" I borrow Poe's opinion, says: "Poe boldly asserted that the conspicuously ideal scaffoldings of Hawthorne's stories were but the monstrous fruits of the bad transcendental atmosphere which he breathed so long." But I hope this way of putting it is not Poe's. "Ideal scaffoldings," are odd enough, but when scaffoldings turn out to be "fruits" of an "atmosphere," and monstrous fruits of a "bad transcendental atmosphere," the brain reels in the fumes of mixed metaphors. "Let him mend his pen," cried Poe, "get a bottle of visible ink, come out from the Old Manse, cut Mr. Alcott," and, in fact, write about things less impalpable, as Mr. Mallock's heroine preferred to be loved, "in a more human sort of way."

Hawthorne's way was never too ruddily and robustly human. Perhaps, even in "The Scarlet Letter," we feel too distinctly that certain characters are moral conceptions, not warmed and wakened out of the allegorical into the real. The persons in an allegory may be real enough, as Bunyan has proved by examples. But that culpable clergyman, Mr. Arthur Dimmesdale, with his large, white brow, his melancholy eyes, his hand on his heart, and his general resemblance to the High Church Curate in Thackeray's "Our Street," is he real? To me he seems very unworthy to be Hester's lover, for she is a beautiful woman of flesh and blood. Mr. Dimmesdale was not only immoral; he was unsportsmanlike. He had no more pluck than a church-mouse. His miserable passion was degraded by its brevity; how could he see this woman's disgrace for seven long years, and never pluck up heart either to share her shame or peccare forliter? He is a lay figure, very cleverly, but somewhat conventionally made and painted. The vengeful husband of Hester, Roger Chillingworth, is a Mr. Casaubon stung into jealous anger. But his attitude, watching ever by Dimmesdale, tormenting him, and yet in his confidence, and ever unsuspected, reminds one of a conception dear to Dickens. He uses it in "David Copperfield," where Mr. Micawber (of all people!) plays this trick on Uriah Heep; he uses it in "Hunted Down"; he was about using it in "Edwin Drood"; he used it (old Martin and Pecksniff) in "Martin Chuzzlewit." The person of Roger Chillingworth and his conduct are a little too melodramatic for Hawthorne's genius.

In Dickens's manner, too, is Hawthorne's long sarcastic address to Judge Pyncheon (in "The House of the Seven Gables"), as the judge sits dead in his chair, with his watch ticking in his hand. Occasionally a chance remark reminds one of Dickens; this for example: He is talking of large, black old books of divinity, and of their successors, tiny books, Elzevirs perhaps. "These little old volumes impressed me as if they had been intended for very large ones, but had been unfortunately blighted at an early stage of their growth." This might almost deceive the elect as a piece of the true Boz. Their widely different talents did really intersect each other where the perverse, the grotesque, and the terrible dwell.

To myself "The House of the Seven Gables" has always appeared the most beautiful and attractive of Hawthorne's novels. He actually gives us a love story, and condescends to a pretty heroine. The curse of "Maule's Blood" is a good old romantic idea, terribly handled. There is more of lightness, and of a cobwebby dusty humour in Hepzibah Pyncheon, the decayed lady shopkeeper, than Hawthorne commonly cares to display. Do you care for the "first lover," the Photographer's Young Man? It may be conventional prejudice, but I seem to see him going about on a tricycle, and I don't think him the right person for Phoebe. Perhaps it is really the beautiful, gentle, oppressed Clifford who haunts one's memory most, a kind of tragic and thwarted Harold Skimpole. "How pleasant, how delightful," he murmured, but not as if addressing any one. "Will it last? How balmy the atmosphere through that open window! An open window! How beautiful that play of sunshine. Those flowers, how very fragrant! That young girl's face, how cheerful, how blooming. A flower with the dew on it, and sunbeams in the dewdrops . . . " This comparison with Skimpole may sound like an unkind criticism of Clifford's character and place in the story—it is only a chance note of a chance resemblance.

Indeed, it may be that Hawthorne himself was aware of the resemblance. "An individual of Clifford's character," he remarks, "can always be pricked more acutely through his sense of the beautiful and harmonious than through his heart." And he suggests that, if Clifford had not been so long in prison, his æsthetic zeal "might have eaten out or filed away his affections." This was what befell Harold Skimpole—himself "in prisons often"—at Coavinses! The Judge Pyncheon of the tale is also a masterly study of swaggering black-hearted respectability, and then, in addition to all the poetry of his style, and the charm of his haunted air, Hawthorne favours us with a brave conclusion of the good sort, the old sort. They come into money, they marry, they are happy ever after. This is doing things handsomely, though some of our modern novelists think it coarse and degrading. Hawthorne did not think so, and they are not exactly better artists than Hawthorne.

Yet he, too, had his economies, which we resent. I do not mean his not telling us what it was that Roger Chillingworth saw on Arthur Dimmesdale's bare breast. To leave that vague is quite legitimate. But what had Miriam and the spectre of the Catacombs done? Who was the spectre? What did he want? To have told all this would have been better than to fill the novel with padding about Rome, sculpture, and the Ethics of Art. As the silly saying runs: "the people has a right to know" about Miriam and her ghostly acquaintance.[10] But the "Marble Faun" is not of Hawthorne's best period, beautiful as are a hundred passages in the tale.

Beautiful passages are as common in his prose as gold in the richest quartz. How excellent are his words on the first faint but certain breath of Autumn in the air, felt, perhaps, early in July. "And then came Autumn, with his immense burthen of apples, dropping them continually from his overladen shoulders as he trudged along." Keats might have written so of Autumn in the orchards—if Keats had been writing prose.

There are geniuses more sunny, large, and glad than Hawthorne's, none more original, more surefooted, in his own realm of moonlight and twilight.

---

[10] I know, now, who Miriam was and who was the haunter of the Catacombs. But perhaps the people is as well without the knowledge of an old and "ower true tale" that shook a throne.

CHAPTER XI

THE PARADISE OF POETS

We were talking of Love, Constancy, the Ideal. "Who ever loved like the poets?" cried Lady Violet Lebas, her pure, pale cheek flushing. "Ah, if ever I am to love, he shall be a singer!"

"Tenors are popular, very," said Lord Walter.

"I mean a poet," she answered witheringly.

Near them stood Mr. Witham, the author of "Heart's Chords Tangled."

"Ah," said he, "that reminds me. I have been trying to catch it all the morning. That reminds me of my dream."

"Tell us your dream," murmured Lady Violet Lebas, and he told it.

"It was through an unfortunate but pardonable blunder," said Mr. Witham, "that I died, and reached the Paradise of Poets. I had, indeed, published volumes of verse, but with the most blameless motives. Other poets were continually sending me theirs, and, as I could not admire them, and did not like to reply by critical remarks, I simply printed some rhymes for the purpose of sending them to the gentlemen who favoured me with theirs. I always wrote on the fly-leaf a quotation from the 'Iliad,' about giving copper in exchange for gold; and the few poets who could read Greek were gratified, while the others, probably, thought a compliment was intended. Nothing could be less culpable or pretentious, but, through some mistake on the part of Charon, I was drafted off to the Paradise of Poets.

"Outside the Golden Gate a number of Shadows were waiting, in different attitudes of depression and languor. Bavius and Maevius were there, still complaining of 'cliques,' railing at Horace for a mere rhymer of society, and at Virgil as a plagiarist, 'Take away his cribs from Homer and Apollonius Rhodius,' quoth honest Maevius, 'and what is there left of him?' I also met a society of gentlemen, in Greek costume, of various ages, from a half-naked minstrel with a tortoiseshell lyre in his hand to an elegant of the age of Pericles. They all consorted together, talking various dialects of Aeolic, Ionian, Attic Greek, and so forth, which were plainly not intelligible to each other. I ventured to ask one of the company who he was, but he, with a sweep of his hand, said, 'We are Homer!' When I expressed my regret and surprise that the Golden Gate had not yet opened for so distinguished, though collective, an artist, my

126

friend answered that, according to Fick, Peppmüller, and many other learned men, they were Homer. 'But an impostor from Chios has got in somehow,' he said; 'they don't pay the least attention to the Germans in the Paradise of Poets.'

"At this moment the Golden Gates were thrown apart, and a fair lady, in an early Italian costume, carrying a laurel in her hand, appeared at the entrance. All the Shadows looked up with an air of weary expectation, like people waiting for their turn in a doctor's consulting-room. She beckoned to me, however, and I made haste to follow her. The words 'Charlatan!' 'You a poet!' in a variety of languages, greeted me by way of farewell from the Shadows.

"'The renowned Laura, if I am not mistaken,' I ventured to remark, recognising her, indeed, from the miniature in the Laurentian library at Florence.

"She bowed, and I began to ask for her adorer, Petrarch.

"'Excuse me,' said Laura, as we glided down a mossy path, under the shade of trees particularly dear to poets, 'excuse me, but the sonneteer of whom you speak is one whose name I cannot bear to mention. His conduct with Burns's Clarinda, his heartless infatuation for Stella—'

"'You astonish me,' I said. 'In the Paradise of Poets—'

"'They are poets still—incorrigible!' answered the lady; then slightly raising her voice of silver, as a beautiful appearance in a toga drew near, she cried 'Catullo mio!'

"The greeting between these accomplished ghosts was too kindly to leave room for doubt as to the ardour of their affections.

"'Will you, my Catullus,' murmured Laura, 'explain to this poet from the land of fogs, any matters which, to him, may seem puzzling and unfamiliar in our Paradise?'

"The Veronese, with a charming smile, took my hand, and led me to a shadowy arbour, whence we enjoyed a prospect of many rivers and mountains in the poets' heaven. Among these I recognised the triple crest of the Eildons, Grongar Hill, Cithaeron and Etna; while the reed-fringed waters of the Mincius flowed musically between the banks and braes o' bonny Doon to join the Tweed. Blithe ghosts were wandering by, in all varieties of apparel, and I distinctly observed Dante's Beatrice, leaning loving on the arm of Sir Philip Sidney, while Dante was closely engaged in conversation with the lost Lenore, celebrated by Mr. Edgar Allan Poe.

"'In what can my knowledge of the Paradise of Poets be serviceable to you, sir?' said Catullus, as he flung himself at the feet of Laura, on the velvet grass.

"'I am disinclined to seem impertinently curious,' I answered,

127

'but the ladies in this fair, smiling country—have the gods made them poetical?'

"'Not generally,' replied Catullus. 'Indeed, if you would be well with them, I may warn you never to mention poetry in their hearing. They never cared for it while on earth, and in this place it is a topic which the prudent carefully avoid among ladies. To tell the truth, they have had to listen to far too much poetry, and too many discussions on the caesura. There are, indeed, a few lady poets—very few. Sappho, for example; indeed I cannot recall any other at this moment. The result is that Phaon, of all the shadows here, is the most distinguished by the fair. He was not a poet, you know; he got in on account of Sappho, who adored him. They are estranged now, of course.'

"'You interest me deeply,' I answered. 'And now, will you kindly tell me why these ladies are here, if they were not poets?'

"'The women that were our ideals while we dwelt on earth, the women we loved but never won, or, at all events, never wedded, they for whom we sighed while in the arms of a recognised and legitimate affection, have been chosen by the Olympians to keep us company in Paradise!'

"'Then wherefore,' I interrupted, 'do I see Robert Burns loitering with that lady in a ruff,—Cassandra, I make no doubt— Ronsard's Cassandra? And why is the incomparable Clarinda inseparable from Petrarch; and Miss Patty Blount, Pope's flame, from the Syrian Meleager, while his Heliodore is manifestly devoted to Mr. Emerson, whom, by the way, I am delighted, if rather surprised, to see here?'

"'Ah,' said Catullus, 'you are a new-comer among us. Poets will be poets, and no sooner have they attained their desire, and dwelt in the company of their earthly Ideals, than they feel strangely, yet irresistibly drawn to Another. So it was in life, so it will ever be. No Ideal can survive a daily companionship, and fortunate is the poet who did not marry his first love!'

"'As far as that goes,' I answered, 'most of you were highly favoured; indeed, I do not remember any poet whose Ideal was his wife, or whose first love led him to the altar.'

"'I was not a marrying man myself,' answered the Veronese; 'few of us were. Myself, Horace, Virgil—we were all bachelors.'

"'And Lesbia!'

"I said this in a low voice, for Laura was weaving bay into a chaplet, and inattentive to our conversation.

"'Poor Lesbia!' said Catullus, with a suppressed sigh. 'How I misjudged that girl! How cruel, how causeless were my reproaches,' and wildly rending his curled locks and laurel crown, he fled into a thicket, whence there soon arose the melancholy notes of the Ausonian lyre.'

"'He is incorrigible,' said Laura, very coldly; and she deliberately began to tear and toss away the fragments of the chaplet she had been weaving. 'I shall never break him of that habit of versifying. But they are all alike.'

"'Is there nobody here,' said I, 'who is happy with his Ideal— nobody but has exchanged Ideals with some other poet?'

"'There is one,' she said. 'He comes of a northern tribe; and in his life-time he never rhymed upon his unattainable lady, or if rhyme he did, the accents never carried her name to the ears of the vulgar. Look there.'

"She pointed to the river at our feet, and I knew the mounted figure that was riding the ford, with a green-mantled lady beside him like the Fairy Queen.

"Surely I had read of her, and knew her—

"'She whose blue eyes their secret told,
Though shaded by her locks of gold.'

"'They are different; I know not why. They are constant,' said Laura, and rising with an air of chagrin, she disappeared among the boughs of the trees that bear her name.

"'Unhappy hearts of poets,' I mused. 'Light things and sacred they are, but even in their Paradise, and among their chosen, with every wish fulfilled, and united to their beloved, they cannot be at rest!'

"Thus moralising, I wended my way to a crag, whence there was a wide prospect. Certain poets were standing there, looking down into an abyss, and to them I joined myself.

"'Ah, I cannot bear it!' said a voice, and, as he turned away, his brow already clearing, his pain already forgotten, I beheld the august form of Shakespeare.

"Marking my curiosity before it was expressed, he answered the unuttered question.

"'That is a sight for Pagans,' he said, 'and may give them pleasure. But my Paradise were embittered if I had to watch the sorrows of others, and their torments, however well deserved. The others are gazing on the purgatory of critics and commentators.'

"He passed from me, and I joined the 'Ionian father of the rest'—Homer, who, with a countenance of unspeakable majesty, was seated on a throne of rock, between the Mantuan Virgil of the laurel crown, Hugo, Sophocles, Milton, Lovelace, Tennyson, and Shelley.

"At their feet I beheld, in a vast and gloomy hall, many an

129

honest critic, many an erudite commentator, an army of reviewers. Some were condemned to roll logs up insuperable heights, whence they descended thundering to the plain. Others were set to impositions, and I particularly observed that the Homeric commentators were obliged to write out the 'Iliad' and 'Odyssey' in their complete shape, and were always driven by fiends to the task when they prayed for the bare charity of being permitted to leave out the 'interpolations.' Others, fearful to narrate, were torn into as many fragments as they had made of these immortal epics. Others, such as Aristarchus, were spitted on their own critical signs of disapproval. Many reviewers were compelled to read the books which they had criticised without perusal, and it was terrible to watch the agonies of the worthy pressmen who were set to this unwonted task. 'May we not be let off with the preface?' they cried in piteous accents. 'May we not glance at the table of contents and be done with it?' But the presiding demons (who had been Examiners in the bodily life) drove them remorseless to their toils.

"Among the condemned I could not but witness, with sympathy, the punishment reserved for translators. The translators of Virgil, in particular, were a vast and motley assemblage of most respectable men. Bishops were there, from Gawain Douglas downwards; Judges, in their ermine; professors, clergymen, civil servants, writhing in all the tortures that the blank verse, the anapaestic measure, the metre of the 'Lay of the Last Minstrel,' the heroic couplet and similar devices can inflict. For all these men had loved Virgil, though not wisely: and now their penance was to hear each other read their own translations."

"That must have been more than they could bear," said Lady Violet

"Yes," said Mr. Witham; "I should know, for down I fell into Tartarus with a crash, and writhed among the Translators."

"Why?" asked Lady Violet.

"Because I have translated Theocritus!"

"Mr. Witham," said Lady Violet, "did you meet your ideal woman when you were in the Paradise of Poets?"

"She yet walks this earth," said the bard, with a too significant bow.

Lady Violet turned coldly away.

* * *

Mr. Witham was never invited to the Blues again—the name of Lord Azure's place in Kent.

The Poet is shut out of Paradise.

CHAPTER XII

PARIS AND HELEN

The first name in romance, the most ancient and the most enduring, is that of Argive Helen. During three thousand years fair women have been born, have lived, and been loved, "that there might be a song in the ears of men of later time," but, compared to the renown of Helen, their glory is dim. Cleopatra, who held the world's fate in her hands, and lay in the arms of Cæsar; Mary Stuart (Maria Verticordia), for whose sake, as a northern novelist tells, peasants have lain awake, sorrowing that she is dead; Agnes Sorel, Fair Rosamond, la belle Stuart, "the Pompadour and the Parabère," can still enchant us from the page of history and chronicle. "Zeus gave them beauty, which naturally rules even strength itself," to quote the Greek orator on the mistress of them all, on her who, having never lived, can never die, the Daughter of the Swan.

While Helen enjoys this immortality, and is the ideal of beauty upon earth, it is curious to reflect on the modernité of her story, the oldest of the love stories of the world. In Homer we first meet her, the fairest of women in the song of the greatest of poets. It might almost seem as if Homer meant to justify, by his dealing with Helen, some of the most recent theories of literary art. In the "Iliad" and "Odyssey" the tale of Helen is without a beginning and without an end, like a frieze on a Greek temple. She crosses the stage as a figure familiar to all, the poet's audience clearly did not need to be told who Helen was, nor anything about her youth.

The famous judgment of Paris, the beginning of evil to Achaeans and Ilian men, is only mentioned once by Homer, late, and in a passage of doubtful authenticity. Of her reconciliation to her wedded lord, Menelaus, not a word is said; of her end we are told no more than that for her and him a mansion in Elysium is prepared—

"Where falls not hail, or rain, or any snow."

We leave her happy in Argos, a smile on her lips, a gift in her hands, as we met her in Troy, beautiful, adored despite her guilt, as sweet in her repentance as in her unvexed Argive home. Women seldom mention her, in the epic, but with horror and anger; men never address her but in gentle courtesy. What is her secret? How did she leave her home with Paris—beguiled by love, by magic, or driven by the implacable Aphrodite? Homer is silent on all of these things; these things, doubtless, were known by his audience. In his poem Helen moves as a thing of simple grace, courtesy, and kindness, save when she rebels against her doom, after seeing her lover fly from her husband's spear. Had we only Homer, by far our earliest literary source, we should know little of the romance of Helen; should only know that a lawless love brought ruin on Troy and sorrow on the Achaeans; and this is thrown out, with no moral comment, without praise or blame. The end, we learn, was peace, and beauty was reconciled to life. There is no explanation, no dénouement; and we know how much dénouement and explanations hampered Scott and Shakespeare. From these trammels Homer is free, as a god is free from mortal limitations.

All this manner of telling a tale—a manner so ancient, so original—is akin, in practice, to recent theories of what art should be, and what art seldom is, perhaps never is, in modern hands.

Modern enough, again, is the choice of a married woman for the heroine of the earliest love tale. Apollonius Rhodius sings (and no man has ever sung so well) of a maiden's love; Virgil, of a widow's; Homer, of love that has defied law, blindly obedient to destiny, which dominates even Zeus. Once again, Helen is not a very young girl; ungallant chronologists have attributed to her I know not what age. We think of her as about the age of the Venus of Milo; in truth, she was "ageless and immortal." Homer never describes her beauty; we only see it reflected in the eyes of the old men, white and weak, thin-voiced as cicalas: but hers is a loveliness "to turn an old man young." "It is no marvel," they say, "that for her sake Trojans and Achaeans slay each other."

She was embroidering at a vast web, working in gold and scarlet the sorrows that for her sake befell mankind, when they called her to the walls to see Paris fight Menelaus, in the last year of the war. There she stands, in raiment of silvery white, her heart yearning for her old love and her own city. Already her thought is far from Paris. Was her heart ever with Paris? That is her secret. A very old legend, mentioned by the Bishop of Thessalonica, Eustathius, tells us that Paris magically beguiled her, disguised in the form of Menelaus, her lord, as Uther beguiled Ygerne. She sees the son of Priam play the dastard in the fight; she turns in wrath on Aphrodite, who would lure her back to his arms; but to his arms she must go, "for the daughter of Zeus was afraid." Violence is put upon beauty; it is soiled, or seems soiled, in its way through the world. Helen urges Paris again into the war. He has a heart invincibly light and gay; shame does not weigh on him. "Not every man is valiant every day," he says; yet once engaged in battle, he bears him bravely, and his arrows rain death among the mail-clad Achaeans.

What Homer thinks of Paris we can only guess. His beauty is the bane of Ilios; but Homer forgives so much to beauty. In the end of the "Iliad," Helen sings the immortal dirge over Hector, the stainless knight, "with thy loving kindness and thy gentle speech."

In the "Odyssey," she is at home again, playing the gracious part of hostess to Odysseus's wandering son, pouring into the bowl the magic herb of Egypt, "which brings forgetfulness of sorrow." The wandering son of Odysseus departs with a gift for his bride, "to wear upon the day of her desire, a memorial of the hands of Helen," the beautiful hands, that in Troy or Argos were never idle.

Of Helen, from Homer, we know no more. Grace, penitence in exile, peace at home, these are the portion of her who set East and West at war and ruined the city of Priam of the ashen spear. As in the strange legend preserved by Servius, the commentator on Virgil, who tells us that Helen wore a red "star-stone," whence fell gouts of blood that vanished ere they touched her swan's neck; so all the blood shed for her sake leaves Helen stainless. Of Homer's Helen we know no more.

The later Greek fancy, playing about this form of beauty, wove a myriad of new fancies, or disinterred from legend old beliefs untouched by Homer. Helen was the daughter of the Swan—that is, as was later explained, of Zeus in the shape of a swan. Her loveliness, even in childhood, plunged her in many adventures. Theseus carried her off; her brothers rescued her. All the princes of Achaea competed for her hand, having first taken an oath to avenge whomsoever she might choose for her husband. The choice fell on the correct and honourable, but rather inconspicuous, Menelaus, and they dwelt in Sparta, beside the Eurotas, "in a hollow of the rifted hills." Then, from across the sea, came the beautiful and fatal Paris, son of Priam, King of Troy. As a child, Paris had been exposed on the mountains, because his mother dreamed that she brought forth a firebrand. He was rescued and fostered by a shepherd; he tended the flocks; he loved the daughter of a river god, Œnone. Then came the naked Goddesses, to seek at the hand of the most beautiful of mortals the prize of beauty. Aphrodite won the golden apple from the queen of heaven, Hera, and from the Goddess of war and wisdom, Athena, bribing the judge by the promise of the fairest wife in the world. No incident is more frequently celebrated in poetry and art, to which it lends such gracious opportunities. Paris was later recognised as of the royal blood of Troy. He came to Lacedaemon on an embassy, he saw Helen, and destiny had its way.

Concerning the details in this most ancient love-story, we learn nothing from Homer, who merely makes Paris remind Helen of their bridal night in the isle of Cranaë. But from Homer we learn that Paris carried off not only the wife of Menelaus, but many of his treasures. To the poet of the "Iliad," the psychology of the wooing would have seemed a simple matter. Like the later vase-painters, he would have shown us Paris beside Helen, Aphrodite standing near, accompanied by the figure of Peitho—Persuasion.

Homer always escapes our psychological problems by throwing the weight of our deeds and misdeeds on a God or a Goddess, or on destiny. To have fled from her lord and her one child, Hermione, was not in keeping with the character of Helen as Homer draws it. Her repentance is almost Christian in its expression, and repentance indicates a consciousness of sin and of shame, which Helen frequently professes. Thus she, at least, does not, like Homer, in his chivalrous way, throw all the blame on the Immortals and on destiny. The cheerful acquiescence of Helen in destiny makes part of the comic element in La Belle Hélène, but the mirth only arises out of the incongruity between Parisian ideas and those of ancient Greece.

Helen is freely and bitterly blamed in the "Odyssey" by Penelope, chiefly because of the ruinous consequences which followed her flight. Still, there is one passage, when Penelope prudently hesitates about recognising her returned lord, which makes it just possible that a legend chronicled by Eustathius was known to Homer,—namely, the tale already mentioned, that Paris beguiled her in the shape of Menelaus. The incident is very old, as in the story of Zeus and Amphitryon, and might be used whenever a lady's character needed to be saved. But this anecdote, on the whole, is inconsistent with the repentance of Helen, and is not in Homer's manner.

The early lyric poet, Stesichorus, is said to have written harshly against Helen. She punished him by blindness, and he indited a palinode, explaining that it was not she who went to Troy, but a woman fashioned in her likeness, by Zeus, out of mist and light. The real Helen remained safely and with honour in Egypt. Euripides has made this idea, which was calculated to please him, the groundwork of his "Helena," but it never had a strong hold on the Greek imagination. Modern fancy is pleased by the picture of the cloud-bride in Troy, Greeks and Trojans dying for a phantasm. "Shadows we are, and shadows we pursue."

Concerning the later feats, and the death of Paris, Homer says very little. He slew Achilles by an arrow-shot in the Scaean gate, and prophecy was fulfilled. He himself fell by another shaft, perhaps the poisoned shaft of Philoctetes. In the fourth or fifth century of our era a late poet, Quintus Smyrnaeus, described Paris's journey, in quest of a healing spell, to the forsaken Œnone, and her refusal to aid him; her death on his funeral pyre. Quintus is a poet of extraordinary merit for his age, and scarcely deserves the reproach of laziness affixed on him by Lord Tennyson.

On the whole, Homer seems to have a kind of half-contemptuous liking for the beautiful Paris. Later art represents him as a bowman of girlish charms, wearing a Phrygian cap. There is a late legend that he had a son, Corythus, by Œnone, and that he killed the lad in a moment of jealousy, finding him with Helen and failing to recognise him. On the death of Paris, perhaps by virtue of the custom of the Levirate, Helen became the wife of his brother, Deïphobus.

How her reconciliation with Menelaus was brought about we do not learn from Homer, who, in the "Odyssey," accepts it as a fact. The earliest traditional hint on the subject is given by the famous "Coffer of Cypselus," a work of the seventh century, B.C., which Pausanias saw at Olympia, in A.D. 174. Here, on a band of ivory, was represented, among other scenes from the tale of Troy, Menelaus rushing, sword in hand, to slay Helen. According to Stesichorus, the army was about to stone her after the fall of Ilios, but relented, amazed by her beauty.

Of her later life in Lacedaemon, nothing is known on really ancient authority, and later traditions vary. The Spartans showed her sepulchre and her shrine at Therapnae, where she was worshipped. Herodotus tells us how Helen, as a Goddess, appeared in her temple and healed a deformed child, making her the fairest woman in Sparta, in the reign of Ariston. It may, perhaps, be conjectured that in Sparta, Helen occupied the place of a local Aphrodite. In another late story she dwells in the isle of Leuke, a shadowy bride of the shadowy Achilles. The mocking Lucian, in his Vera Historia, meets Helen in the Fortunate Islands, whence she elopes with one of his companions. Again, the sons of Menelaus, by a concubine, were said to have driven Helen from Sparta on the death of her lord, and she was murdered in Rhodes, by the vengeance of Polyxo, whose husband fell at Troy. But, among all these inventions, that of Homer stands out pre-eminent. Helen and Menelaus do not die, they are too near akin to Zeus; they dwell immortal, not among the shadows of heroes and of famous ladies dead and gone, but in Elysium, the paradise at the world's end, unvisited by storms.

"Beyond these voices there is peace."

It is plain that, as a love-story, the tale of Paris and Helen must to modern readers seem meagre. To Greece, in every age, the main interest lay not in the passion of the beautiful pair, but in its world-wide consequences: the clash of Europe and Asia, the deaths of kings, the ruin wrought in their homes, the consequent fall of the great and ancient Achaean civilisation. To the Greeks, the Trojan war was what the Crusades are in later history. As in the Crusades, the West assailed the East for an ideal, not to recover the Holy Sepulchre of our religion, but to win back the living type of beauty and of charm. Perhaps, ere the sun grows cold, men will no more believe in the Crusades, as an historical fact, than we do in the siege of Troy. In a sense, a very obvious sense, the myth of Helen is a parable of Hellenic history. They sought beauty, and they found it; they bore it home, and, with beauty, their bane. Wherever Helen went "she brought calamity," in this a type of all the famous and peerless ladies of old days, of Cleopatra and of Mary Stuart. Romance and poetry have nothing less plausible than the part which Cleopatra actually played in the history of the world, a world well lost by Mark Antony for her sake. The flight from Actium might seem as much a mere poet's dream as the gathering of the Achaeans at Aulis, if we were not certain that it is truly chronicled.

From the earliest times, even from times before Homer (whose audience is supposed to know all about Helen), the imagination of Greece, and later, the imagination of the civilised world, has played around Helen, devising about her all that possibly could be devised. She was the daughter of Zeus by Nemesis, or by Leda; or the daughter of the swan, or a child of the changeful moon, brooding on "the formless and multi-form waters." She could speak in the voices of all women, hence she was named "Echo," and we might fancy that, like the witch of the Brocken, she could appear to every man in the likeness of his own first love. The ancient Egyptians either knew her, or invented legends of her to amuse the inquiring Greeks. She had touched at Sidon, and perhaps Astaroth is only her Sidonian name. Whatever could be told of beauty, in its charm, its perils, the dangers with which it surrounds its lovers, the purity which it retains, unsmirched by all the sins that are done for beauty's sake, could be told of Helen.

Like a golden cup, as M. Paul de St. Victor says, she was carried from lips to lips of heroes, but the gold remains unsullied and unalloyed. To heaven she returns again, to heaven which is her own, and looks down serenely on men slain, and women widowed, and sinking ships, and burning towns. Yet with death she gives immortality by her kiss, and Paris and Menelaus live, because they have touched the lips of Helen. Through the grace of Helen, for whom he fell, Sarpedon's memory endures, and Achilles and Memnon, the son of the Morning, and Troy is more imperishable than Carthage, or Rome, or Corinth, though Helen

136

"Burnt the topless towers of Ilium."

In one brief passage, Marlowe did more than all poets since Stesichorus, or, at least since the epithalamium of Theocritus, for the glory of Helen. Roman poets knew her best as an enemy of their fabulous ancestors, and in the "Æneid," Virgil's hero draws his sword to slay her. Through the Middle Ages, in the romances of Troy, she wanders as a shining shadow of the ideally fair, like Guinevere, who so often recalls her in the Arthurian romances. The chivalrous mediæval poets and the Celts could understand better than the Romans the philosophy of "the world well lost" for love. Modern poetry, even in Goethe's "Second part of Faust," has not been very fortunately inspired by Helen, except in the few lines which she speaks in "The Dream of Fair Women."

"I had great beauty; ask thou not my name."

Mr. William Morris's Helen, in the "Earthly Paradise," charms at the time of reading, but, perhaps, leaves little abiding memory. The Helen of "Troilus and Cressida" is not one of Shakespeare's immortal women, and Mr. Rossetti's ballad is fantastic and somewhat false in tone—a romantic pastiche. Where Euripides twice failed, in the "Troades" and the "Helena," it can be given to few to succeed. Helen is best left to her earliest known minstrel, for who can recapture the grace, the tenderness, the melancholy, and the charm of the daughter of Zeus in the "Odyssey" and "Iliad"? The sightless eyes of Homer saw her clearest, and Helen was best understood by the wisdom of his unquestioning simplicity.

As if to prove how entirely, though so many hands paltered with her legend, Helen is Homer's alone, there remains no great or typical work of Greek art which represents her beauty, and the breasts from which were modelled cups of gold for the service of the gods. We have only paintings on vases, or work on gems, which, though graceful, is conventional and might represent any other heroine, Polyxena, or Eriphyle. No Helen from the hands of Phidias or Scopas has survived to our time, and the grass may be growing in Therapnae over the shattered remains of her only statue.

As Stesichorus fabled that only an eidolon of Helen went to Troy, so, except in the "Iliad" and "Odyssey," we meet but shadows of her loveliness, phantasms woven out of clouds, and the light of setting suns.

CHAPTER XIII

ENCHANTED CIGARETTES

To dream over literary projects, Balzac says, is like "smoking enchanted cigarettes," but when we try to tackle our projects, to make them real, the enchantment disappears. We have to till the soil, to sow the seed, to gather the leaves, and then the cigarettes must be manufactured, while there may be no market for them after all. Probably most people have enjoyed the fragrance of these enchanted cigarettes, and have brooded over much which they will never put on paper. Here are some of "the ashes of the weeds of my delight"—memories of romances whereof no single line is written, or is likely to be written.

Of my earliest novel I remember but little. I know there had been a wreck, and that the villain, who was believed to be drowned, came home and made himself disagreeable. I know that the heroine's mouth was not "too large for regular beauty." In that respect she was original. All heroines are "muckle-mou'd," I know not why. It is expected of them. I know she was melancholy and merry; it would not surprise me to learn that she drowned herself from a canoe. But the villain never descended to crime, the first lover would not fall in love, the heroine's own affections were provokingly disengaged, and the whole affair came to a dead stop for want of a plot. Perhaps, considering modern canons of fiction, this might have been a very successful novel. It was entirely devoid of incident or interest, and, consequently, was a good deal like real life, as real life appears to many cultivated authors. On the other hand, all the characters were flippant. This would never have done, and I do not regret novel No. I., which had not even a name.

The second story had a plot, quantities of plot, nothing but plot. It was to have been written in collaboration with a very great novelist, who, as far as we went, confined himself to making objections. This novel was stopped (not that my friend would ever have gone on) by "Called Back," which anticipated part of the idea. The story was entitled "Where is Rose?" and the motto was—

"Rosa quo locorum
Sera moratur."

The characters were—(1) Rose, a young lady of quality. (2) The Russian Princess, her friend (need I add that, to meet a public demand, her name was Vera?). (3) Young man engaged to Rose. (4) Charles, his friend. (5) An enterprising person named "The Whiteley of Crime," the universal Provider of Iniquity. In fact, he anticipated Sir Arthur Doyle's Professor Moriarty. The rest were detectives, old ladies, mob, and a wealthy young Colonial larrikin. Neither my friend nor I was fond of describing love scenes, so we made the heroine disappear in the second chapter, and she never turned up again till chapter the last. After playing in a comedy at the house of an earl, Rosa and Vera entered her brougham. Soon afterwards the brougham drew up, empty, at Rose's own door. Where was Rose? Traces of her were found, of all places, in the Haunted House in Berkeley Square, which is not haunted any longer. After that Rose was long sought in vain.

This, briefly, is what had occurred. A Russian detective "wanted" Vera, who, to be sure, was a Nihilist. To catch Vera he made an alliance with "The Whiteley of Crime." He was a man who would destroy a parish register, or forge a will, or crack a crib, or break up a Pro-Boer meeting, or burn a house, or kidnap a rightful heir, or manage a personation, or issue amateur bank-notes, or what you please. Thinking to kill two birds with one stone, he carried off Rose for her diamonds and Vera for his friend, the Muscovite police official, lodging them both in the Haunted House. But there he and the Russian came to blows, and, in the confusion, Vera made her escape, while Rose was conveyed, as Vera, to Siberia. Not knowing how to dispose of her, the Russian police consigned her to a nunnery at the mouth of the Obi. Her lover, in a yacht, found her hiding-place, and got a friendly nun to give her some narcotic known to the Samoyeds. It was the old truc of the Friar in "Romeo and Juliet." At the mouth of the Obi they do not bury the dead, but lay them down on platforms in the open air. Rose was picked up there by her lover (accompanied by a chaperon, of course), was got on board the steam yacht, and all went well. I forget what happened to "The Whiteley of Crime." After him I still rather hanker—he was a humorous ruffian. Something could be made of "The Whiteley of Crime." Something has been made, by the author of "Sherlock Holmes."

In yet another romance, a gentleman takes his friend, in a country place, to see his betrothed. The friend, who had only come into the neighbourhood that day, is found dead, next morning, hanging to a tree. Gipsies and others are suspected. But the lover was the murderer. He had been a priest, in South America, and the lady was a Catholic (who knew not of his Orders). Now the friend fell in love with the lady at first sight, on being introduced to her by the lover. As the two men walked home, the friend threatened to

139

reveal the lover's secret—his tonsure—which would be fatal to his hopes. They quarrelled, parted, and the ex-priest lassoed his friend. The motive, I think, is an original one, and not likely to occur to the first comer. The inventor is open to offers.

The next novel, based on a dream, was called "In Search of Qrart."

What is Qrart? I decline to divulge this secret beyond saying that Qrart was a product of the civilisation which now sleeps under the snows of the pole. It was an article of the utmost value to humanity. Farther I do not intend to commit myself. The Bride of a God was one of the characters.

The next novel is, at present, my favourite cigarette. The scene is partly in Greece, partly at the Parthian Court, about 80-60 B.C. Crassus is the villain. The heroine was an actress in one of the wandering Greek companies, splendid strollers, who played at the Indian and Asiatic Courts. The story ends with the representation of the "Bacchae," in Parthia. The head of Pentheus is carried by one of the Bacchae in that drama. Behold, it is not a mask, but the head of Crassus, and thus conveys the first news of the Roman defeat. Obviously, this is a novel that needs a great deal of preliminary study, as much, indeed, as "Salammbo."

Another story will deal with the Icelandic discoverers of America. Mr. Kipling, however, has taken the wind out of its sails with his sketch, "The Finest Story in the World." There are all the marvels and portents of the Eyrbyggja Saga to draw upon, there are Skraelings to fight, and why should not Karlsefni's son kill the last mastodon, and, as Quetzalcoatl, be the white-bearded god of the Aztecs? After that a romance on the intrigues to make Charles Edward King of Poland sounds commonplace. But much might be made of that, too, if the right man took it in hand. Believe me, there are plenty of stories left, waiting for the man who can tell them. I have said it before, but I say it again, if I were king I would keep court officials, Mr. Stanley Weyman, Mr. Mason, Mr. Kipling, and others, to tell me my own stories. I know the kind of thing which I like, from the discovery of Qrart to that of the French gold in the burn at Loch Arkaig, or in "the wood by the lochside" that Murray of Broughton mentions.

Another cigarette I have, the adventures of a Poet, a Poet born in a Puritan village of Massachusetts about 1670. Hawthorne could have told me my story, and how my friend was driven into the wilderness and lived among the Red Men. I think he was killed in an attempt to warn his countrymen of an Indian raid; I think his MS. poems have a bullet-hole through them, and blood on the leaves. They were in Carew's best manner, these poems.

Another tale Hawthorne might have told me, the tale of an excellent man, whose very virtues, by some baneful moral chemistry, corrupt and ruin the people with whom he comes in contact. I do not mean by goading them into the opposite extremes, but rather something like a moral jettatura. This needs a great deal of subtlety, and what is to become of the hero? Is he to plunge into vice till everybody is virtuous again? It wants working out. I have omitted, after all, a schoolboy historical romance, explaining why Queen Elizabeth was never married. A Scottish paper offered a prize for a story of Queen Mary Stuart's reign. I did not get the prize—perhaps did not deserve it, but my story ran thus: You must know that Queen Elizabeth was singularly like Darnley in personal appearance. What so natural as that, disguised as a page, her Majesty should come spying about the Court of Holyrood? Darnley sees her walking out of Queen Mary's room, he thinks her an hallucination, discovers that she is real, challenges her, and they fight at Faldonside, by the Tweed, Shakespeare holding Elizabeth's horse. Elizabeth is wounded, and is carried to the Kirk of Field, and laid in Darnley's chamber, while Darnley goes out and makes love to my rural heroine, the lady of Fernilee, a Kerr. That night Bothwell blows up the Kirk of Field, Elizabeth and all. Darnley has only one resource. Borrowing the riding habit of the rural heroine, the lady of Fernilee, he flees across the Border, and, for the rest of his life, personates Queen Elizabeth. That is why Elizabeth, who was Darnley, hated Mary so bitterly (on account of the Kirk of Field affair), and that is why Queen Elizabeth was never married. Side-lights on Shakespeare's Sonnets were obviously cast. The young man whom Shakespeare admired so, and urged to marry, was—Darnley. This romance did not get the prize (the anachronism about Shakespeare is worthy of Scott), but I am conceited enough to think it deserved an honourable mention.

Enough of my own cigarettes. But there are others of a more fragrant weed. Who will end for me the novel of which Byron only wrote a chapter; who, as Bulwer Lytton is dead? A finer opening, one more mysteriously stirring, you can nowhere read. And the novel in letters, which Scott began in 1819, who shall finish it, or tell us what he did with his fair Venetian courtezan, a character so much out of Sir Walter's way? He tossed it aside—it was but an enchanted cigarette—and gave us "The Fortunes of Nigel" in its place. I want both. We cannot call up those who "left half told" these stories. In a happier world we shall listen to their endings, and all our dreams shall be coherent and concluded. Meanwhile, without trouble, and expense, and disappointment, and reviews, we can all smoke our cigarettes of fairyland. Would that many people were content to smoke them peacefully, and did not rush on pen, paper, and ink!

CHAPTER XIV

STORIES AND STORY-TELLING
(From STRATH NAVER)

We have had a drought for three weeks. During a whole week this northern strath has been as sunny as the Riviera is expected to be. The streams can be crossed dry-shod, kelts are plunging in the pools, but even kelts will not look at a fly. Now, by way of a pleasant change, an icy north wind is blowing, with gusts of snow, not snow enough to swell the loch that feeds the river, but just enough snow (as the tourist said of the water in the River Styx) "to swear by," or at! The Field announces that a duke, who rents three rods on a neighbouring river, has not yet caught one salmon. The acrimoniously democratic mind may take comfort in that intelligence, but, if the weather will not improve for a duke, it is not likely to change for a mere person of letters. Thus the devotee of the Muses is driven back, by stress of climate, upon literature, and as there is nothing in the lodge to read he is compelled to write.

Now certainly one would not lack material, if only one were capable of the art of fiction. The genesis of novels and stories is a topic little studied, but I am inclined to believe that, like the pearls in the mussels of the river, fiction is a beautiful disease of the brain. Something, an incident or an experience, or a reflection, gets imbedded, incrusted, in the properly constituted mind, and becomes the nucleus of a pearl of romance. Mr. Marion Crawford, in a recent work, describes his hero, who is a novelist, at work. This young gentleman, by a series of faults or misfortunes, has himself become a centre of harrowing emotion. Two young ladies, to each of whom he has been betrothed, are weeping out their eyes for him, or are kneeling to heaven with despairing cries, or are hardening their hearts to marry men for whom they "do not care a bawbee." The hero's aunt has committed a crime; everybody, in fact, is in despair, when an idea occurs to the hero. Indifferent to the sorrows of his nearest and dearest, he sits down with his notion and writes a novel—writes like a person possessed.

He has the proper kind of brain, the nucleus has been dropped into it, the pearl begins to grow, and to assume prismatic hues. So he is happy, and even the frozen-out angler might be happy if he could write a novel in the absence of salmon. Unluckily, my brain is not capable of this æsthetic malady, and to save my life, or to "milk a fine warm cow rain," as the Zulus say, I could not write

142

a novel, or even a short story. About The Short Story, as they call it, with capital letters, our critical American cousins have much to say. Its germ, one fancies, is usually an incident, or a mere anecdote, according to the nature of the author's brain; this germ becomes either the pearl of a brief conte, or the seed of a stately tree, in three volumes. An author of experience soon finds out how he should treat his material. One writer informs me that, given the idea, the germinal idea, it is as easy for him to make a novel out of it as a tale—as easy, and much more satisfactory and remunerative. Others, like M. Guy de Maupassant, for example, seem to find their strength in brevity, in cutting down, not in amplifying; in selecting and reducing, not in allowing other ideas to group themselves round the first, other characters to assemble about those who are essential. That seems to be really the whole philosophy of this matter, concerning which so many words are expended. The growth of the germinal idea depends on the nature of an author's talent—he may excel in expansion, or in reduction; he may be economical, and out of an anecdote may spin the whole cocoon of a romance; or he may be extravagant, and give a capable idea away in the briefest form possible.

These ideas may come to a man in many ways, as we said, from a dream, from a fragmentary experience (as most experiences in life are fragmentary), from a hint in a newspaper, from a tale told in conversation. Not long ago, for example, I heard an anecdote out of which M. Guy de Maupassant could have made the most ghastly, the most squalid, and the most supernaturally moving of all his contes. Indeed, that is not saying much, as he did not excel in the supernatural. Were it written in French, it might lie in my lady's chamber, and, as times go, nobody would be shocked. But, by our curious British conventions, this tale cannot be told in an English book or magazine. It was not, in its tendency, immoral; those terrible tales never are. The events were rather calculated to frighten the hearer into the paths of virtue. When Mr. Richard Cameron, the founder of the Cameronians, and the godfather of the Cameronian Regiment, was sent to his parish, he was bidden by Mr. Peden to "put hell-fire to the tails" of his congregation. This vigorous expression was well fitted to describe the conte which I have in my mind (I rather wish I had it not), and which is not to be narrated here, nor in English.

For a combination of pity and terror, it seemed to me unmatched in the works of the modern fancy, or in the horrors of modern experience; whether in experience or in imagination it had its original source. But even the English authors, who plume themselves on their audacity, or their realism, or their contempt for

143

"the young person," would not venture this little romance, much less, then, is a timidly uncorrect pen-man likely to tempt Mr. Mudie with the conte. It is one of two tales, both told as true, which one would like to be able to narrate in the language of Molière. The other is also very good, and has a wonderful scene with a corpse and a chapelle ardente, and a young lady; it is historical, and of the last generation but one.

Even our frozen strath here has its modern legend, which may be told in English, and out of which, I am sure, a novelist could make a good short story, or a pleasant opening chapter of a romance. What is the mysterious art by which these things are done? What makes the well-told story seem real, rich with life, actual, engrossing? It is the secret of genius, of the novelist's art, and the writer who cannot practise the art might as well try to discover the Philosopher's Stone, or to "harp fish out of the water." However, let me tell the legend as simply as may be, and as it was told to me.

The strath runs due north, the river flowing from a great loch to the Northern sea. All around are low, undulating hills, brown with heather, and as lonely almost as the Sahara. On the horizon to the south rise the mountains, Ben this and Ben that, real mountains of beautiful outline, though no higher than some three thousand feet. Before the country was divided into moors and forests, tenanted by makers of patent corkscrews, and boilers of patent soap, before the rivers were distributed into beats, marked off by white and red posts, there lived over to the south, under the mountains, a sportsman of athletic frame and adventurous disposition. His name I have forgotten, but we may call him Dick Lindsay. It is told of him that he once found a poacher in the forest, and, being unable to catch the intruder, fired his rifle, not at him, but in his neighbourhood, whereon the poacher, deliberately kneeling down, took a long shot at Dick. How the duel ended, and whether either party flew a flag of truce, history does not record.

At all events, one stormy day in late September, Dick had stalked and wounded a stag on the hills to the south-east of the strath. Here, if only one were a novelist, one could weave several pages of valuable copy out of the stalk. The stag made for the strath here, and Dick, who had no gillie, but was an independent sportsman of the old school, pursued on foot. Plunging down the low, birch-clad hills, the stag found the flooded river before him, black and swollen with rain. He took the water, crossing by the big pool, which looked almost like a little loch, tempestuous under a north wind blowing up stream, and covered with small white, vicious crests. The stag crossed and staggered up the bank, where

144

he stood panting. It is not a humane thing to leave a deer to die slowly of a rifle bullet, and Dick, reaching the pool, hesitated not, but threw off his clothes, took his skene between his teeth, plunged in, and swam the river.

All naked as he was he cut the stag's throat in the usual manner, and gralloched him with all the skill of Bucklaw. This was very well, and very well it would be to add a description of the stag at bay; but as I never happened to see a stag at bay, I omit all that. Dick had achieved success, but his clothes were on one side of a roaring river in spate, and he and the dead stag were on the other. There was no chance of fording the stream, and there was then no bridge. He did not care to swim back, for the excitement was out of him. He was trembling with cold, and afraid of cramp. "A mother-naked man," in a wilderness, with a flood between him and his raiment, was in a pitiable position. It did not occur to him to flay the stag, and dress in the hide, and, indeed, he would have been frozen before he could have accomplished that task. So he reconnoitred.

There was nobody within sight but one girl, who was herding cows. Now for a naked man, with a knife, and bedabbled with blood, to address a young woman on a lonely moor is a delicate business. The chances were that the girl would flee like a startled fawn, and leave Dick to walk, just as he was, to the nearest farmhouse, about a mile away. However, Dick had to risk it; he lay down so that only his face appeared above the bank, and he shouted to the maiden. When he had caught her attention he briefly explained the unusual situation. Then the young woman behaved like a trump, or like a Highland Nausicaa, for students of the "Odyssey" will remember how Odysseus, simply clad in a leafy bough of a tree, made supplication to the sea-king's daughter, and how she befriended him. Even if Dick had been a reader of Homer, which is not probable, there were no trees within convenient reach, and he could not adopt the leafy covering of Odysseus.

"You sit still; if you move an inch before I give you the word, I'll leave you where you are!" said Miss Mary. She then cast her plaid over her face, marched up to the bank where Dick was crouching and shivering, dropped her ample plaid over him, and sped away towards the farmhouse. When she had reached its shelter, and was giving an account of the adventure, Dick set forth, like a primeval Highlander, the covering doing duty both for plaid and kilt. Clothes of some kind were provided for him at the cottage, a rickety old boat was fetched, and he and his stag were rowed across the river to the place where his clothes lay.

That is all, but if one were a dealer in romance, much play

might be made with the future fortunes of the sportsman and the maiden, happy fortunes or unhappy. In real life, the lassie "drew up with" a shepherd lad, as Miss Jenny Denison has it, married him, and helped to populate the strath. As for Dick, history tells no more of his adventures, nor is it alleged that he ever again visited the distant valley, or beheld the face of his Highland Nausicaa.

Now, if one were a romancer, this mere anecdote probably would "rest, lovely pearl, in the brain, and slowly mature in the oyster," till it became a novel. Properly handled, the incident would make a very agreeable first chapter, with the aid of scenery, botany, climate, and remarks on the manners and customs of the red deer stolen from St. John, or the Stuarts d'Albanie. Then, probably, one would reflect on the characters of Mary and of Richard; Mary must have parents, of course, and one would make them talk in Scottish. Probably she already had a lover; how should she behave to that lover? There is plenty of room for speculation in that problem. As to Dick, is he to be a Lothario, or a lover pour le bon motif? What are his distinguished family to think of the love affair, which would certainly ensue in fiction, though in real life nobody thought of it at all? Are we to end happily, with a marriage or marriages, or are we to wind all up in the pleasant, pessimistic, realistic, fashionable modern way? Is Mary to drown the baby in the Muckle Pool? Is she to suffer the penalty of her crime at Inverness? Or, happy thought, shall we not make her discarded rival lover meet Dick in the hills on a sunny day and then—are they not (taking a hint from facts) to fight a duel with rifles? I see Dick lying, with a bullet in his brow, on the side of a corrie; his blood crimsons the snow, an eagle stoops from the sky. That makes a pretty picturesque conclusion to the unwritten romance of the strath.

Another anecdote occurs to me; good, I think, for a short story, but capable, also, of being dumped down in the middle of a long novel. It was in the old coaching days. A Border squire was going north, in the coach, alone. At a village he was joined by a man and a young lady: their purpose was manifest, they were a runaway couple, bound for Gretna Green. They had not travelled long together before the young lady, turning to the squire, said, "Vous parlez français, Monsieur?" He did speak French—it was plain that the bridegroom did not—and, to the end of the journey, that remarkable lady conducted a lively and affectionate conversation with the squire in French! Manifestly, he had only to ask and receive, but, alas! he was an unadventurous, plain gentleman; he alighted at his own village; he drove home in his own dogcart; the fugitive pair went forward, and the Gretna blacksmith united them in holy matrimony. The rest is silence.

146

I would give much to know what that young person's previous history and adventures had been, to learn what befell her after her wedding, to understand, in brief, her conduct and her motives. Were I a novelist, a Maupassant, or a Meredith, the Muse, "from whatsoever quarter she chose," would enlighten me about all, and I would enlighten you. But I can only marvel, only throw out the hint, only deposit the grain of sand, the nucleus of romance, in some more fertile brain. Indeed the topic is much more puzzling than the right conclusion for my Highland romance. In that case fancy could find certain obvious channels, into one or other of which it must flow. But I see no channels for the lives of these three queerly met people in the coach.

As a rule, fancies are capable of being arranged in but a few familiar patterns, so that it seems hardly worth while to make the arrangement. But he who looks at things thus will never be a writer of stories. Nay, even of the slowly unfolding tale of his own existence he may weary, for the combinations therein have all occurred before; it is in a hackneyed old story that he is living, and you, and I. Yet to act on this knowledge is to make a bad affair of our little life: we must try our best to take it seriously. And so of story-writing. As Mr. Stevenson says, a man must view "his very trifling enterprise with a gravity that would befit the cares of empire, and think the smallest improvement worth accomplishing at any expense of time and industry. The book, the statue, the sonata, must be gone upon with the unreasoning good faith and the unflagging spirit of children at their play."

That is true, that is the worst of it. The man, the writer, over whom the irresistible desire to mock at himself, his work, his puppets and their fortunes has power, will never be a novelist. The novelist must "make believe very much"; he must be in earnest with his characters. But how to be in earnest, how to keep the note of disbelief and derision "out of the memorial"? Ah, there is the difficulty, but it is a difficulty of which many authors appear to be insensible. Perhaps they suffer from no such temptations.

CHAPTER XV

THE SUPERNATURAL IN FICTION

It is a truism that the supernatural in fiction should, as a general rule, be left in the vague. In the creepiest tale I ever read, the horror lay in this—there was no ghost! You may describe a ghost with all the most hideous features that fancy can suggest—saucer eyes, red staring hair, a forked tail, and what you please—but the reader only laughs. It is wiser to make as if you were going to describe the spectre, and then break off, exclaiming, "But no! No pen can describe, no memory, thank Heaven, can recall, the horror of that hour!" So writers, as a rule, prefer to leave their terror (usually styled "The Thing") entirely in the dark, and to the frightened fancy of the student. Thus, on the whole, the treatment of the supernaturally terrible in fiction is achieved in two ways, either by actual description, or by adroit suggestion, the author saying, like cabmen, "I leave it to yourself, sir." There are dangers in both methods; the description, if attempted, is usually overdone and incredible: the suggestion is apt to prepare us too anxiously for something that never becomes real, and to leave us disappointed.

Examples of both methods may be selected from poetry and prose. The examples in verse are rare enough; the first and best that occurs in the way of suggestion is, of course, the mysterious lady in "Christabel."

> "She was most beautiful to see,
> Like a lady of a far countrée."

Who was she? What did she want? Whence did she come? What was the horror she revealed to the night in the bower of Christabel?

> "Then drawing in her breath aloud
> Like one that shuddered, she unbound
> The cincture from beneath her breast.
> Her silken robe and inner vest
> Dropt to her feet, and full in view
> Behold her bosom and half her side—
> A sight to dream of, not to tell!
> O shield her! shield sweet Christabel!"

148

And then what do her words mean?

> "Thou knowest to-night, and wilt know to-morrow,
> This mark of my shame, this seal of my sorrow."

What was it—the "sight to dream of, not to tell?"

Coleridge never did tell, and, though he and Mr. Gilman said he knew, Wordsworth thought he did not know. He raised a spirit that he had not the spell to lay. In the Paradise of Poets has he discovered the secret? We only know that the mischief, whatever it may have been, was wrought.

> "O sorrow and shame! Can this be she—
> The lady who knelt at the old oak tree?"
>
> . . .
>
> "A star hath set, a star hath risen,
>   O Geraldine, since arms of thine
> Have been the lovely lady's prison.
>   O Geraldine, one hour was thine."[11]

If Coleridge knew, why did he never tell? And yet he maintains that "in the very first conception of the tale, I had the whole present to my mind, with the wholeness no less than with the liveliness of a vision," and he expected to finish the three remaining parts within the year. The year was 1816, the poem was begun in 1797, and finished, as far as it goes, in 1800. If Coleridge ever knew what he meant, he had time to forget. The chances are that his indolence, or his forgetfulness, was the making of "Christabel," which remains a masterpiece of supernatural suggestion.

For description it suffices to read the "Ancient Mariner." These marvels, truly, are speciosa miracula, and, unlike Southey, we believe as we read. "You have selected a passage fertile in unmeaning miracles," Lamb wrote to Southey (1798), "but have passed by fifty passages as miraculous as the miracles they celebrate." Lamb appears to have been almost alone in appreciating this masterpiece of supernatural description. Coleridge himself shrank from his own wonders, and wanted to call the piece "A Poet's Reverie." "It is as bad as Bottom the weaver's declaration that he is not a lion, but only the scenical representation of a lion. What new idea is gained by this title but one subversive of all credit—which the tale should force upon us—of its truth?" Lamb himself was forced, by the temper of the time, to declare that he "disliked all the

---

[11] Cannot the reader guess? I am afraid that I can!

miraculous part of it," as if it were not all miraculous! Wordsworth wanted the Mariner "to have a character and a profession," perhaps would have liked him to be a gardener, or a butler, with "an excellent character!" In fact, the love of the supernatural was then at so low an ebb that a certain Mr. Marshall "went to sleep while the 'Ancient Mariner' was reading," and the book was mainly bought by seafaring men, deceived by the title, and supposing that the "Ancient Mariner" was a nautical treatise.

In verse, then, Coleridge succeeds with the supernatural, both by way of description in detail, and of suggestion. If you wish to see a failure, try the ghost, the moral but not affable ghost, in Wordsworth's "Laodamia." It is blasphemy to ask the question, but is the ghost in "Hamlet" quite a success? Do we not see and hear a little too much of him? Macbeth's airy and viewless dagger is really much more successful by way of suggestion. The stage makes a ghost visible and familiar, and this is one great danger of the supernatural in art. It is apt to insist on being too conspicuous. Did the ghost of Darius, in "Æschylus," frighten the Athenians? Probably they smiled at the imperial spectre. There is more discretion in Cæsar's ghost—

> "I think it is the weakness of mine eyes
> That shapes this monstrous apparition,"

says Brutus, and he lays no very great stress on the brief visit of the appearance. For want of this discretion, Alexandre Dumas's ghosts, as in "The Corsican Brothers," are failures. They make themselves too common and too cheap, like the spectre in Mrs. Oliphant's novel, "The Wizard's Son." This, indeed, is the crux of the whole adventure. If you paint your ghost with too heavy a hand, you raise laughter, not fear. If you touch him too lightly, you raise unsatisfied curiosity, not fear. It may be easy to shudder, but it is difficult to teach shuddering.

In prose, a good example of the over vague is Miriam's mysterious visitor—the shadow of the catacombs—in "Transformation; or, The Marble Faun." Hawthorne should have told us more or less; to be sure his contemporaries knew what he meant, knew who Miriam and the Spectre were. The dweller in the catacombs now powerfully excites curiosity, and when that curiosity is unsatisfied, we feel aggrieved, vexed, and suspect that Hawthorne himself was puzzled, and knew no more than his readers. He has not—as in other tales he has—managed to throw the right atmosphere about this being. He is vague in the wrong way, whereas George Sand, in Les Dames Vertes, is vague in the right

150

way. We are left in Les Dames Vertes with that kind of curiosity which persons really engaged in the adventure might have felt, not with the irritation of having a secret kept from us, as in "Transformation."

In "Wandering Willie's Tale" (in "Redgauntlet"), the right atmosphere is found, the right note is struck. All is vividly real, and yet, if you close the book, all melts into a dream again. Scott was almost equally successful with a described horror in "The Tapestried Chamber." The idea is the commonplace of haunted houses, the apparition is described as minutely as a burglar might have been; and yet we do not mock, but shudder as we read. Then, on the other side—the side of anticipation—take the scene outside the closed door of the vanished Dr. Jekyll, in Mr. Stevenson's well-known apologue:

They are waiting on the threshold of the chamber whence the doctor has disappeared—the chamber tenanted by what? A voice comes from the room. "Sir," said Poole, looking Mr. Utterson in the eyes, "was that my master's voice?"

A friend, a man of affairs, and a person never accused of being fanciful, told me that he read through the book to that point in a lonely Highland chateau, at night, and that he did not think it well to finish the story till next morning, but rushed to bed. So the passage seems "well-found" and successful by dint of suggestion. On the other side, perhaps, only Scotsmen brought up in country places, familiar from childhood with the terrors of Cameronian myth, and from childhood apt to haunt the lonely churchyards, never stirred since the year of the great Plague choked the soil with the dead, perhaps they only know how much shudder may be found in Mr. Stevenson's "Thrawn Janet." The black smouldering heat in the hills and glens that are commonly so fresh, the aspect of the Man, the Tempter of the Brethren, we know them, and we have enough of the old blood in us to be thrilled by that masterpiece of the described supernatural. It may be only a local success, it may not much affect the English reader, but it is of sure appeal to the lowland Scot. The ancestral Covenanter within us awakens, and is terrified by his ancient fears.

Perhaps it may die out in a positive age—this power of learning to shudder. To us it descends from very long ago, from the far-off forefathers who dreaded the dark, and who, half starved and all untaught, saw spirits everywhere, and scarce discerned waking experience from dreams. When we are all perfect positivist philosophers, when a thousand generations of nurses that never heard of ghosts have educated the thousand and first generation of children, then the supernatural may fade out of fiction. But has it

151

not grown and increased since Wordsworth wanted the "Ancient Mariner" to have "a profession and a character," since Southey called that poem a Dutch piece of work, since Lamb had to pretend to dislike its "miracles"? Why, as science becomes more cock-sure, have men and women become more and more fond of old follies, and more pleased with the stirring of ancient dread within their veins?

As the visible world is measured, mapped, tested, weighed, we seem to hope more and more that a world of invisible romance may not be far from us, or, at least, we care more and more to follow fancy into these airy regions, et inania regna. The supernatural has not ceased to tempt romancers, like Alexandre Dumas, usually to their destruction; more rarely, as in Mrs. Oliphant's "Beleaguered City," to such success as they do not find in the world of daily occupation. The ordinary shilling tales of "hypnotism" and mesmerism are vulgar trash enough, and yet I can believe that an impossible romance, if the right man wrote it in the right mood, might still win us from the newspapers, and the stories of shabby love, and cheap remorses, and commonplace failures.

"But it needs Heaven-sent moments for this skill."

CHAPTER XVI

AN OLD SCOTTISH PSYCHICAL RESEARCHER

ADVERTISEMENT

"If any Gentlemen, and others, will be pleased to send me any relations about Spirits, Witches, and Apparitions, In any part of the Kingdom; or any Information about the Second Sight, Charms, Spells, Magic, and the like, They shall oblige the Author, and have them publisht to their satisfaction.

"Direct your Relations to Alexander Ogstouns, Shop Stationer, at the foot of the Plain-stones, at Edinburgh, on the North-side of the Street."

Is this not a pleasing opportunity for Gentlemen, and Others, whose Aunts have beheld wraiths, doubles, and fetches? It answers very closely to the requests of the Society for Psychical Research, who publish, as some one disparagingly says, "the dreams of the middle classes." Thanks to Freedom, Progress, and the decline of Superstition, it is now quite safe to see apparitions, and even to publish the narrative of their appearance.

But when Mr. George Sinclair, sometime Professor of Philosophy in Glasgow, issued the invitation which I have copied, at the end of his "Satan's Invisible World Discovered,"[12] the vocation of a seer was not so secure from harm. He, or she, might just as probably be burned as not, on the charge of sorcery, in the year of grace, 1685. However, Professor Sinclair managed to rake together an odd enough set of legends, "proving clearly that there are Devils," a desirable matter to have certainty about. "Satan's Invisible World Discovered" is a very rare little book; I think Scott says in a MS. note that he had great difficulty in procuring it, when he was at work on his "infernal demonology." As a copy fell in my way, or rather as I fell in its way, a helpless victim to its charms and its blue morocco binding, I take this chance of telling again the old tales of 1685.

Mr. Sinclair began with a long dedicatory Epistle about nothing at all, to the Lord Winton of the period. The Earl dug coal-mines, and constructed "a moliminous rampier for a harbour." A

---

[12] Edinburgh, 1685.

"moliminous rampier" is a choice phrase, and may be envied by novelists who aim at distinction of style. "Your defending the salt pans against the imperious waves of the raging sea from the NE. is singular," adds the Professor, addressing "the greatest coal and salt-master in Scotland, who is a nobleman, and the greatest nobleman who is a Coal and Salt Merchant." Perhaps it is already plain to the modern mind that Mr. George Sinclair, though a Professor of Philosophy, was not a very sagacious character.

Mr. Sinclair professes that his proofs of the existence of Devils "are no old wife's trattles about the fire, but such as may bide the test." He lived, one should remember, in an age when faith was really seeking aid from ghost stories. Glanvil's books—and, in America, those of Cotton Mather—show the hospitality to anecdotes of an edifying sort, which we admire in Mr. Sinclair. Indeed, Sinclair borrows from Glanvil and Henry More, authors who, like himself, wished to establish the existence of the supernatural on the strange incidents which still perplex us, but which are scarcely regarded as safe matter to argue upon. The testimony for a Ghost would seldom go to a jury in our days, though amply sufficient in the time of Mr. Sinclair. About "The Devil of Glenluce" he took particular care to be well informed, and first gave it to the world in a volume on—you will never guess what subject—Hydrostatics! In the present work he offers us

> "The Devil of Glenluce Enlarged
> With several Remarkable Additions
> from an Eye and Ear Witness,
> A Person of undoubted
> Honesty."

Mr. Sinclair recommends its "usefulness for refuting Atheism." Probably Mr. Sinclair got the story, or had it put off on him rather, through one Campbell, a student of philosophy in Glasgow, the son of Gilbert Campbell, a weaver of Glenluce, in Galloway; the scene in our own time, of a mysterious murder. Campbell had refused alms to Alexander Agnew, a bold and sturdy beggar, who, when asked by the Judge whether he believed in a God, answered: "He knew no God but Salt, Meal, and Water." In consequence of the refusal of alms, "The Stirs first began." The "Stirs" are ghostly disturbances. They commenced with whistling in the house and out of it, "such as children use to make with their small, slender glass whistles." "About the Middle of November," says Mr. Sinclair, "the Foul Fiend came on with his extraordinary assaults." Observe that he takes the Foul Fiend entirely for granted, and that he never tells us the date of the original quarrel, and the early agitation. Stones were thrown down the chimney and in at the windows, but nobody was hurt.

Naturally Gilbert Campbell carried his tale of sorrow to the parish Minister. This did not avail him. His warp and threads were cut on his loom, and even the clothes of his family were cut while they were wearing them. At night something tugged the blankets off their beds, a favourite old spiritual trick, which was played, if I remember well, on a Roman Emperor, according to Suetonius. Poor Campbell had to remove his stock-in-trade, and send his children to board out, "to try whom the trouble did most follow." After this, all was quiet (as perhaps might be expected), and quiet all remained, till a son named Thomas was brought home again. Then the house was twice set on fire, and it might have been enough to give Thomas a beating. On the other hand, Campbell sent Thomas to stay with the Minister. But the troubles continued in the old way. At last the family became so accustomed to the Devil, "that they were no more afraid to keep up the Clash" (chatter) "with the Foul Fiend than to speak to each other." They were like the Wesleys, who were so familiar with the fiend Jeffrey, that haunted their home.

The Minister, with a few of the gentry, heard of their unholy friendship, and paid Campbell a visit. "At their first coming in the Devil says: 'Quum Literarum is good Latin.'" These are the first words of the Latin rudiments which scholars are taught when they go to the Grammar School. Then they all prayed, and a Voice came from under the bed: "Would you know the Witches of Glenluce?" The Voice named a few, including one long dead. But the Minister, with rare good sense, remarked that what Satan said was not evidence.

Let it be remarked that "the lad Tom" had that very day "come back with the Minister." The Fiend then offered terms. "Give me a spade and shovel, and depart from the house for seven days, and I will make a grave, and lie down in it, and trouble you no more." Hereon Campbell, with Scottish caution, declined to give the Devil the value of a straw. The visitors then hunted after the voice, observing that some of the children were in bed. They found nothing, and then, as the novelists say, "a strange thing happened."

There appeared a naked hand and an arm, from the elbow down, beating upon the floor till the house did shake again. "The Fiend next exclaimed that if the candle were put out he would appear in the shape of Fireballs."

Let it be observed that now, for the first time, we learn that all the scene occurred in candle-light. The appearance of floating balls of fire is frequent (if we may believe the current reports) at spiritualistic séances. But what a strange, ill-digested tale is Mr. Sinclair's! He lets slip an expression which shows that the investigators were in one room, the But, while the Fiend was diverting himself in the other room, the Ben! The Fiend (nobody going Ben) next chaffed a gentleman who wore a fashionable broad-brimmed hat, "whereupon he presently imagined that he felt a pair of shears going about his hat," but there was no such matter. The voice asked for a piece of bread, which the others were eating, and said the maid gave him a crust in the morning. This she denied, but admitted that something had "clicked" a piece of bread out of her hand.

The séance ended, the Devil slapping a safe portion of the children's bodies, with a sound resembling applause. After many months of this really annoying conduct, poor Campbell laid his case before the Presbyters, in 1655, thirty years before the date of publication. So a "solemn humiliation" was actually held all through the bounds of the synod. But to little purpose did Glenluce sit in sackcloth and ashes. The good wife's plate was snatched away before her very eyes, and then thrown back at her. In similar "stirs," described by a Catholic missionary in Peru soon after Pizarro's conquest, the cup of an Indian chief was lifted up by an invisible hand, and set down empty. In that case, too, stones were thrown, as by the Devil of Glenluce.

And what was the end of it all? Mr. Sinclair has not even taken the trouble to inquire. It seems by some conjuration or other, the Devil suffered himself to be put away, and gave the weaver a habitation. The weaver "has been a very Odd man that endured so long these marvellous disturbances."

This is the tale which Mr. Sinclair offers, without mentioning his authority. He complains that Dr. Henry More had plagiarised it, from his book of Hydrostatics. Two points may be remarked. First: modern Psychical Inquirers are more particular about evidence than Mr. Sinclair. Not for nothing do we live in an age of science. Next: the stories of these "stirs" are always much the same everywhere, in Glenluce, at Tedworth, where the Drummer came, in Peru, in Wesley's house, in heroic Iceland, when Glam, the vampire, "rode the roofs." It is curious to speculate on how the tradition of making themselves little nuisances in this particular manner has been handed down among children, if we are to suppose that children do the trick. Last autumn a farmer's house in Scotland was annoyed exactly as the weaver's home was, and that within a quarter of a mile of a well-known man of science. The mattress of the father was tenanted by something that wriggled like a snake. The mattress was opened, nothing was found, and the disturbance began again as soon as the bed was restored to its place. This occurred when the farmer's children had been sent to a distance.

One cannot but be perplexed by the problem which these tales suggest. Almost bare of evidence as they are, their great number, their wide diffusion, in many countries and in times ancient and modern, may establish some substratum of truth. Scott mentions a case in which the imposture was detected by a sheriff's officer. But a recent anecdote makes me almost distrust the detection.

Some English people, having taken a country house in Ireland, were vexed by the usual rappings, stone-throwings, and all the rest of the business. They sent to Dublin for two detectives, who arrived. On their first night, the lady of the house went into a room, where she found one of the policemen asleep in his chair. Being a lively person, she rapped twice or thrice on the table. He awakened, and said: "Ah, so I suspected. It was hardly worth while, madam, to bring us so far for this." And next day the worthy men withdrew in dudgeon, but quite convinced that they had discovered the agent in the hauntings.

But they had not!

On the other hand, Scott (who had seen one ghost, if not two, and had heard a "warning") states that Miss Anne Robinson managed the Stockwell disturbances by tying horsehairs to plates and light articles, which then demeaned themselves as if possessed.

Here we have vera causa, a demonstrable cause of "stirs," and it may be inferred that all the other historical occurrences had a similar origin. We have, then, only to be interested in the persistent tradition, in accordance with which mischievous persons always do exactly the same sort of thing. But this is a mere example of the identity of human nature.

It is curious to see how Mr. Sinclair plumes himself on this Devil of Glenluce as a "moliminous rampier" against irreligion. "This one Relation is worth all the price that can be given for the Book." The price I have given for the volume is Ten Golden Guineas, and perhaps the Foul Thief of Glenluce is hardly worth the money.

"I believe if the Obdurest Atheist among men would seriously and in good earnest consider that relation, and ponder all the circumstances thereof, he would presently cry out, as a Dr. of Physick did, hearing a story less considerable, 'I believe I have been in the wrong all the time—if this be true.'"

Mr. Sinclair is also a believer in the Woodstock devils, on which Scott founded his novel. He does not give the explanation that Giles Sharp, alias Joseph Collins of Oxford, alias Funny Joe, was all the Devil in that affair. Scott had read the story of Funny

Joe, but could never remember "whether it exists in a separate collection, or where it is to be looked for."

Indifferent to evidence, Mr. Sinclair confutes the Obdurest Atheists with the Pied Piper of Hamelin, with the young lady from Howells' "Letters," whose house, like Rahab's, was "on the city wall," and with the ghost of the Major who appeared to the Captain (as he had promised), and scolded him for not keeping his sword clean. He also gives us Major Weir, at full length, convincing us that, as William Erskine said, "The Major was a disgusting fellow, a most ungentlemanlike character." Scott, on the other hand, remarked, long before "Waverley," "if I ever were to become a writer of prose romances, I think I would choose Major Weir, if not for my hero, at least for an agent and a leading one, in my production." He admitted that the street where the Major lived was haunted by a woman "twice the common length," "but why should we set him down for an ungentlemanly fellow?" Readers of Mr. Sinclair will understand the reason very well, and it is not necessary, nor here even possible, to justify Erskine's opinion by quotations. Suffice it that, by virtue of his enchanted staff, which was burned with him, the Major was enabled "to commit evil not to be named, yea, even to reconcile man and wife when at variance." His sister, who was hanged, had Redgauntlet's horse-shoe mark on her brow, and one may marvel that Scott does not seem to have remembered this coincidence. "There was seen an exact Horse-shoe, shaped for nails, in her wrinkles. Terrible enough, I assure you, to the stoutest beholder!"

Most modern readers will believe that both the luckless Major and his sister were religious maniacs. Poverty, solitude, and the superstition of their time were the true demon of Major Weir, burned at the stake in April 1670. Perhaps the most singular impression made by "Satan's Invisible World Discovered" is that in Sinclair's day, people who did not believe in bogies believed in nothing, while people who shared the common creed of Christendom were capable of believing in everything.

Atheists are as common as ghosts in his marvellous relations, and the very wizards themselves were often Atheists.

NOTE.—I have said that Scott himself had seen one ghost, if not two, and heard a "warning." The ghost was seen near Ashestiel, on an open spot of hillside, "please to observe it was before dinner." The anecdote is in Gillis's, "Recollections of Sir Walter Scott," p. 170. The vision of Lord Byron standing in the great hall of Abbotsford is described in the "Demonology and Witchcraft." Scott alleges that it resolved itself into "great coats, shawls, and plaids"—a hallucination. But Lockhart remarks ("Life," ix. p. 141) that he did not care to have the circumstance discussed in general. The "stirs" in Abbotsford during the night when his architect, Bullock, died in London, are in Lockhart, v. pp. 309-315. "The noise resembled half-a-dozen men hard at work putting up boards and furniture, and nothing can be more certain than that there was nobody on the premises at the time." The noise, unluckily, occurred twice, April 28 and 29, 1818, and Lockhart does not tell us on which of these two nights Mr. Bullock died. Such is the casualness of ghost story-tellers. Lockhart adds that the coincidence made a strong impression on Sir Walter's mind. He did not care to ascertain the point in his own mental constitution "where incredulity began to waver," according to his friend, Mr. J. L. Adolphus.

CHAPTER XVII

THE BOY

As a humble student of savage life, I have found it necessary to make researches into the manners and customs of boys. Boys are not what a vain people supposes. If you meet them in the holidays, you find them affable and full of kindness and good qualities. They will condescend to your weakness at lawn-tennis, they will aid you in your selection of fly-hooks, and, to be brief, will behave with much more than the civility of tame Zulus or Red Men on a missionary settlement. But boys at school and among themselves, left to the wild justice and traditional laws which many generations of boys have evolved, are entirely different beings. They resemble that Polynesian prince who had rejected the errors of polytheism for those of an extreme sect of Primitive Seceders. For weeks at a time this prince was known to be "steady," but every month or so he disappeared, and his subjects said he was "lying off." To adopt an American idiom, he "felt like brandy and water"; he also "felt like" wearing no clothes, and generally rejecting his new conceptions of duty and decency. In fact, he had a good bout of savagery, and then he returned to his tall hat, his varnished boots, his hymn-book, and his edifying principles. The life of small boys at school (before they get into long-tailed coats and the upper-fifth) is often a mere course of "lying-off"—of relapse into native savagery with its laws and customs.

If any one has so far forgotten his own boyhood as to think this description exaggerated, let him just fancy what our comfortable civilised life would be, if we could become boys in character and custom. Let us suppose that you are elected to a new club, of which most of the members are strangers to you. You enter the doors for the first time, when two older members, who have been gossiping in the hall, pounce upon you with the exclamation, "Hullo, here's a new fellow! You fellow, what's your name?" You reply, let us say, "Johnson." "I don't believe it, it's such a rum name. What's your father?" Perhaps you are constrained to answer "a Duke" or (more probably) "a solicitor." In the former case your friends bound up into the smoking-room, howling, "Here's a new fellow says his father is a Duke. Let's take the cheek out of him." And they "take it out" with umbrellas, slippers, and other surgical instruments. Or, in the latter case (your parent being a solicitor) they reply, "Then your father must be a beastly cad. All solicitors are sharks. My father says so, and he knows. How many sisters have you?" The new member answers, "Four." "Any of them married?" "No." "How awfully awkward for you."

By this time, perhaps, luncheon is ready, or the evening papers come in, and you are released for a moment. You sneak up into the library, where you naturally expect to be entirely alone, and you settle on a sofa with a novel. But an old member bursts into the room, spies a new fellow, and puts him through the usual catechism. He ends with, "How much tin have you got?" You answer "twenty pounds," or whatever the sum may be, for perhaps you had contemplated playing whist. "Very well, fork it out; you must give a dinner, all new fellows must, and you are not going to begin by being a stingy beast?" Thus addressed, as your friend is a big bald man, who looks mischievous, you do "fork out" all your ready money, and your new friend goes off to consult the cook. Meanwhile you "shed a blooming tear," as Homer says, and go home heart-broken. Now, does any grown-up man call this state of society civilisation? Would life be worth living (whatever one's religious consolations) on these terms? Of course not, and yet this picture is a not overdrawn sketch of the career of some new boy, at some schools new or old. The existence of a small schoolboy is, in other respects, not unlike that of an outsider in a lawless "Brotherhood," as the Irish playfully call their murder clubs.

The small boy is in the society, but not of it, as far as any benefits go. He has to field out (and I admit that the discipline is salutary) while other boys bat. Other boys commit the faults, and compel him to copy out the impositions—say five hundred lines of Virgil—with which their sins are visited. Other boys enjoy the pleasures of football, while the small boy has to run vaguely about, never within five yards of the ball. Big boys reap the glories of paperchases, the small boy gets lost in the bitter weather, on the open moors, or perhaps (as in one historical case) is frozen to death within a measurable distance of the school playground. And the worst of it is that, as a member of the great school secret society, the small boy can never complain of his wrongs, or divulge the name of his tormentors. It is in this respect that he resembles a harmless fellow, dragged into the coils of an Anarchist "Inner Brotherhood." He is exposed to all sorts of wrongs from his neighbours, and he can only escape by turning "informer," by breaking the most sacred law of his society, losing all social status, and, probably, obliging his parents to remove him from school. Life at school, as among the Celtic peoples, turns on the belief that law and authority are natural enemies, against which every one is banded.

The chapter of bullying among boys is one on which a man enters with reluctance. Boys are, on the whole, such good fellows,

161

and so full of fine unsophisticated qualities, that the mature mind would gladly turn away its eyes from beholding their iniquities. Even a cruel bully does not inevitably and invariably develop into a bad man. He is, let us hope, only passing through the savage stage, in which the torture of prisoners is a recognised institution. He has, perhaps, too little imagination to understand the pain he causes. Very often bullying is not physically cruel, but only a perverted sort of humour, such as Kingsley, in "Hypatia," recognised among his favourite Goths. I remember a feeble foolish boy at school (feeble he certainly was, and was thought foolish) who became the subject of much humorous bullying. His companions used to tie a thin thread round his ear, and attach this to a bar at such a height that he could only avoid breaking it by standing on tiptoe. But he was told that he must not break the thread. To avoid infringing this commandment, he put himself to considerable inconvenience and afforded much enjoyment to the spectators.

Men of middle age, rather early middle age, remember the two following species of bullying to which they were subjected, and which, perhaps, are obsolescent. Tall stools were piled up in a pyramid, and the victim was seated on the top, near the roof of the room. The other savages brought him down from this bad eminence by hurling other stools at those which supported him. Or the victim was made to place his hands against the door, with the fingers outstretched, while the young tormentors played at the Chinese knife-trick. They threw knives, that is to say, at the door between the apertures of the fingers, and, as a rule, they hit the fingers and not the door. These diversions I know to be correctly reported, but the following pretty story is, perhaps, a myth. At one of the most famous public schools, a praepostor, or monitor, or sixth-form boy having authority, heard a pistol-shot in the room above his own. He went up and found a big boy and a little boy. They denied having any pistol. The monitor returned to his studies, again was sure he heard a shot, went up, and found the little boy dead. The big boy had been playing the William Tell trick with him, and had hit his head instead of the apple. That is the legend. Whether it be true or false, all boys will agree that the little victim could not have escaped by complaining to the monitor. No. Death before dishonour. But the side not so seamy of this picture of school life is the extraordinary power of honour among boys. Of course the laws of the secret society might well terrify a puerile informer. But the sentiment of honour is even more strong than fear, and will probably outlast the very disagreeable circumstances in which it was developed.

People say bullying is not what it used to be. The much

abused monitorial system has this in it of good, that it enables a clever and kindly boy who is high up in the school to stop the cruelties (if he hears of them) of a much bigger boy who is low in the school. But he seldom hears of them. Habitual bullies are very cunning, and I am acquainted with instances in which they carry their victims off to lonely torture cells (so to speak) and deserted places fit for the sport. Some years ago a small boy, after a long course of rope's-ending in out-of-the-way dens, revealed the abominations of some naval cadets. There was not much sympathy with him in the public mind, and perhaps his case was not well managed. But it was made clear that whereas among men an unpopular person is only spoken evil of behind his back, an unpopular small boy among boys is made to suffer in a more direct and very unpleasant way.

Most of us leave school with the impression that there was a good deal of bullying when we were little, but that the institution has died out. The truth is that we have grown too big to be bullied, and too good-natured to bully ourselves. When I left school, I thought bullying was an extinct art, like encaustic painting (before it was rediscovered by Sir William Richmond). But a distinguished writer, who was a small boy when I was a big one, has since revealed to me the most abominable cruelties which were being practised at the very moment when I supposed bullying to have had its day and ceased to be. Now, the small boy need only have mentioned the circumstances to any one of a score of big boys, and the tormentor would have been first thrashed, and then, probably, expelled.

A friend of my own was travelling lately in a wild and hilly region on the other side of the world, let us say in the Mountains of the Moon. In a mountain tavern he had thrust upon him the society of the cook, a very useless young man, who astonished him by references to one of our universities, and to the enjoyments of that seat of learning. This youth (who was made cook, and a very bad cook too, because he could do nothing else) had been expelled from a large English school. And he was expelled because he had felled a bully with a paving-stone, and had expressed his readiness to do it again. Now, there was no doubt that this cook in the mountain inn was a very unserviceable young fellow. But I wish more boys who have suffered things literally unspeakable from bullies would try whether force (in the form of a paving stone) is really no remedy.

The Catholic author of a recent book ("Schools," by Lieut.-Col. Raleigh Chichester), is very hard on "Protestant Schools," and thinks that the Catholic system of constant watching is a remedy for bullying and other evils. "Swing-doors with their upper half glazed, might have their uses," he says, and he does not see why a boy should not be permitted to complain, if he is roasted, like Tom Brown, before a large fire. The boys at one Catholic school described by Colonel Raleigh Chichester, "are never without surveillance of some sort." This is true of most French schools, and any one who wishes to understand the consequences (there) may read the published confessions of a pion—an usher, or "spy." A more degraded and degrading life than that of the wretched pion, it is impossible to imagine. In an English private school, the system of espionnage and tale bearing, when it exists, is probably not unlike what Mr. Anstey describes in Vice Versâ. But in the Catholic schools spoken of by Colonel Raleigh Chichester, the surveillance may be, as he says, "that of a parent; an aid to the boys in their games rather than a check." The religious question as between Catholics and Protestants has no essential connection with the subject. A Protestant school might, and Grimstone's did, have tale-bearers; possibly a Catholic school might exist without parental surveillance. That system is called by its foes a "police," by its friends a "paternal" system. But fathers don't exercise the "paternal" system themselves in this country, and we may take it for granted that, while English society and religion are as they are, surveillance at our large schools will be impossible. If any one regrets this, let him read the descriptions of French schools and schooldays, in Balzac's Louis Lambert, in the "Memoirs" of M. Maxime du Camp, in any book where a Frenchman speaks his mind about his youth. He will find spying (of course) among the ushers, contempt and hatred on the side of the boys, unwholesome and cruel punishments, a total lack of healthy exercise; and he will hear of holidays spent in premature excursions into forbidden and shady quarters of the town.

No doubt the best security against bullying is in constant occupation. There can hardly (in spite of Master George Osborne's experience in "Vanity Fair") be much bullying in an open cricket-field. Big boys, too, with good hearts, should not only stop bullying when they come across it, but make it their business to find out where it exists. Exist it will, more or less, despite all precautions, while boys are boys—that is, are passing through a modified form of the savage state.

There is a curious fact in the boyish character which seems, at first sight, to make good the opinion that private education, at home, is the true method. Before they go out into school life, many little fellows of nine, or so, are extremely original, imaginative, and almost poetical. They are fond of books, fond of nature, and, if you can win their confidence, will tell you all sorts of pretty thoughts and fancies which lie about them in their infancy. I have known a little boy who liked to lie on the grass and to people the alleys and glades of that miniature forest with fairies and dwarfs, whom he seemed actually to see in a kind of vision. But he went to school, he instantly won the hundred yards race for boys under twelve, and he came back a young barbarian, interested in "the theory of touch" (at football), curious in the art of bowling, and no more capable than you or I of seeing fairies in a green meadow. He was caught up into the air of the boy's world, and his imagination was in abeyance for a season.

This is a common enough thing, and rather a melancholy spectacle to behold. One is tempted to believe that school causes the loss of a good deal of genius, and that the small boys who leave home poets, and come back barbarians, have been wasted. But, on the other hand, if they had been kept at home and encouraged, the chances are that they would have blossomed into infant phenomena and nothing better. The awful infancy of Mr. John Stuart Mill is a standing warning. Mr. Mill would probably have been a much happier and wiser man if he had not been a precocious linguist, economist, and philosopher, but had passed through a healthy stage of indifference to learning and speculation at a public school. Look again, at the childhood of Bishop Thirlwall. His Primitiae were published (by Samuel Tipper, London, 1808), when young Connop was but eleven years of age. His indiscreet father "launched this slender bark," as he says, and it sailed through three editions between 1808 and 1809. Young Thirlwall was taught Latin at three years of age, "and at four read Greek with an ease and fluency which astonished all who heard him." At seven he composed an essay, "On the Uncertainty of Human Life," but "his taste for poetry was not discovered till a later period." His sermons, some forty, occupy most of the little volume in which these Primitiae were collected.

He was especially concerned about Sabbath desecration. "I confess," observes this sage of ten, "when I look upon the present and past state of our public morals, and when I contrast our present luxury, dissipation, and depravity, with past frugality and virtue, I feel not merely a sensation of regret, but also of terror, for the result of the change." "The late Revolution in France," he adds, "has afforded us a remarkable lesson how necessary religion is to a State, and that from a deficiency on that head arise the chief evils which can befall society." He then bids us "remember that the Nebuchadnezzar who may destroy our Israel is near at hand," though it might be difficult to show how Nebuchadnezzar destroyed Israel.

As to the uncertainty of life, he remarks that "Edward VI died in his minority, and disappointed his subjects, to whom he had promised a happy reign." Of this infant's thirty-nine sermons (just as many as the Articles), it may be said that they are in no way inferior to other examples of this class of literature. But sermons are among the least "scarce" and "rare" of human essays, and many parents would rather see their boy patiently acquiring the art of wicket-keeping at school than moralising on the uncertainty of life at home. Some one "having presented to the young author a copy of verses on the trite and familiar subject of the Ploughboy," he replied with an ode on "The Potboy."

> "Bliss is not always join'd to wealth,
>   Nor dwells beneath the gilded roof
> For poverty is bliss with health,
>   Of that my potboy stands a proof."

The volume ends with this determination,

> "Still shall I seek Apollo's shelt'ring ray,
> To cheer my spirits and inspire my lay."

If any parent or guardian desires any further information about Les Enfans devenus célèbres par leurs écrits, he will find it in a work of that name, published in Paris in 1688. The learned Scioppius published works at sixteen, "which deserved" (and perhaps obtained) "the admiration of dotards." M. Du Maurier asserts that, at the age of fifteen, Grotius pleaded causes at the Bar. At eleven Meursius made orations and harangues which were much admired. At fifteen, Alexandre le Jeune wrote anacreontic verses, and (less excusably) a commentary on the Institutions of Gaius. Grevin published a tragedy and two comedies at the age of thirteen, and at fifteen Louis Stella was a professor of Greek. But no one reads Grevin now, nor Stella, nor Alexandre le Jeune, and perhaps their time might have been better occupied in being "soaring human boys" than in composing tragedies and commentaries. Monsieur le Duc de Maine published, in 1678, his Œuvres d'un Auteur de Sept Ans, a royal example to be avoided by all boys. These and several score of other examples may perhaps reconcile us to the spectacle of puerile genius fading away in the existence of the common British schoolboy, who is nothing of a poet, and still less of a jurisconsult.

The British authors who understand boys best are not those who have written books exclusively about boys. There is Canon Farrar, for example, whose romances of boyish life appear to be very popular, but whose boys, somehow, are not real boys. They are too good when they are good, and when they are bad, they are not perhaps too bad (that is impossible), but they are bad in the wrong way. They are bad with a mannish and conscious vice, whereas even bad boys seem to sin less consciously and after a ferocious fashion of their own. Of the boys in "Tom Brown" it is difficult to speak, because the Rugby boy under Arnold seems to have been of a peculiar species. A contemporary pupil was asked, when an undergraduate, what he conceived to be the peculiar characteristic of Rugby boys. He said, after mature reflection, that "the differentia of the Rugby boy was his moral thoughtfulness." Now the characteristic of the ordinary boy is his want of what is called moral thoughtfulness.

He lives in simple obedience to school traditions. These may compel him, at one school, to speak in a peculiar language, and to persecute and beat all boys who are slow at learning this language. At another school he may regard dislike of the manly game of football as the sin with which "heaven heads the count of crimes." On the whole this notion seems a useful protest against the prematurely artistic beings who fill their studies with photographs of Greek fragments, vases, etchings by the newest etcher, bits of China, Oriental rugs, and very curious old brass candlesticks. The "challenge cup" soon passes away from the keeping of any house in a public school where Bunthorne is a popular and imitated character. But when we reach æsthetic boys, we pass out of the savage stage into hobbledehoyhood. The bigger boys at public schools are often terribly "advanced," and when they are not at work or play, they are vexing themselves with the riddle of the earth, evolution, agnosticism, and all that kind of thing. Latin verses may not be what conservatives fondly deem them, and even cricket may, it is said, become too absorbing a pursuit, but either or both are better than precocious freethinking and sacrifice on the altar of the Beautiful.

A big boy who is tackling Haeckel or composing virelais in playtime is doing himself no good, and is worse than useless to the society of which he is a member. The small boys, who are the most ardent of hero-worshippers, either despise him or they allow him to address them in chansons royaux, and respond with trebles in triolets. At present a great many boys leave school, pass three years or four at the universities, and go back as masters to the place where some of their old schoolfellows are still pupils. It is through these very young masters, perhaps, that "advanced" speculations and tastes get into schools, where, however excellent in themselves, they are rather out of place. Indeed, the very young master, though usually earnest in his work, must be a sage indeed if he can avoid talking to the elder boys about the problems that interest him, and so forcing their minds into precocious attitudes. The advantage of

167

Eton boys used to be, perhaps is still, that they came up to college absolutely destitute of "ideas," and guiltless of reading anything more modern than Virgil. Thus their intellects were quite fallow, and they made astonishing progress when they bent their fresh and unwearied minds to study. But too many boys now leave school with settled opinions derived from the very latest thing out, from the newest German pessimist or American socialist. It may, however, be argued that ideas of these sorts are like measles, and that it is better to take them early and be done with them for ever.

While schools are reformed and Latin grammars of the utmost ingenuity and difficulty are published, boys on the whole change very little. They remain the beings whom Thackeray understood better than any other writer: Thackeray, who liked boys so much and was so little blind to their defects. I think he exaggerates their habit of lying to masters, or, if they lied in his day, their character has altered in that respect, and they are more truthful than many men find it expedient to be. And they have given up fighting; the old battles between Berry and Biggs, or Dobbin and Cuff (major) are things of the glorious past. Big boys don't fight, and there is a whisper that little boys kick each other's shins when in wrath. That practice can hardly be called an improvement, even if we do not care for fisticuffs. Perhaps the gloves are the best peacemakers at school. When all the boys, by practice in boxing, know pretty well whom they can in a friendly way lick, they are less tempted to more crucial experiments "without the gloves."

But even the ascertainment of one's relative merits with the gloves hurts a good deal, and one may thank heaven that the fountain of youth (as described by Pontus de Tyarde) is not a common beverage. By drinking this liquid, says the old Frenchman, one is insensibly brought back from old to middle age, and to youth and boyhood. But one would prefer to stop drinking of the fountain before actually being reduced to boy's estate, and passing once more through the tumultuous experiences of that period. And of these, not having enough to eat is by no means the least common. The evidence as to execrable dinners is rather dispiriting, and one may end by saying that if there is a worse fellow than a bully, it is a master who does not see that his boys are supplied with plenty of wholesome food. He, at least, could not venture, like a distinguished headmaster, to preach and publish sermons on "Boys' Life: its Fulness." A schoolmaster who has boarders is a hotel-keeper, and thereby makes his income, but he need not keep a hotel which would be dispraised in guide books. Dinners are a branch of school economy which should not be left to the wives of schoolmasters. They have never been boys.